PRAISE FOR *ROLLING BACK THE RIVER*

"In *Rolling Back the River*, Paul Guernsey crafts a moving, elegiac portrait of a man—and a world—struggling to hold onto what matters most. As Vincent Mapp fights to preserve wild waters, native fish, and old loyalties, he discovers that some currents cannot be reversed, no matter how fiercely we row against them. A powerful meditation on loss, resilience, and the beauty of letting go, *Rolling Back the River* speaks to anyone who's ever loved a place—or a person—enough to mourn its passing."—**Joshua Caldwell**, fly fisher and director of the feature film *Mending the Line*

"A thoroughly enjoyable, absorbing, and darkly comic novel about the delicate balance of the natural world."—**David Coggins**, author of *The Believer: A Year in the Fly Fishing Life*

"*Rolling Back the River* is great fun, a crisp and rollicking read that artfully mixes humor and meaningful contemplation, often on the very same page."—**Monte Burke**, author of *Lords of the Fly*, *Saban*, and *Rivers Always Reach the Sea*

"I've never read anything quite like this. It grabbed me, compelled me, and made me assess all the reasons why I care so much about fly-fishing. The writing is nothing short of masterful and laden with legitimate substance. It is so deeply honest and imaginative, it left me speechless." —**Kirk Deeter**, editor of *TROUT* magazine

"Imagine Carl Hiaasen's environmental urgency crossed with John Gierach's dry wit and Norman Maclean's quiet reverence for trout water. That's the sweet spot Paul Guernsey hits in *Rolling Back the River*—a terrific novel celebrating friendship, fly fishing, and the tangled comedy of growing older and wiser on a rapidly changing planet."—**Tim Schulz**, author of *A Cast Away in Montana*

"In *Rolling Back the River*, Paul Guernsey has written a novel of nuance and meaning that brought me moments of laughter, joy, curiosity, and almost sentimental reflection. I loved this story."—**Steve Ramirez**, author of *Casting Forward* and the Lyons Press Casting series

"Great fishing novels capture anglers and non-anglers. They're scarce as coelacanths, but one has surfaced here. With wit and superb writing, Guernsey takes us to beautiful places and develops characters who are real people, most of whom we want to know, all of whom we get to know."—**Ted Williams**, conservation journalist, author, and guide

"It doesn't take more than a few sentences to realize that Paul Guernsey is a writer who fly fishes, rather than the other way around. When he is describing time on the water, the authenticity is clear, but what really carries the narrative are his skills as a writer—a fine eye for detail, an acute sense of life's absurdities, and a profound sense of humanity. While anglers will certainly enjoy this book, its appeal goes far beyond its sporting subject."—**Phil Monahan**, editor in chief of *MidCurrent*

"A delightful book. The characters and their relationships are honest and believable. Well-known names in the fly-fishing community are seamlessly woven into the tapestry of the story, and there are rich literary allusions throughout. Most importantly, the descriptions of fishing are truthful and not overdone. I found myself rooting for the hero, and hope he makes a comeback in future books, like Joseph Heywood's Bowie Rhodes, or Jim Harrison's Brown Dog."—**Bob White**, sporting artist, author, and Argentina and Alaska fishing guide

"I've known Paul Guernsey since his days with *Fly Rod & Reel* magazine. Paul was promoting wild native fish and real conservation when doing so put readership and advertising at risk due to potential blowback from the industry and angling community. But Paul is also a fly fisherman, and he manages to find a balance between fish and fishing in his book, which is important."—**Bob Mallard**, writer, former fly-shop owner, fly-fishing guide, and founding member and executive director of the Native Fish Coalition

Rolling Back the River

Rolling Back the River

A NOVEL

Paul Guernsey

STACKPOLE
BOOKS
Essex, Connecticut

STACKPOLE BOOKS
The Globe Pequot Publishing Group, Inc.
64 South Main Street
Essex, CT 06426
www.globepequot.com

British Library Cataloguing in Publication Information available

Library of Congress Cataloging-in-Publication Data available

ISBN 9780811777865 (paperback) | ISBN 9780811777872 (epub)

For the gauchos, guides, and tango dancers.
For every fishing friend I've had.
And most of all, for all the fish.

CONTENTS

One of the penalties of an ecological education is that one lives alone in a world of wounds.

—ALDO LEOPOLD

I agree with a friend of mine who says that if fishing is really like sex, then he's doing one of them wrong.

—JOHN GIERACH, *DANCES WITH TROUT*

CHAPTER ONE

Maps and Mazes

VINCENT MAPP WAS FREQUENTLY IMPULSIVE. IT WAS A QUALITY THAT, over the course of his long life, had brought him adventure and adversity in roughly equal measure—and often at the same time. Just now, it caused him to pause partway through the story he was telling and begin thrashing against his shoulder harness as he wrestled the phone from his pants pocket, abruptly curious to see who had called him earlier, while they were still humming along on pavement. It was Jimmy Dunlevy—which was unusual and therefore a surprise. Jimmy had left a text message: *Need to talk to you about Argentina. Need to talk to you about J. T. Allman.*

"Hmm," said Vincent.

Argentina: South American country with fine fly fishing—as long as one didn't mind that the trout were not native to its rivers.

J. T. Allman: Reclusive rich guy, getting far on in years now. Global wildlife conservationist. Passionate angler. Owned ranches everywhere, including a vast one in Argentina. A river ran through it.

By then, Vincent and Sean—Master Maine Fishing Guide Sean Rideout—were shuddering down a muddy gravel track so far up-country that cell reception would be unreliable. It was likely no use trying to call him back. Anyway, it was only Dunlevy.

"Dunlevy," said Vincent, toggling the phone in his hand.

Sean grunted. He curled one edge of his upper lip and kept his eyes on the rutted road.

"Something about Argentina."

Sean whispered a curse and jerked the wheel to avoid a pair of yellow rocks that erupted like fangs from the roadbed ahead of them.

Dunlevy: Vincent had hired him green, right out of journalism school, to work as his associate editor, back when Vincent was running the magazine—a decade and a half ago now when not only did magazines still exist but people thought they were important. Smart, Dunlevy. Decent writer. Halfway decent fisherman. More than a bit of a wiseass. After their magazine ceased publication, Vincent started teaching college, and Dunlevy ... drifted back out West to spend several years doing this and that before eventually launching a fly-fishing website, which was connected in some way to a fly-fishing podcast, which was connected in some way to several fly-fishing social media accounts, which in turn were connected to a tangle of things online that Vincent not only did not completely understand but also did not care about. He hoped Jimmy was making a living from it all, at least.

Vincent himself, as a writer and editor: through and through still hopelessly loyal to and enamored of the idea of print on paper. An armored knight in the age of the longbow and therefore—as he well understood—a tragic and fading figure. So be it.

One of Vincent's finest moments as an editor: giving his magazine's annual conservation award to J. T. Allman. Allman had applied rotenone to thirty miles of a highly regarded trout creek that ran through his Montana property. Caused every single brown trout, rainbow trout, and bastardized rainbow/cutthroat hybrid trout in that creek to turn its pale belly to the Montana sky. Replaced them all with pure Westslope cutthroat trout—the fish that had evolved in the Rocky Mountains, that belonged in those sacred aboriginal waters. In the wake of Allman's award, a hail of hate mail poured in from anglers who had enjoyed fishing for those alien species. They called Allman a Nazi. They called Vincent a communist. But Vincent stood strong and weathered it. He came out of it a better editor. A more committed conservationist. A tougher person. He never learned what Allman thought of all the turmoil. Meanwhile, in Allman's stream, absent brown trout constantly bullying them and eating all their food and without rainbow trout constantly having sex with them, the cutthroat trout survived and thrived. It was glorious. It was also a very long time ago.

"Anyway," Vincent said as he jammed the phone back into his pocket. "Remind me, now: What I was telling you?" Sean filled his cheeks with air and gave him a sideways look.

Vincent outwaited him, and finally, after the weight of silence and expectation finally tipped the scales, Sean exhaled and said, "You were saying some shit about how your subconscious mind is a subterranean river, with brook trout swimming all through it."

"Yes. And so, the best illustration of that was this dream I had. A long time ago. After my father died."

"We're about two miles from the bridge," Sean said. "I'm thinking we'll start out with a two-fly rig. Elk Hair Caddis with a Pheasant Tail dropper."

"Brookies were the first fish my father taught me to catch when I was just a kid. I became imprinted on them. They became an actual part of me. He wasn't a fly fisherman. We caught them on garden hackle. But, still."

"You could write all this down," Sean suggested. "Like you used to. Then I could read it . . . or not."

"Anyway, this dream. Exactly a year to the night he died. I woke up—in the dream—and I was in the house where I grew up. I went to the window and looked out. Back lawn, instead of being a back lawn, was a pond."

"Prone to flooding, no doubt?"

"No! Always dry as a bone. Not a big pond. Not a deep pond. You could still see the tips of the green grass poking through the surface. But, water standing on it. The surface quivered like quicksilver. It reflected the clouds. Like never before and never again."

"So, I'm employing my psychotic powers here . . . and I'm gonna predict that in this dream you went and got your fly rod."

"I *did* get my fly rod. Strung it up. Tied on an Adams. Size 16, as I remember. Greased it up. Made a cast, landed that little Adams right out there in the middle of a cloud with barely a ripple, and out of nowhere—out of the wet lawn—up comes a snout and a brook trout takes the fly. Brought him in; ten inches, maybe eleven. Nice for a brookie. The most vivid spots I'd ever seen on a fish. Yellow and red; brilliant blue halos around the red ones. Glowing. Shimmering. Otherworldly. When I put him back into the water, it wasn't like he swam off. He just vanished. I mean, it was like he dematerialized back into that flooded grass."

"And you cast again."

"Of course I did. And another fish. Same size. Same eerie iridescence. Same spooky disappearance when I released him."

"In all the fairy tales, magic always happens in threes," Sean said. He allowed himself a twitch of a smile.

"That's right. Caught the third fish. Just the same as the other two, and when I put it back, a little tremble of its tail and then, *poof.* After that, I reeled up and went into the house. And there, waiting for me in the living room—my childhood living room—there were three beings. Three supernatural beings. *Luminous* beings sitting side by side on the couch. No hair at all on their heads or their faces; I couldn't tell whether they were male or female. All three wore matching robes that were the same pattern and color of a brook trout's skin. Each one held a scepter in their hand—although I had never seen scepters like these before."

Sean couldn't suppress a snort of laughter. "You've made a study of scepters?"

"Each scepter was a golden bamboo fly rod—a short one, maybe six feet—each rod with different colored wraps: one with red wraps, one with yellow wraps, one with blue wraps. Each one attached to a jewel-encrusted fly reel."

"Must've cost some money, those reels." Vincent ignored him.

"Right away I knew who these beings were. I knew *what* they were. I said to them, 'Where did you come from?'"

"And the being on the left—the one with the red-wrapped fly rod—answered, 'We came from the water.'"

"I asked, 'But where did the water come from?'"

"And the being on the right—blue rod wraps—answered, 'The water comes from the earth.'"

"And so, I said, 'But there's never been water where the water is now. When there is no water, where do you go?'"

"And the luminous being in the middle, the one with the yellow-wrapped rod, they looked at the luminous being to their right, and then

4

they looked at the luminous being to their left. And then the one in the middle said to me, 'We can't tell you that.'"

"And I said, 'You have to tell me. I *need* to know.'"

"And at that, they all three shook their shiny heads. And the one in the middle told me, 'If you *really* need to know, you have two choices. Your first choice is as follows: it is written that in the river, there are words beneath the rocks. Keep looking.'"

"I said, 'That would take a long time.'"

"He said, 'The second choice is . . . wait until you see your father. Then ask *him*.'"

"I said, 'My father's been dead for a year.'"

"He said, 'Those are the choices; choose one, choose both, or choose none. Whichever way, it is not for us to tell you.' Then they all three vanished into the air, the same way those three trout dematerialized into the water."

They juddered along in silence. Sean, his expression flinty once again, finally said, "Is that it?"

"What do you mean, is that *it*? What do you think?"

"What do I think?" Sean paused for a long moment, and Vincent began to wonder whether he would answer his own question. Finally, Sean said, "I guess I think a couple of things. The first one is, what the fuck have you been smoking?"

Vincent laughed and was about to respond when Sean continued, "But to be honest, the second thing is that, once you've heard one fly fisherman's story about his dead dad, you've really heard them all. Come to think of it, same goes for dead brothers, dead dogs, and dead best fishing buddies. If you ever wind up writing anything else ever again, don't do that. Fish some new water. Don't keep rowing the boat back up the river."

After Vincent had blinked away his astonishment, he said, "I can't say that I was asking you for a literary critique . . . of my dream. Nonetheless, thanks for your advice."

"I mean it. Give us something without a bunch of boo-hoo dripping off of it. And how about some *sex*, for Christ's sake? How come fishing stories never have any sex?"

"Sean, it was a dream, not a first draft."

Sean took one hand from the wheel and lifted it into the air. "*Life* is a first draft," he said.

Vincent snickered and was about to ask him what the hell he knew about first drafts in the first place when ahead of them loomed the half-rotted wooden bridge that was their destination.

On all the maps, the gravel-bottomed, tannin-tinted stream had a name, but Vincent and Sean never spoke it, even to each other. They did have words for each of the stream's discrete and singular features—its pools, its runs, its riffles—but these were names that had never been put to paper, which they themselves had conjured through a blend of long familiarity and imagination and which therefore comprised a litany, an incantation, that served only to deepen rather than unmask the mystery of the stream. Just upstream of the bridge was the First Pool—which they never fished because it sat within view of the derelict bridge and the nearly abandoned gravel road. Beyond the First Pool in ascending order: the Road Riffle, the Boulder Pool, the Long Riffle, the Hot Corner, Leaning Tree, the Glide, the Black Run, the Alder Tunnel, the Short Riffle, the Pocket, the High Bank, the Bend, the Blackfly Pool, the Top Run, and finally, at the end of every upstream quest, the Meeting Pool, where two tea-colored brooks that spilled from swamps and springs to the northeast and the northwest came eddying together to give birth to the stream.

They loved this stream because there were brook trout in it, there had always been brook trout, and there had never been anything but brook trout. The trout were not large; any specimen that reached a length in double digits they considered a good one (most were smaller). But these were fish that unquestionably belonged here, the ones whose ancestors had remained behind in the barren wake of retreating glaciers and had gone on to swim and spawn through the millennia as all around them feathery, gray-green lichens took hold on the naked, ice-scoured bed-rock, only to be overtaken by emerald mosses—which themselves were succeeded by an eruption of grasses that carpeted a broad and welcoming path for the forests that rose and fell and changed and rose again . . . all amid thousands of years of flooding and droughts and hard, snow-blasted freezes that sometimes lasted for almost a year, and the jaws of myriad, still-evolving predators and the ravenous claws and beaks of birds and the apocalyptic feet of mammoths and the sharp hooves of migrating caribou and solitary, plodding moose and the woven fish traps and stone spear-points of the First peoples, who passed through from the North and the West in wave after wave, and, finally, the depredations and degradations of the Final people: the clear-cutters and the gravel-road builders. And the anglers.

While in many other waters populations of brook trout had faded and been replaced, in this fortunate flowage, the cycle of unending challenges seemed only to have made each generation of spotted fish a little stronger and a bit better suited to survival in this specific place—where they fit so well and belonged so completely that each individual was a living mani-festation of the stream itself—of its amber flow and the sound of its water in the riffles and drops, and the wind bending the alders along its winding banks, and the shadows in its depths and the transient fingers of sunlight that reached down to its bed of dark and shifting gravel, and its swamps and its unseen icy springs and the whispering forest all around.

Each season, Vincent and Sean fished the stream throughout a single day—fished it hard and thoroughly, and then they rested it for the remainder of the year. Rather than each of them carrying a rod and leapfrogging one another from pool to upstream pool the way two dry-fly anglers would do on almost any other small river or creek, here they fished side by side and took turns casting with a single seven-and-a-half-foot, four-weight F. E. Thomas split-cane fly rod that Sean had inherited from his father. Although they knew that other people occasionally vis-ited the place—they sometimes found tangles of discarded monofilament spinning line and Styrofoam worm containers and other trash near the pool by the bridge—the stream had no paths along its banks, and it was a difficult wade, and in all their years of coming, they had never encoun-tered another angler.

They parked near the wooden bridge and tugged on their waders and their wading boots, and then Vincent walked out onto the bridge to watch the hypnotic spurl of the water as it passed beneath him while

Sean rigged their rod. To himself, Vincent recited what he could recall of one of his favorite literary passages, from Cormac McCarthy's *The Road*:

> *Once there were brook trout in the streams. You could see them standing in the amber current where the white edges of their fins wimpled softly in the flow. They smelled of moss in your hand. On their backs were vermiculate patterns that were maps of the world in its becoming. Maps and mazes. Of a thing which could not be put back. Not be made right again. In the deep glens where they lived all things were older than man and they hummed of mystery.*

To the tippet, Sean tied a bushy, tan caddisfly, a pattern that, with its flaring wing of elk-hair bristles, invariably put Vincent in mind of an old-fashioned shaving brush. To the bend of the hook, Sean knotted another light length of monofilament, and to its end he attached a smaller dropper fly. The dropper was a dull-colored nymph with a wing case and tail crafted with fibers from a pheasant's feather—a fly tied to represent the larva of an aquatic insect—and just below its hook eye, it bore a tiny brass bead to give it weight that would pull it below the surface of the water.

Once the rigging was accomplished, the two anglers put on their hats, slipped on their worn fishing vests, and clambered down the sloping bank below the bridge. Their boots in two feet of water, with branch tips of dense alder trees brushing their shoulders as they moved, they skirted the edge of the First Pool and worked their way up to the Road Riffle. Sean made the first cast, and no sooner did the flies touch the water than a nine-inch brook trout lifted from the bottom to hammer the dry fly. They whooped, and, after a brief fight, Vincent netted and released the fish. Then it was his turn, and he hooked another, slightly smaller trout that came swirling after the nymph. Sean caught one more trout in the Road Riffle, then they moved upstream, catching trout as they went.

They found four trout in the Boulder Pool—two for each of them, with Sean's eleven-incher, caught on the caddisfly, the largest. In this way they worked toward the Meeting Pool, the rod changing hands each time a fish was caught. Within the leafy, tangled tube of the Alder Tunnel, a conventional cast of any kind was impossible—not an overhead, a side-arm, or even a roll cast could go forth without wrapping in branches. But there had always been a good fish or two in that mysterious, shadowy spot, and so rather than skirting it and moving up to the relative openness and easiness of the Short Riffle, they took turns twanging out a bow-and-arrow cast: they would draw back the leader like a bowstring until the tip of the rod arced severely and then release it so that, in springing straight again, the rod tip rocketed the flies upstream, the leader and several feet of fly line unrolling behind them. In this way, they each took a decent brook trout in the Alder Tunnel.

They caught fish in every one of their named places, and they lifted none of them from the water but always removed the hook while cradling the trout in the cold flow of its element. One of them would gently hold the fish while the other slipped the barbless hook from its jaw, then the two of them would quietly celebrate the trout, honoring its vitality and its beauty, until it finally and suddenly realized it was free and, with a frenzied thrash of its tail, shot down to the depths. So perfectly matched were these trout to the colors and the shifting patterns of gravel and light at the bottom of the stream that rather than escaping back into the flow, they seemed to dissolve in it, vanishing as completely as had the three trout in Vincent's long-ago dream.

It was a near-perfect day until they reached the High Bank. It was there that, just after Sean had finished untangling the two-fly rig from an alder branch that Vincent had snagged on his backcast, they heard movement and turned their eyes to the top of the bank. There on the High Bank stood not the first but the first *three* other anglers they had ever encountered on this stream: three much younger fishermen . . . three fishing *Bros*, each Bro with a backpack rather than a fishing vest, each wearing a longish Bro beard. There was Black Beard Bro, Brown Beard Man-Bun Bro, and Little Runty Red Beard Bro. Black Beard Bro and Brown Beard Man-Bun Bro had their cell phones out—these people videoed *everything*—and they were recording Sean and Vincent. As for Red Beard Bro . . . a set of large white ear buds bloomed beneath his hat, and he was jerking his head and twitching his shoulders to a tune that only he could hear. At the feet of Brown Beard Man-Bun Bro sat a blue fabric beer cooler that bulged like a tick. These people *drank* while they fly fished.

Most worrisome: their fly rods were not rigged; instead, each Bro clenched a fistful of multipiece graphite fly-rod sections, suggesting that rather than fishing the entire stream as they followed it toward its sources, they were likely headed to one particular spot on the stream—the stream's *last* fishable place before it divided out into the swamps and the best place on the entire stream in terms of size and number of fish.

Vincent heard Sean swear under his breath. He felt a vague tug against his right wading boot, and when he looked down, he saw that, following his last cast, as he'd shifted his attention to the Bros on the bank, the flies and the fly line had drifted back down to him, the line somehow wrapping his lower shin before passing between his legs. Line now hung from him, twin V-wakes coming off the flies as they dragged in the current twenty feet downstream—and this awkwardness was what the Bros were recording with their cell phones.

Abruptly, Red Beard Bro pirouetted away from the stream and crashed off into the brush. Although they could no longer see him, they continued to hear him and to see the tops of alders swaying above him as he thrashed his way down from the high bank and continued upstream. The other two Bros lowered their phones.

"Hail fellows well met," called Black Beard Bro, a bright grin slicing his face. Sean and Vincent continued to stare. After a moment, Black Beard added, "Say, is this a bamboo fly rod which I see before me?"

Vincent glanced down at the elegant rod. Sean said, "Thomas split cane. Might be worth more than your car."

Brown Beard Man-Bun said, "Well, he's got a Tesla, so . . ."

"Well maybe two of his cars, then." The two Bros laughed. Sean did not.

Black Beard said, "Seriously though, I've always wanted to cast one. Never had the pleasure."

"Is that so?" said Sean. There was an uneasy silence.

Black Beard said, "We read about this brook on the forum. Decided to give it a try."

Sean, after the shock had worn off, said, "On a forum, did you?"

Vincent noticed that the water around their feet had grown cloudy. He turned his eyes upstream to the bottom of the Bend, and there stood Red Beard Bro, in the middle of the stream, dancing. His shuffling feet kicked up a ribbon of silt that wound its way down to them.

"Hey!" yelled Vincent.

Sean saw what was happening, and he too yelled. "Hey, asshole!"

Vincent felt the loop of fly line tighten against his shin, and when he looked downstream, he saw that a small brook trout had hooked itself on the nymph and was now doing a dance of its own as it struggled.

Back upstream, Red Beard Bro laughed and waved, obviously unable to hear them over the sound of his music. Only after Sean raised his hands above his head and scissored them maniacally did he unplug an earbud and cup a hand to his ear.

"Quit that shit!"

Black Beard Bro had his phone in hand again, and he was videoing as Vincent hunched down over the water, rod tucked beneath his arm, and began awkwardly drawing in the little trout, hand over hand.

"Bro," Brown Beard Man-Bun Bro said to Sean. "Tucker's only trying to help. He's only booting a few bugs off the bottom in order to get the fish turned on for you."

Sean said, "We don't want Tucker's fucking help. We don't need Tucker to turn the fucking fish on for us."

"And it seems to me like he's done you a good turn. I'd bet that's the first fish you venerable gents have caught all day long."

"That's not the way we fish. That's not the way *anybody* fishes. You guys need to get lost."

"I believe the two words you're actually struggling so hard to find right now might be 'thank you.'"

"Actually, the two words I'm finding for you right now . . ."

"Sean," Vincent said. He was feeling a little sick to his stomach. So much wrong here, all at once. As he removed the hook from the tiny trout's mouth, he was imagining things getting very ugly. "Let's let it go.

These guys are here; there's no rolling that back. And they're different. They have different ideas. He likely did think he was helping."

Sean dropped his gaze from the men on the bank. "Fucking clowns," he muttered.

"Yeah."

When the accidental fish had been freed and they returned their eyes to the bank, the two Bros and their cooler were gone. They looked upstream, and Red Beard Bro was gone as well. But the three of them were not *really* gone, they knew.

Dreading what lay ahead of them, they resumed moving upstream, bypassing the Bend, which had been ruined for them by Red Beard Bro and his shuffling dance. They caught a couple in the Blackfly Pool, three in the Top Run. Ten minutes after their final fish in the Top Run, Sean reeled up and said, "Maybe they went right past it and kept going."

"They'd have to be blind," Vincent responded. "And stupid."

"Maybe they just kept walking right past it and fell into a swamp and drowned." Vincent drew in a ragged breath. His stomach was still queasy.

At that point, they would have been wise to go back to the bridge. But they couldn't help themselves. The horror that awaited them ahead was irresistible; it drew them onward. As quietly as they were able, because they now were the interlopers, they approached the Meeting Pool. They heard the Bros laughing from a long way off, and as they came within sight, they stopped and knelt in the woods. Brown Beard and Red Beard were sitting on a bleached tree trunk that rested parallel to the stream. Each held a can of beer, and the two of them were throwing out wry comments as they observed Black Beard working the pool with an extremely long graphite rod. It was a ten-footer at least.

"That's not a fly line coming off of that thing," Sean said after a moment.

"Nope. Looks like monofilament."

At the end of each downstream swing, Black Beard lifted his arm and passed the rod over his head to plop a team of weighted flies back above him. Then, keeping the rod high and the line taut, he followed the swinging flies with the rod tip. The visible part of his line consisted of three colored sections of mono—green, yellow, red, maybe six feet in all—knotted between a short, transparent leader at the terminal end and stouter, colorless mono that ran all the way back through the line guides and disappeared into his reel. All in all, he had no more than a dozen feet of line off the rod tip. After every couple of casts, Black Beard shifted his position in the pool.

"He's not even *casting*," Sean said quietly.

"Nope."

"He's just dunking the damn flies."

"He is."

Sean clawed a pair of compact binoculars from his vest and lifted them to his eyes. After a minute, he said, "Yup. As we might have guessed, we've got what appears to be a red Squirmy Wormy as the point fly and a chartreuse thing that looks to be maybe a Mop Fly as the dropper."

"In other words, a rubber tube and a piece of carpet fuzz."

Sean said, "So, what an awesome day this has been. Not only do we learn that our undercover brook trout stream has been burned on a forum, and not only do we have to run into other anglers here for the first time in twenty years, but . . . those fucking anglers just have to be a fucking Three Stooges team of fucking bearded Euro-nymphers. They have to be using this ridiculous technique and this ridiculous gear that's not even real fly fishing."

Vincent was about to say, "It could hardly be worse" when Black Beard Bro jerked his fly rod skyward and yelped. The long rod bent deeply, the tip pulsing as he stripped in line, and after a minute, the fish came thrashing to the surface.

When the fight was finished and the trout lay arcing against the bankside gravel, the three Bros yipped and gathered around it like hyenas at a kill. They drew out their cell phones and videoed each other holding the fish, and they interviewed one another about the experience of having caught it. About the intense emotions each of them was feeling. Their high-fives and fist bumps were recorded for posterity and online publication. It was the best thing, the best thing ever. It was indescribable. It was *fuckinawesomebro*. Sean groaned when Red Beard Bro stared into the compound lenses of two cell phones and announced to the world the name of their stream.

To their credit, the Bros held their hostage underwater for revival between each new round of exaggerated, self-conscious celebration. When they finally released it, it still was more or less alive.

And really, Vincent found it hard to blame them very much. If he'd caught that trout, even though it had been years since he'd taken his last trophy photo, he might have wanted a picture of it. It was a fine fish. An extraordinary fish, given the water it had come from. It had to be a good sixteen inches—definitely larger than any brook trout either he or Sean had taken in twenty years of fishing this very stream.

Sean gave him a nudge. "Come on," he said. "It's time for us to go."

CHAPTER TWO

The Magic of Three

VINCENT WENT HOME THAT NIGHT TO AN ENJOYABLY EMPTY HOUSE. Caroline was away with her friend, Naya. The two of them were on one of their semiannual trips together—this most recent one a cruise around a constellation of Caribbean islands. Eating. Shopping. Whale watching. Swimming in some lagoon with a herd of dog-paddling pigs. That was the deal: Vincent got to fish—a pastime to which Caroline was, at best, indifferent, and Caroline got to take cruises and spa vacations with her friend—which was fine, as even the thought of participating himself in any sort of conventional tourist activities made Vincent's stomach slither. Naya had inherited a lot of money, and she was generous with it, so Caroline's trips didn't even put much of a dent in their bank account. A great arrangement all around.

His teaching year having ended a couple of weeks back, Vincent had been spending his solo time fishing, eating poorly, visiting pubs, and fishing again. This was the season when striped bass and shad were following herring up the rivers from the ocean. In addition, in the lake, right off the dock behind his house, there was decent angling to be had for several scaly invasive species. In Caroline's absence, he had been taking full advantage.

The following morning Dunlevy called again. Vincent had not forgotten Dunlevy's phone message; he just had been in no hurry to respond to it.

"Jimmy," said Vincent. "I was just on my way out onto the pond."

"Chief," said Jimmy as he invariably greeted Vincent in spite of the fact that the two of them had not worked together for almost fifteen years. "How are things? All good?"

"Never better. You?"

"Perfect. Getting married next year."

"Hah! About time. Congratulations."

"Listen, Vincent. A little bit of a hurry here . . . we can catch up later. I'm in touch right now because I've got kind of an idea thing for you. I think you'll like it. Tell me, do you still speak Spanish?"

"Jimmy, Spanish is one of the subjects I teach."

"Yeah, I thought so. That's what I thought. Great. So, you know, one of your stories—you always told the best fishing stories—but the one I always remember—well *one* of the ones—is about the landlocked salmon. About how the first fish you caught on a fly you tied yourself was a big landlocked salmon." A warm feeling filled Vincent.

"Not *all* that big, really. Maybe a little over twenty. The fly . . . was a Gray Ghost. And that was a long time ago; we're talking around thirty-five years. And that was here in Maine. And so, what's the connection . . ."

". . . and you hooked this monster right in the narrows of that lake—what's the name of it? The one you took me to that time, north of Augusta? It's been so long—and right in front of that sporting camp there. And while you're fighting the fish, word gets out, and unbeknownst to you, the dining room of the sporting camp empties out, and when you finally scoop that salmon into your net, you hear applause and—you look up onto the bank behind you, and there's a couple dozen people gathered along the road looking down at you—an entire audience—all of them clapping for your accomplishment."

Vincent shivered; after all this time, this remained a major experience in his career as an angler. Then came a flicker of sadness as he realized that, at this point, Dunlevy was probably the only other person who remembered it—and Dunlevy's memory was secondhand, through Vincent's own story.

"Like I said. A long time ago."

"Well, you know, they've got landlockeds in Argentina."

"They do, or at least, they did. I'm not sure what's going on there now."

"No, supposedly they still do. In the Río Perca. And they grow really huge down there, for some reason—like silver submarines. Some they've caught have been almost as big as regular sea-run Atlantic salmon."

"I didn't know where, exactly. And I haven't heard any accounts of really big ones recently. Not in years, in fact. And so . . ."

"And the salmon eggs they took there in the early nineteen hundreds to get the population started? All originally from Maine."

"Makes sense. Where else would they come from?"

"Well, so, get this. Río Perca Lodge—it's on the opposite side of the river from the big ranch J. T. Allman owns down there—and their U.S. booking agency told me they'd host, a . . . they'll host a writer next season at the lodge. And of course, I right away thought of you. How cool would that be: a Maine fisherman with these incredible memories of Maine landlocked salmon fishing traveling to Argentina to catch a fish that originally *came* from Maine . . . you could do that thing you're so good at. The thing you always did when you wrote travel pieces for the magazine. And . . . extra points, *big* extra points, if you manage to score an interview with Allman."

"I thought Allman was spending all his time in Africa lately. Shuffling rhinos from one country to another or some shit. And, *what* thing I did? What thing I'm so good at?"

"You know . . . what I mean is . . . you could—like nobody else, in fact—always make trying to catch one fish seem so fucking . . . important. Even to people who didn't care about fishing. Like your heart would literally break, and your entire life would take a dark turn if you didn't get it done. They were never *just* fishing stories, and that's what I'm looking for on this."

There was a long silence between them. Eventually, Dunlevy said, "Cards on the table here: I think my website and the podcast stand to get some Argentina sponsorship money out of it. I mean, not enough to *pay* you anything other than the trip itself. But Aerolíneas Argentinas is willing to comp business-class airfare provided we give them a mention or two. When's the last time you flew business class, Chief?"

Another silence before Vincent drew in a shallow breath and said, "A *writer*? Since when do you use actual writers, anyway? On your . . . *thing*, your *things*, whatever the fuck they are?"

"What do you mean? Of course, there'd be some writing involved. For just one example, you'd have to loosely script some scenes, you know? Sure, you'd need to video pretty much everything you did. And you'd need to have somebody else—your guide or whoever—video *you* from time to time. There's where the writing comes in: asides to the camera and so forth. But all you'd require equipment-wise would be a cell phone with good photo lenses. Maybe a tripod to attach it to sometimes. A selfie stick, perhaps. And if you don't have an up-to-date cell phone . . ."

"Jimmy. What I'm trying to say is, I'm a writer, not a fucking porn star." Dunlevy laughed—laughter in which Vincent thought he detected a tone of derision. Condescension.

"Listen, Chief. Not for nothing: like you always told me, you can't roll back a river. By which I believe you meant you can't return to what you remember as a better time; you just have to keep riding downstream. But . . . and I hope you don't take this the wrong way . . . I don't think you're too old to learn a few new things. You're not too old to row back out into the current and keep on floating, if you know what I mean. I think you still have some important things to say; you just need to start saying them in a more contemporary way." A current of anger surged through Vincent and almost erupted from him in the form of words, but he fought it back. There was no gain in that. He kept his voice calm.

"And you know what, Jimmy? Fishing-wise, what I've cared about most for a long time is *native* fish. Appreciating them in the aquatic environments in which they evolved and where they belong. Fish are worth encountering and appreciating so long as they're an organic part of an ecosystem that shaped them and which they themselves have helped to shape. As much as I love landlocked salmon, in Argentina, landlocked salmon are none of those things."

"And you know what, Chief? As skillful a communicator as you are—as skillful a *teacher* as you are, you could weave that exact lesson into this Argentina story. While you're having a good time catching fish, you could explain the whole ecological galaxy: native fish versus wild, non-native fish, and both of those versus hatchery fish . . ."

"I'm a *writer*, not a *communicator*. And I don't think so. If you were talking about something natural . . . roosterfish in Mexico, maybe, or permit in Belize, I might be a little more tempted. Provided that the airfare. . . ."

"Come on, Chief, you know how this business works: the assignment I've got for you is the assignment I've got for you. And I'm excited about it, to tell you the truth. I'm pumped. Listen, I'll give you some time to think. I could send somebody else, but you're the perfect one. I don't like to think of anyone else doing this."

"Thanks anyway, Jim. Congratulations on the upcoming marriage. From the photos you've posted and everything . . . you're a lucky man. Beyond that, I won't give you any advice; you wouldn't listen anyway."

"I'll shoot you and Caroline an invitation. *We* will. Bozeman. It'll be a good excuse for you to come to Montana again. Afterwards, fish the Madison, maybe. Not with me though, because . . . honeymoon, you know. . . ."

"Yeah, okay. Thank you, Jimmy."

"But, hey. This trip I'm talking about is not until next April—Argentina, I mean—so you've got some time to reconsider."

"Terrific. Not that I need time to reconsider."

"I'm betting you'll change your mind. I'll leave the door open for a while."

"Up to you. Good talking. I miss you, sometimes. Boat's waiting at the end of the dock; speaking of doors, I'm on my way out of one."

While talking to Dunlevy, he'd heard a message zing into his phone. As soon as the call was over, he checked his messages and saw the new one was from Caroline:

Hi! Back tomorrow late PM. If you're not out fishing or pubbing it, we've got something important we need to discuss with you. It would be good if you were home.

We. The word ignited his imagination. Anxiety, followed by a bonfire in his brain. Heat that sizzled down the fuse of his spine and into his loins. A conversation, with him, that Naya was going to be part of.

This was an echo of something that had happened previously, a long time before, back when he'd still had the magazine. The two women had both been there at the house with him, having just that evening returned from a weekend trip. The three of them had carried drinks out onto the screened-in back porch where, after a few minutes, Caroline and Naya exchanged a mysterious look. Naya had stepped through the groaning screen door and in her bare feet padded over the lawn through the darkness and out to the end of the dock. For an instant, she illuminated her face with the flare from a lighter, and then all Vincent could see of her was her vague silhouette and the slow, trembling rise and fall of her glowing cigarette.

He'd been afraid at first. He wondered whether certain minor dissatisfactions with him that Caroline had been expressing recently might have accumulated to a point at which she was ready to ask him for a separation. A divorce, even, with Naya there in the house with them for moral support during a difficult conversation. His fear only increased when Caroline reached to take his hand.

She said, "Naya's thinking of having a baby."

"Oh," said Vincent. Although Vincent and Caroline had met many of Naya's male companions over the years, she was not currently in a relationship with anyone. Had not been in a relationship with anyone for at least a year at that point. Then, because he sensed that something further was expected of him, he added, "She'd be a good mother, I think."

"Well, so. She's wondering—she asked me, and *we're* wondering—if you might not be willing to be the . . . to donate . . . to, to, to . . . furnish . . . the seed for her child." *Furnish* the seed. Vincent's head whirled. He set down his drink, and his hand drifted to his forehead.

Such a sudden torrent going through him. When he continued to be unable to speak, Caroline said, "It's a big thing to think about, I know."

"And you, you'd be okay with this?"

"That's what I told her, yes. As long as it was okay with you." His hand found his drink, and he drank until the ice cubes rattled against his front teeth.

He drew in a breath and said, "We don't even have our own kid. We decided that. A long time ago."

"I'm still okay with it."

"So, if Naya . . . you wouldn't have . . . strange feelings?"

"No."

"And so." He paused to suck in another breath. "And so . . . if . . . would I be the . . . would I be considered to be . . . would I have the *role* . . ."

"None of that has been decided. I guess we'd all three need to talk about it, wouldn't we? But . . . I think I'm hearing you say that you're willing to think about it?"

"To think about it," he said. "It's a lot, all at once."

"It is," she said. "I know."

They sat in silence for a time. Out at the end of the dock, Naya lit another cigarette, and Vincent watched as her ember rose and fell and rose again. His mind continued to whirlpool, unexpected things rising to the surface. He found himself thinking about how, in spite of the fact that he and Caroline were perfectly happy—arguably happier—without children, there might be something very satisfying in having a tiny, somewhat darker version of himself out here in the world. A vague vision came to him: casting lessons off the dock, his hand surrounding a tiny fist that was wrapped around the cork handle of a fly rod. Further emotional swirling, and what next emerged was this: he'd always found Naya attractive. If he were being honest with himself . . . he'd entertained himself with fantasies about her. And the fact that, of all the men in the world, including all the husbands of all her other friends and all the men in New York City, where Naya lived, who were husbands of no one . . . she had chosen Vincent . . . did that not mean that she imagined him in a particular way—that a certain physical longing—perhaps unspoken, even to Caroline—drove her to crave a child of her own that would also be his creation? Feeling slightly guilty, he looked over at his wife—who smiled a reassuring smile and gave his hand a squeeze.

Of methods, for what they were requesting of him, there were only two, as far as he knew. One being clinical. The other being biblical. He found it potentially significant that Caroline had not spoken on this matter. One would think a wife might do that, in an initial conversation. Unless . . . that was yet another thing to talk about. Something that needed to be worked out, to the satisfaction of everyone. His tumbling imagination tumbled forth a warm bed in which he was nestled between the two of them. He found himself beginning to get an erection.

Naya finished her cigarette and came back to the porch. He glanced up at her and gave her a tight, self-conscious smile, and from the corner of his eye, he saw Caroline give her a single, slight nod. Looking directly at Vincent, Naya smiled.

"Well, I'm tired," Naya said. "I'm going to turn in. Goodnight . . . all." As she went past Vincent, she brushed her hand against his shoulder. Then she entered the house and made her way up the stairs to the guest bedroom.

Ten minutes later, Caroline went up to bed as well, leaving Vincent on the porch to deal with an erection that failed to subside.

Naya drove back to New York the following afternoon. As days passed, Vincent, for his part, grew increasingly enthusiastic. His imagination, when he wasn't thinking about helping to raise a little fisherman, was pornographic. Of course, alone now with Caroline in their home, he made no further mention of what had been discussed. He knew it was not his place to do so—that seeming at all eager rather than merely high-minded and generous might be a cause for suspicion, even alarm, on her part. He needed to wait. He needed to pretend he'd almost forgotten about it.

But more days passed, then weeks. Then months. Caroline spoke frequently to Naya, but as far as Vincent knew, the subject of his potential fertility never arose again. Ever, in any context. Caroline did not bring it up with Vincent, and Naya apparently did not return to the topic with Caroline. Or did she? Something had changed, and Vincent ached to know what it was. Meanwhile, time continued to pass without Naya announcing a pregnancy or plans to seek a pregnancy and without Vincent's learning what had happened. He went years without assembling the courage to ask Caroline about it, while it seemingly never occurred to her to broach the topic on her own. Had he done something wrong—proven himself unworthy in some way? Or, worse than unworthy, *unfit*?

With a shudder of horror and shame, Vincent recalled that, as the three of them were preparing breakfast on the morning following that brain-spinning conversation with Caroline, Naya had handed him a jar of applesauce, then stood watching as, in spite of many desperate, grunting attempts, he'd been unable to twist the lid off of it. That little twitch of her lower lip—had that been the dawning of disappointment? Of disillusionment? Of contempt sliding toward rejection? Or could the answer have been as simple as that one of them had changed her mind? Why hadn't they ever *talked* to him? He recalled that, by the following summer, he had begun to wonder whether he hadn't merely fallen asleep on the porch that previous summer's night and experienced an extraordinarily vivid middle-aged midsummer night's dream.

Now, far downriver from that place in time, it was yet another midsummer, and Caroline's text message was causing Vincent to dream again. Naya was beyond the age when most women would be thinking about trying to have a child. Nonetheless, who knew? Nonetheless, whatever thoughts or feelings had driven her to imagine giving birth to his baby all those years ago . . . perhaps they were still lingering though no longer necessarily connected to literal reproduction. Perhaps back then, the two women had at least briefly collaborated and now were collaborating again . . . in a fantasy similar to his own . . . of the three of them sharing affection between a set of sheets. Why not? Wilder, more exciting things than that happened in the world every single day—just not to Vincent. Just not yet, in any case.

The day after he'd talked to Dunlevy and then received Caroline's intriguing message, in order to kill the time before Caroline and Naya came home, he once again gathered his fishing gear and climbed off the dock and into his green aluminum Jon boat. He clipped in a freshly charged battery and started the electric motor and buzzed his way out to his favorite island and its surrounding boulders and weed beds.

It was ironic: much as Vincent prized fish that lived and reproduced in their own aboriginal environment, the lake beside which he made his home had long been a murky aquarium of the alien and the ugly. He'd known about that even before he and Caroline bought the place. Any trout that still swam there was a pale and nearly finless product of the concrete raceways in the state's fish-hatchery system. Meanwhile, the predominant, naturally reproducing game fish was the largemouth bass—a green, scaly invader from the South whose primary virtue was that, unlike the trout, it thrived in dirty and overfertilized waters—an enthusiastic denizen of environmental ruins.

Yes, a lot of anglers, including many of Vincent's neighbors, loved the largemouth—particularly the majority of those who were spin or bait fishers rather than fly anglers. The virtues of the bass—in their estimation—were that not only was it plentiful, but it grew to good size, it was indiscriminately voracious and therefore easy to catch, and it generally provided some excitement by jumping a couple of times when hooked. The bass had become so abundant in Vincent's lake that on one day each summer, contestants in a national largemouth tournament came swooping in from the direction of the public boat launch, the water suddenly swarming with glitzy bass boats carrying uniformed, professional spin fishermen from around the country, each angler wearing a bright ball cap and a zippered jumpsuit festooned with patches representing his myriad sponsors, each aiming to stuff the live well of his boat with heavy bass as he competed for cash prizes. Often the overpowered boats would sit rocking in the ripples just off of Vincent's back lawn, the anglers slinging their metal lures and their rubber worms directly beneath his dock. They were, to a person, very precise spin casters; Vincent had to give them that. Two or three snapping, sidearm casts followed by retrieves without a hit, and they would fire their engines and rocket off to the next likely spot. On tournament day, Vincent would sit on his screen porch with a drink in his hand, by turns amused, horrified, and—in spite of himself— impressed at the spectacle of anglers in such a rush to catch such a fish at such great expense.

Not that Vincent was above fishing frequently for largemouth himself. Not that he didn't spend a significant amount of time each winter at his fly-tying table, spinning colorfully dyed deer hair onto hooks and then trimming it down into the multicolored, tightly packed popping flies he preferred for bass fishing. Not that he didn't own a Jon boat specifically for the purpose of penetrating the weedy shallows where the largemouth were most likely to be lurking. But . . . he felt that his attitude about this kind of fishing distinguished him from many of its other practitioners. Unlike most people who fished the lakes, including the majority of his neighbors, not only did he know what largemouth were, but he also knew what they *weren't*. Whenever he found himself trapped in conversation with anyone who was actually serious about bass fishing—who was passionate about it rather than viewing it as bit of mild amusement and a convenient way to stay in tune for the kind of fishing that really counted—he not only had to be mindful of his words, but he needed to keep conscious control over his facial expressions—in particular, over the rogue right corner of his mouth, which even under the best of circumstances was often on the verge of twisting in a way that betrayed a disinterest that edged toward contempt. It would not do to have people getting the idea that he was some kind of insufferable trout snob.

The south side of the small island, with its protruding boulders and its weed beds, was his favorite spot on the lake for his least favorite fish. In deeper water, it was usually necessary to fish for them with a sinking line and a leech or a baitfish imitation, but here, he could fish the surface with his popping flies, working them among the rocks and weeds where bass lay in ambush. He anchored his boat, tied on a frog-colored popper, and with his fingers massaged a generous dollop of liquid floatant into the trimmed deer hair. He stood, spent a moment adjusting his balance in the boat, and then made a long, open-looped cast that plopped the popper into a weed bed between two rocks. Although this was dry-fly fishing, there was no need for subtle casting; largemouth were the dull thugs of the freshwater-fish world, and a splash, such as a real frog or a dragonfly might make, would actually attract rather than frighten one. After letting the fly sit for a moment, he tugged it out into a clearing, where it sat bobbing. He began stripping in line ten inches at a time, the broad, concave face of the fly noisily shoving water ahead of it with each forceful strip. His second cast landed adjacent to a rock; he stripped just once, and a largemouth rose from the depths to engulf it. Vincent laughed as the fish struggled in an arc around the boat, jumped three times, and then, in the way of largemouth, surrendered and allowed itself to be drawn to the boat and released.

Over the course of the morning and afternoon, Vincent changed flies, changed locations around the island, and ultimately netted and released seven or eight decent bass, along with a few smaller ones. In the midafternoon, he stopped for a sandwich and a soft drink, and when he resumed fishing, the action seemed to have fallen off. Things were quiet. He switched to a much smaller popper, a gaudy little bug with floppy rubber legs, and when a fish came to take it, he saw right away that it wasn't a bass. It was a black crappie, a big, dark, sunfish-looking thing, yet another invader from the South. He had heard they'd gotten into his lake, some bucket-toting idiot having dumped in at least one randy pair of them, but until this moment, he had never seen one himself. His first thought was to pitch this fish onto the island for the eagles, which was the same fate he and Sean inflicted on all the smallmouth bass they caught whenever they were out on one of the bigger rivers, fishing for trout from Sean's drift boat. "Red-eyed bastards" Sean called the small-mouths; the two of them invariably snapped their necks and threw them onto the bank to feed the birds.

Nonetheless, however satisfying it felt, at least for a moment—killing one bass that otherwise might spawn a thousand more—smallmouth infested all the rivers now; they were there to stay, just as largemouth swarmed irreversibly in so many of the lakes, and he and Sean were only kidding themselves if they ever actually believed that snuffing half a dozen smallies every time they fished actually did much to diminish the population. Likely it would be no different with the crappie; they were a species that bred furiously and doubtlessly had spread all through the entire lake by now. There would be no getting them out; extinguishing this one individual would fail to make a bit of difference, and therefore there would not be much downside to allowing the pathetic creature to keep its life. Vincent tossed the fish back into the water and watched it swim away.

By the time the sun had begun to slide behind the shoreline trees, Vincent had caught two more crappie, and he was feeling tired as well as a little bit anxious. He also felt the heat of a sunburn on the back of his neck. He motored to his dock, went into the house for a shower, and, as twilight deepened outside, whipped up a simple spaghetti for his dinner, with a bit left over in case Caroline and Naya were hungry when they came in. Afterward, he did his dishes and tidied the kitchen—all except for the empty, unrinsed spaghetti-sauce jar, which he left on the counter beside its lid as if it were an artistic display.

He decided it would be a poor strategy to drink alcohol ahead of whatever conversation among the three of them there would be, and instead, he brewed coffee and tried to read. But his concentration was poor, and eventually, he took a nighttime walk along the gravel road that intersected his driveway, then returned to the house to organize some of his fishing gear, after which he flopped onto the couch to watch part of a nature documentary on television. By coincidence, someone was interviewing a young wildlife biologist who worked for J. T. Allman. The show had to do with the North American tallgrass prairie—vanished habitat of the late, great herds of bison—and the biologist was describing, with just the hint of an accent that Vincent guessed was either German or Dutch, the Allman team's efforts to reconstruct the prairie ecosystem on one of his huge ranches out West. The goal was to end up with grasses, grazers, flowers, bugs, birds, rodents, even wolves, all working like an orchestra to restore at least a sliver of America to its long-lost purity and aboriginal innocence.

Because of his tiredness and his distraction, Vincent found himself struggling to follow what was being said on the flickering flat-screen. Eventually, he dozed.

He awoke only when automobile headlights shone through the front windows and swept all around the house. Caroline and Naya were home.

CHAPTER THREE

A World of Wounds

AT FIRST, IT WAS A DREAMLIKE REPLAY OF THAT SHIMMERING NIGHT SO many years before. Vincent and Caroline carried drinks onto the porch. A barefoot Naya padded to the end of the dock and stood smoking against a backdrop of stars.

Caroline, with a shake in her voice, said, "Vincent. What I have to tell you. I'm sure it's not going to come as a complete surprise."

"I'm listening." Vincent felt slightly sick with anticipation.

"Naya and I are a couple."

After a moment, in a flat tone, he said, "A couple of what?" Caroline drew a ragged breath.

"Oh, Vincent. We're a romantic couple. We're in love. You must have had an idea." He felt a sensation of falling. Of being upside down and grabbing at the air.

Sometime later: "Are you going to say something, Vincent?" Her voice was that thing he could hold.

He heard himself say, "Is there a place for me in there somewhere?" It came out as a whine, and he immediately hated himself for it. Felt shame. For that weakness, goddamn him. Caroline sniffled, and he looked over at her. She was touching her face with a tissue. But she was looking right at him.

"Of course you have a place. We love you, Vincent. *I* love you. But Naya and I? We're a couple."

In other words, there was a place, but there was no place.

"Wow." He finished his drink in two swallows. Went to set his glass on the little table but instead released it to crash onto the wooden floor. She reached to put her hand on his arm, but he said, "Don't do that." She drew her hand away.

He rehearsed a few further reactions that were swirling in his head. Nothing but broken nonsense. Finally, he asked her, "How long?"

"How long have we been . . . a *long* time, Vincent. At first, it was just an occasional thing. Just play. Just guilty fun. But then we fell in love. At one point long ago, we were considering having a baby together. But then, we decided against."

"That was *you* and Naya? Considering having a baby? *Together?*"

"I wish I'd been brave and . . . good enough to tell you all of this much, much earlier. I'm so very sorry if this has hurt you."

"If?"

"I'm so, so sorry, Vincent."

Naya finished her cigarette and came back onto the porch. She glanced at Caroline but did not look at Vincent. As she passed by on her way into the house, she brushed Vincent's shoulder with her fingers as she had all those years ago. Vincent shuddered. He felt his face contort. He heard Naya walk upstairs to the guest bedroom.

Vincent, a catch in his voice, said, "Well, but, are you going to keep living here?"

"Please, Vincent. How could that be?" The future emptiness spooled out to infinity in his imagination.

"Well," he said. His fingers swept the air for the drink that was no longer there. The drink he had finished before dropping the empty glass on the floor. Something was in him that wanted to come out. Was it tears? Anger? He wasn't sure. His chest felt tight; he had to work at bringing in a breath. He wanted another drink, but he thought that if he stood to get one, he might fall. Staying put seemed to be the thing to do.

"Vincent?"

"Yeah?"

"Do you ever regret that we never had children?"

After a while, she left the porch. Vincent continued to sit. Sometime during the night, he felt the will-o'-the-wisp warmth of a hope that perhaps she would change her mind. That perhaps in some way he had misheard. Misunderstood. When he finally went upstairs, he found that his bed—his and Caroline's—was empty. The door to the guest bedroom was closed.

—⟨◦⟩

Caroline went back to New York with Naya. For the rest of late spring and summer, Vincent tried to fill the hole with fishing. There were herring. By mid-June, blueback herring had almost entirely replaced the alewife herring in the rivers and streams; Vincent fished for them with a light fly rod by casting a tiny, weighted nymph downstream and across the current before stripping it through their migrating silver schools. Every so often, a herring would take the fly, and then, being a twelve-inch cousin of the giant tarpon, it would dance on the water as Vincent drew it in to release it.

With a much stouter rod—a nine-weight—he fished the bigger rivers for striped bass by swinging and stripping large flies that imitated herring, and over the course of a week, he was able to land several stripers that were nearly as long as his arm. In those same rivers, with that same rod, he would switch to a sinking-tip line and a smaller, weighted, brightly colored fly in order to take shad that had come in from the ocean to spawn.

Fishing with an eight-weight rod and a wire leader, using an assortment of baitfish flies, Vincent caught invasive, razor-toothed northern pike in streams where they had devoured most of the trout and salmon—and he murdered every murderous pike he caught.

In early July, he traveled up-country with Sean and two other friends to camp on a remote pond and fish the *Hexagenia* mayfly hatch for brook trout. Every day, in the late afternoon, after hours of relative indolence, the anglers would paddle their canoes onto the pond's reflective stillness and wait for the inch-long insects to crawl from burrows concealed in the sediment below, kick their way up through the water column, and appear as if from nowhere on the darkening mirror of the trembling surface, where each would split its way out of a too-tight jacket of larval skin and sit, nearly motionless, as its new, translucent wings dried and unfurled, soon to endow it with the angelic power of flight. As day moved into evening, the pond would be covered with helpless, not-yet-ready-to-fly Hexes, and trout would cruise among them, their dorsal fins and tail tips slicing the surface as they gulped in the big, unmoving bugs, one after the other. The anglers casted out various imitations of Hex flies—size and color being the most important characteristics—and once the fly was on the water, they would let it sit. Whenever a cruising trout approached, they would tug in an inch or two of line to make the fly give the tiniest of lifelike twitches, then they would wait, ready to set the hook, as the fish took notice and swam slowly over.

After fishing the Hex hatch, Vincent spent a number of days catching largemouth and crappies in the lake beyond his back lawn; he released the bass, but by now having caught far too many crappies, he had turned hard-hearted toward them, and he fed each one to the eagles.

In mid-July, a couple of Sean's Connecticut clients at the last minute canceled two days of guided fishing, so Sean and Vincent spent those days in Sean's drift boat, floating a couple of stretches of big river for brown and rainbow trout. The brown trout had been hatched, raised, and stocked by the State of Maine, but once they were released from the stocking trucks, they thrived and grew, and Vincent and Sean found them more than worthy of being caught. The rainbows, though their progenitors had been brought east from Northern California, reproduced naturally in the tributaries of one large river and were quite wild—and for that reason the two anglers prized them even more highly than they did the browns. Whether angling for rainbows or browns, what the two of them especially liked about this big-river dry-fly fishing was its technicality. Rather than feeding on any insect that came along as brook trout and freshwater bass were inclined to do, these large brown and rainbow trout frequently keyed in on one specific species of caddisfly, mayfly, or stonefly out of the myriad bugs that might appear on the water all at once, and in order to catch them, an angler needed to determine which bug it was they wanted, select an accurate artificial facsimile of that insect, and then present it properly, on a long, fine leader and from a great-enough distance to avoid being detected, to a specific, rising fish. It was fly fishing at its most challenging and its most satisfying.

When they fished for these picky river trout, smallmouth bass would sometimes intercept their flies, and Vincent and Sean were merciless, invariably leaving the bass on a bank or a gravel bar for the eagles to eat. One time, when they were drifting within sight of another angler, a man wading the river close to shore, they observed that he also pitched onto the bank a fish that was not a trout. Sean dropped the anchor with a splash, the anchor rope singing as it rounded the pulley. The boat began to swing in the current.

"Hey, was that a bass you just grounded?" Sean called in a tone that signaled he already knew the answer.

"Fucking chub," the angler said. "That's all I've caught today."

"They're called fallfish. They build pyramids of rocks on the river bottom in the fall when they're getting ready to spawn; they've been doing that for thousands of years. They're just about the only fish left that's native to this river. You should put it back."

"Fuck that. I hate those ugly things."

Sean and Vincent stood in the anchored, swinging boat, both of them loudly berating the angler, until finally he set down his rod, retrieved the fallfish from the bank, and pitched it back into the river. "There," he yelled. "You fucking happy now?" It was likely the fish did not survive—but at least that angler would think twice before killing one again.

Later in July, fishing the Penobscot River from a kayak, Vincent, with a six-weight rod and casting both weighted streamers and popping flies, caught smallmouth bass after smallmouth bass. But these smallies he did not feed to birds. The Penobscot—formerly an important river for Atlantic salmon fishing—now boasted a reputation as a smallmouth river—it was *valued* for being a smallmouth river, with anglers coming from around the country to fish for them—and therefore smallmouth had a different status on that water, a special, elevated status, and all the smallmouth Vincent caught there he released almost as carefully as if they were rainbows. The near-obligatory destruction of Maine smallmouth bass was entirely situational, locational, and—Vincent had to admit when he thought about it—not completely rational.

In August, a friend called to ask if Vincent wanted to join him fishing for carp in Merrymeeting Bay, the estuary where the Kennebec, the

Androscoggin, and four other rivers all came together. Vincent's answer was, "You know, buddy . . . I would never intentionally catch a carp." The old friend laughed.

"You should learn to appreciate them," he said. "The way each summer's been coming in hotter than the last and setting new temperature records and with the water everywhere getting warmer and more deoxygenated, in a few decades, carp will be the only thing we have left to fish for." Vincent thought about that.

"No," he finally said. "We won't be that lucky. No matter how much of a hellscape the world becomes, we'll never be rid of the fucking smallmouths." The friend laughed longer this time.

"See, that's the reason I really want to fish with you. Your dark humor lightens the weight of a heavy world."

"Another day, then, bud. Another fish. And, you know what? By the time carp and other such invasive vermin are all we have left, I truly hope not to be here to witness it."

"Do you have any objection to blue sharks?"

"Why, no. I like sharks. I mean, blues are a little sluggish, but they're 100 percent organic."

"My new fishing friend down in Portland's got a twenty-one-foot Contender. We'll be going out for the toothy ones at the end of next week. Many have been spotted of late. Friday. Why don't you come with us?"

The following week, Vincent and the two other men boated out among the offshore islands to hunt the salt for sharks. They fished big rods—twelve-weights—with leaders of steel wire and floppy flies tied to imitate chunks of mutilated fish, and they carried buckets of chum aboard. Vincent tolerated the chum, which was necessary for shark fishing because these predators hunted primarily by their sense of smell. But when his companions advised him to swish his chum fly in the chum bucket before casting it, he balked. He thought that would be a step too far in the direction of fishing with bait; it was cheating as far as he was concerned, and he couldn't bring himself to do it. The result was that his friends finished the day each having caught a shark—one blue, one tail-dancing mako—while Vincent ended up skunked for the outing.

Late in the chill of a late-August night, by the dark of the moon and all alone, Vincent took a huge brown trout from a small river using a heavy, tightly packed, natural-colored deer-hair fly he'd trimmed up to look like a mouse, casting it from one side of the river into the grass on the opposite bank and then tugging it into the water and stripping it across the current. In that moonless blackness, Vincent never saw the take; he just heard the monstrous gulp, and he set the hook.

One day, Jimmy Dunlevy called. He said, "Are you okay, Chief? I'm a little concerned about you."

"Never better," said Vincent.

"Hey, some good news on the dam-removal front, huh? Looks like at least one more hydropower dam will be taken out on the Pacific coast. Better upstream migration for lots of anadromous fish? So not all the environmental news these days is bad."

After a moment, Vincent said, "At this point, even without any dams at all, I'm not sure all those Pacific salmonid species would make a comeback—the chinooks, the cohos, the sockeyes. The steelhead. Too many of them get commercially harvested out in the ocean. And the ocean itself has been changing. The temperature. The chemistry of it, even. The rivers themselves are overly warm. Overly dirty. They have less water. Those fish may all be just too magical to do well in our blighted contemporary world . . . they're unicorns. We no longer deserve them."

Vincent could hear Dunlevy draw a ragged breath before he finally said, "Anyway, why I'm calling. As you know, as I don't have to tell you, Maine landlocked salmon are actually native only to four lakes there: Grand, Sebago, Green, and Sebec." Vincent detected an annoying tone of triumph in Dunlevy's voice.

"It's true; you *don't* have to tell me. What's your point?"

"Everywhere else they're *not* native. Even in Maine. In fact, in a lot of Maine waters, especially the ones where back in the day they stocked smelts specifically to keep nonnative landlockeds fed, it's brought consequences to the species that *are* native to those waters."

"Jimmy. I continue to hear you regurgitating information that you learned from me a lot of years ago. I repeat, what is your point?"

"That one salmon long ago that was so important to you? Your life-changing *Ur* salmon? Your first salmon—your first fish of any kind—on your own fly? The salmon you caught in front of an audience that watched as your big fish tail-danced across the narrows and then applauded when you landed it? That fish was in water where it really did not belong. Where it was an *invader*."

"Jimmy, you know, it's always good talking to you. I always enjoy it. But I've got my fishing gear all collected, and I'm just on my way out the door here."

"What I'm trying to say, Chief, is that I think you ought to reconsider going to Argentina for us in April. Even if it's not a native fish you'll be trying to catch. I think it'd be good for you. Give you something cool to look forward to for the next few months. I think it might even be *fun*. And it would certainly be a help to me."

"I've been to Argentina. Several times. Fished Patagonia one end to the other and over to the Chilean side. Been there, done that, as you kids like to say. I don't have an urge to go back."

Vincent had a dream that night: he was standing in the parking lot of a topless-dancing club. This was an actual place from his distant past, now long gone, that he had sometimes visited back before he had met Caroline and perhaps even a handful times after they'd begun dating. The strip club was set close by the bank of a narrow tidal river that was bordered by tall marsh grass on either side, and sometimes, on evenings during the spring and the fall when both the tide and the moon were right, Vincent, after stepping out of the noisy club for a breath of air, could stand at the edge of the parking lot, shins pressed against the steel guardrail meant to prevent drunks from rolling their cars down the steep bank and into the river, listening amid the flash of neon lightning and the muffled thumping of music and the whine of the nearby highway as the rest of the heedless world whirled on around his beer-buzzing head—and he could hear striped bass splashing as they fed in the riffle of the retreating current.

In his dream, he turned from his listening, having heard not a thing but the gurgle of water, and found himself facing a trio of luminous beings. The three of them wore high-topped black boxing shoes and broad-sleeved, hooded boxing robes that appeared to have been fashioned from the scaly skins of stripers. Between the black pinstripes on the robes, the broad bars of silver gleamed. Their heads were bowed, and their peaked hoods shadowed their faces; they held their fisted hands before them, their knuckles wound and bound in strips of fish-striped skin.

One being rocked his head several times, loosening his muscular neck. He skipped forward on the balls of his feet and lifted his face so that the flashing neon illuminated his features. A red scar ran along one of his cheeks, and Vincent could see that at some point, his nose had been badly broken. In his lower lip, he wore an ugly piercing—a large and rusted fishhook, and when he spoke, it was in a deep voice, with a thick Slavic accent.

"In your life, you are alone once more," the being said. "And this is all your fault."

"*All* my fault?" Vincent protested. "*Some* of it, sure. Most of it, maybe. But . . ."

"Because you dared to imagine of having two women, you now have none."

"That hardly makes sense."

"You are Midas, so greedy you are now unable to eat even one bite of food. You are Icarus, plunging with your wings of wax melted. You are Ahab, sliding into mouth of whale."

The three beings disappeared before Vincent could express further disagreement. He stood paralyzed in the parking lot, unsure of whether he should go back into the bar or return to listening for stripers.

At the beginning of September, the fall semester began, requiring Vincent to teach and therefore to confine his fishing to his weekends and the ends of his days. Still, he continued to fish obsessively. He also, somehow—on less sleep than he'd ever gotten—put more energy into his teaching than he ever had. In a frenzy of maniacal creativity, he tossed out all but one of his old syllabi and radically revised the curricula for four of his five fall classes.

He decided that, in place of the inane dialogues he'd forced on them for years—*My Mexican Cousin* and *A Restaurant in Madrid*—he would make his most advanced Spanish students read and discuss Part I of *Don Quixote*. They would certainly struggle, but then . . . without struggle, there could be no growth.

He developed a new reading list for his Literature of the Outdoors class, chopping out all the useless Romantic poetry—material that idealized a natural world that was tamed and framed—and setting out to select a few challenging works of prose that would be focused largely on fishing, with some hunting and adventure mixed in, most of it from the twentieth century. Materials that corresponded to actual issues of the world's contemporary reality. His problem was that, every time he thought he had that list nailed down, he found himself drawn back to it—sometimes from out of a sound sleep in the middle of the night—to add just one more title. It was almost as if the spirits of every book or story he had ever read were rising one by one from the haunted well of his memory to possess him.

On the first day of class, he projected his list of books and essays and stories onto the whiteboard: Aldo Leopold: *A Sand County Almanac*. Annie Dillard: *Pilgrim at Tinker Creek*. Ernest Hemingway: *Big Two-Hearted River, The Old Man and the Sea, The Short Happy Life of Francis Macomber*, and *The Snows of Kilimanjaro*. William Faulkner: *The Bear*. James Dickey: *Deliverance*. Norman Maclean: *A River Runs Through It*. Rick Bass and David James Duncan: *The Heart of the Monster*. David James Duncan: *The River Why*. David Quammen: *The Heartbeat of the Wild*. John Gierach: *Trout Bum* and *Sex, Death, and Fly-Fishing*. Pam Houston: *Women on Hunting*. Ted Kerasote: *Bloodties*. Paul Schullery: *If Fish Could Scream*. Herman Melville: *Moby Dick*. That was the first page . . .

The students exchanged glances. One of them raised her hand. Vincent was immediately wary; he knew this student from a couple of his classes during the previous semester. She was one to watch out for. "Vincent," she said. "That's a lot of reading."

"It's only a little more than a book or the equivalent of a book per week." Which seemed absolutely reasonable until the moment he finished speaking and it dawned on him, with a sinking feeling, that a few of them likely had never finished a whole book in their entire lives. This was a different generation. . . .

She said, "This is a one-credit course. We only meet once a week."

Vincent found himself nodding. He stood, turning his face from one side of the class to the other, and continued to nod. He looked up at the whiteboard, then back at the class. Some of the students avoided his eyes;

others stared at him, unblinking. He lifted a finger in the air, and he said, "Every book you read becomes a part of your identity, part of who you are. Everything you read works its way into your very being and changes you for good and for the better. Makes you more imaginative, more adaptable, more knowledgeable, more . . . interesting. The *more* you read . . ."

"I do agree with you on that," the outspoken student said. Blank-ish expressions on the rest of them; they undoubtedly were hoping their classmate would win the argument, but nobody wanted to be caught supporting an insurrection. "On the other hand, if you add up the number of pages represented by this reading list and you divide that number by the number of class hours available to discuss those pages over the course of the semester . . ."

Vincent had always been terrible at math. Terrified of it, in fact. Counted on his fingers when he didn't have a calculator handy. Never managed to memorize his multiplication tables as a child. Some kind of undiagnosed disability: multiplication, division, any of it. Whenever a dispute involving numbers arose, he always quickly folded his hand. He said, "It *is* a lot of reading, isn't it?" Irrationally hoping she might suddenly reverse herself and contradict him.

"Yes it is, Vincent."

"All right. From what's on my list of readings, I suppose I am forced to let each of you make some selections."

In his Environmental Insights class, a course designed to prepare first-year students for the more advanced classes taught by actual scientists, Vincent decided he would focus primarily on invasive species. He would utilize the degradation of ecosystems by alien plants and animals as a lens through which to view every other environmental problem. His larger vision was that, on a planet that was overheated, overpopulated, overexploited, and increasingly subject to wild swings of violent weather, alternately freezing, baking, drenched, and blasted by ferocious winds, only species that were invasive—with no predators and no competition—and/or extraordinarily adaptable would possess the ability to survive. Weeds with leaves and weeds with fins or legs, all thriving amid the ongoing planetary apocalypse.

Vincent had intended, during the opening class of this new semester, to give his environmental students an overview of everything they would be learning. Instead—perhaps because he'd gotten home late from fishing and had slept poorly the previous night—he found himself wandering down a rabbit hole on the topic of cocaine hippos, telling his new students about how, in the 1980s, the drug lord Pablo Escobar had brought a herd of hippopotami to his personal zoo in rural Colombia, inadequate confinement from which they had subsequently escaped, began reproducing, and eventually spread throughout entire Colombian river systems, threatening agriculture and rapidly destroying habitat for numerous native species, including manatees and capybaras.

"And, wow, are they dangerous!" Vincent said. "In their natural habitats—in Africa—hippos are responsible for more attacks on people than any other animal. You can be sure it won't be long before they start injuring and killing people in South America." By the time he was finally ready to move on to another topic, he had scrawled illustrations all over the whiteboard—hippo size compared to human, shape and size of hippo teeth, hippo facing off against a pride of lions—and he had burned through the entire fifty minutes of class time. The students, looking disoriented, were gathering their backpacks and shuffling toward the door.

On the first day of his other Spanish class, his second-year Spanish speakers, Vincent made a big show of dropping a copy of their text book into the trash can. "No more of that," he said. He told the students they would instead spend their class time playing Two Truths and a Lie in the language they were learning. During each class period several students would take turns at the whiteboard writing two truthful, properly spelled and grammatically correct statements about themselves, along with one absolute though properly constructed falsehood, after which they would present those statements orally and answer probing questions from their classmates—all of it facilitated by Vincent, who would break in from time to time to assist with vocabulary and grammar and to offer alternative ways of phrasing things. At the end of each presentation, the class would vote on which claim they thought was the false one, and at the end of every class, the students would vote on which of them had done the best job of lying.

"Okay," said Vincent after he was done explaining the game. "*Dos Verdades y Una Mentira*. I'll start!"

The curriculum for his first-semester composition class was the only one that would remain just as he had always taught it. It was perfect the way it was—but that didn't mean that the class, like any class at any time, could not still generate an unanticipated disaster.

On the first day, Vincent was conducting the routine introductory meet and greet with all the composition students: tell us your name, your hometown, your reason for choosing this college—and give us an example of an experience that changed your life. One young woman's extraordinary experience was that of talking to her father about what he'd seen and heard and felt after his heart had stopped beating on the operating table: the music, the indescribable colors of the celestial lights, the palpable glow of peace, the welcoming embrace of his own parents and the rest of his relatives who had preceded him in death. Then the doctors had jump-started his engine, and he was back among the living, having brought with him a precious gift for his daughter: the assurance that life was eternal and that she should not fear dying.

When she had finished speaking, there were murmurs of appreciation and awe from around the classroom. Vincent, a bit impatiently, said, "That's really nice. And that's a surprisingly common experience people have." He added, "But you know, there *is* a biological explanation for it. Even after the heart stops, brain activity does continue for a few minutes. However, it is *abnormal* activity because without blood circulation and being deprived of oxygen, the cerebral neurons begin short-circuiting, so to speak. After all, they are part of a complex electrical system. And in short-circuiting, they generate great, sparking explosions of electrical activity that result in wild hallucinations: angels, demons, harp music, flying houses like in *The Wizard of Oz*, your dead grandmother offering you a plate of brownies. Think of it all as the grand finale in a fireworks display, just before the sky goes completely and permanently dark."

The class sat in silence. A few people shifted uneasily. Vincent said to the young woman, "I'm very glad your father survived."

She said, "Well. A month later, he died. Again. And he didn't come back." She lifted her purse from the floor and began stirring around inside of it.

Vincent felt hot and slightly faint. Quietly, chastened, he said, "I'm sorry." She nodded without looking up at him.

Vincent pointed to a student who had not yet introduced himself. "Okay. What about you?" he said.

The rest of the class was a struggle. Vincent was a stammering mess. As soon as it was over, he went to stand before the desk of the young woman whose father had died. She was gathering her things now, standing up.

"Hi," he said. He'd been unable to remember what she'd said her name was, and the alphabetized classroom roster had been no help. "Listen, I'm very sorry to hear about your dad. I think I have an idea of how hard that was and continues to be. And I'd like you to know that I didn't mean to suggest that just because there is a biological explanation for the things he told you . . . that doesn't mean there might not also be a spiritual explanation as well."

"It's okay," she said. "You didn't know." She gave him a tight smile that told him her pain was in a place no one else could reach. Helpless to heal the wound he had heedlessly reopened, he watched as she walked out of the classroom.

—☙

Autumn—that heavy metaphor—arrived, and it scared him. The season began, as far as Vincent was concerned, not with the first chilly nights and hints of color in the maple leaves but with the out-migration of baby herring from inland ponds and streams and into the rivers that would carry them to the ocean. Whenever he wasn't teaching or grading papers, he was standing in the current of one of those rivers, casting, swinging, and stripping flies he had tied to look like alewives—in smaller sizes than those he'd used in the spring, when he fished with imitations of their parents—and he had decent luck hooking striped bass that had ascended from the estuaries to eat.

Inevitably, the leaves did change color and begin to fall, the sky and the air did get colder, and the schools of little herring moving tail-first down the rivers thinned. On the first evening when he didn't get so much as a bump on one of his flies, Vincent went home to his silent house, gathered up the printed manuscripts of two novels he had written over the course of the past fifteen years and had never been able to publish, and, as an offering to the fishing gods, burned them in the firepit on his back lawn. The sacrifice seemed to work because he caught a good striped bass the following afternoon, and he continued to catch at least one a day for another eight days, even though, on each of the final two days, light snow fell through the darkness onto the dark waters he fished.

Finally, the last of the herring had gone, either eaten by predators or safely escaped to the coast, and so the stripers also dropped from the upper reaches of the rivers, and then those cold rivers were as empty as Vincent's house by the lake. What further thing could Vincent sacrifice to roll back the river—to restore light and life to his world for another handful of days? To feel the solid pull of just one more miraculous fish?

He filled his car with clothes and toiletries and a pillow and the mattress pad he used for camping and some of his fly-fishing gear and all of his fly-tying gear, and he went to live in his office at the college. Plenty of professors worked late into the night, and he was reasonably certain he would not be caught out by the administration. He'd be comfortable and warm and within easy walking distance of all his classes and no longer inhabiting a place where he was haunted by the echo of his own footsteps. He could return to dealing with all of that once the sun again reanimated the earth.

Another dream, this one dreamt as he lay on the floor of his office: he was fishing for trout on a river that skirted the green edge of a late-summer cornfield. Upstream of him, a diapered toddler emerged from between two rows of tall corn and went staggering toward the river. Vincent dropped his rod into the weeds and ran to intercept the child before he could plunge off the bank. He carried him back to the corn, turned him around, and watched him toddle between the rows to wherever he had come from. He was returning to his fly rod when, beyond it, he saw another baby pop from the corn and head for the current. Vincent leaped over the rod and ran until he had scooped her up; he set her back down onto the furrowed dirt amid stalks of corn, among which she immediately disappeared.

Another child, and another child, and another child. As he raced up and down the river, frantic, his mouth dry, kids now emerged two and three and four at a time, all of them paddling directly for the water like baby turtles on a beach. At one point, he stepped on his rod and felt it snap beneath his boot—a rod that had been an old and faithful friend—but he had no time to stop and grieve.

The final toddler, just before he awoke, he held in the air close to his face. The baby smiled, and Vincent recognized something familiar in her; he thought that this could be a child that he and Naya might have had together. Then he woke up, exhausted. He lay back against the mattress pad, staring at the gray ceiling of his office, and it occurred to him that here he was, far more than halfway through a long life, and he had never done a selfless thing. Plenty of *good* things, certainly—he was a conservationist who had promoted causes and campaigns, who continued to promote conservation as a teacher, and it was possible that some of his work had actually affected the world for the better in some small, indiscernible way. But he'd always gotten something out of it all that went beyond mere satisfaction. At the least, he had earned for himself recognition, praise, attention. Advancement. He had never really done a single thing whose main benefit wasn't largely to himself. And now, old as he was, old and at least partly worn out and beginning to look forward to retiring and doing nothing but fishing—fishing, even as the fish were dwindling and the world was catching fire and the oceans crept ever closer to a boil—what were the odds he would ever get the chance?

One day, he was sitting in his office, feet up on the desk, staring out the window. Snow was falling, and he thought that perhaps classes would be canceled for the remainder of the day. There were footsteps in the hallway; someone knocked on his door. Vincent ignored them. Nobody home.

Another knock and another, and then there was a scraping, rustling sound, a rattle, and the door creaked open. It was Sean standing there, a nylon shopping bag on the floor at his feet.

"Sean. That door was locked."

"I carded it."

"You did what?"

"A lot of doors, you can get them open with a credit card, if you've got the technique."

"No shit? That should be illegal."

"It is, if it's not your door. It's called breaking and entering. Fuck didn't you open it when I knocked?"

"Well, welcome to my office, I guess. How have you been?"

Sean picked up the shopping bag, closed the door behind him as he stepped in, and walked over to drop into the chair Vincent kept beside his desk for his students. On the edge of the desk was a box of tissues that students were welcome to take in order to catch their tears as they talked to him. Sean said, "Called you a bunch of times. No return call. Been by your house. Dark as fuck. Nobody ever there."

"I've been here most of the time. Lots of work. Busy, busy."

"Sleeping here?"

"Yeah."

"Shower at the gym, maybe?"

"Yep."

"Not shaving."

"Sean, I'm growing a fucking beard!"

Sean reached into the shopping bag and drew out two bottles of beer. Handed one to Vincent. They both opened and drank.

Sean said, "So, you ain't doing too fucking well." It was not a question.

"I've never been better," said Vincent. "I've been uncommonly inspired."

"I heard from Dunlevy a few times. He says you're not returning his calls either." Vincent snickered.

"I didn't know you were pals with Dunlevy. I thought you thought he was a punk."

"I thought he was something of a punk seventeen years ago, when he was right out of college. Who isn't at that age, and who the hell knows what he is now that he's all grown up? Anyway, he and I have some common concerns."

"And what might those be?" Sean tipped his head to the side and stared at him.

"For one, we both think you ought to get your fucking head out of your ass. Sure, you've had a rough time recently. Nobody can deny that. But both of us think there might be a fresh start for you in a new perspective. Maybe start working with Dunlevy to plan that trip to Argentina.

That'd be a beginning." Vincent spread his arms toward either side of the narrow office. Except for the fly-tying vise and a scattering of feathers and other materials on his desk, all his personal things were hidden in the closet, and the place was not untidy.

"Look at all this," he said. "I'm doing great. Teaching interesting courses. Students who admire me. Haven't missed a day of work all semester. I appreciate your concern, but, to be honest, I think it's misplaced. And you know what? In my time off, I've been enjoying the fishing right around here. More than ever, maybe. I could show you a picture of the big sea-run brown I caught the other day. I just don't have the urge to get on a plane and fly twelve hours to Argentina. Fifteen or more if you count the domestic flight down to Patagonia. Not for my former assistant—or anybody."

Sean looked up at the ceiling and then back down at Vincent. He shook his head. "You want to come over on Friday night? Have dinner with me and Sharon?"

Vincent said, "You know, thanks. I appreciate it. But I think I've got something planned."

—❧

Following the final faculty meeting before the long winter break—a break during which Vincent would have the college virtually to himself for nearly a month—as he hunched across the campus toward the sanctuary of his office, the college president caught up with him. "Vincent!" she said, striding beside him as a light snow fell around them. "How are you?"

"Dr. Chowdhury," he answered, feigning happiness at seeing her. Until now, throughout the semester, he'd always been fortunate enough to avoid her direct attention. "You know, I've never been better."

"Well, I'm delighted to hear that. And I've actually got some terrific news for you."

"Really?" he said, unable to imagine what news that might be.

"Your sabbatical for next semester has been approved." He stopped and looked at her. She stopped as well and returned his gaze with a tight smile.

"That's interesting, as I did not apply for a sabbatical."

"Well then, I imagine this comes as a pleasant surprise."

"In fact, in my lowly status here as an instructor rather than a professor, I don't believe I'm even eligible for a sabbatical."

"Well isn't it delightful that you're getting one anyway! What do you suppose you'll work on? Another novel, perhaps? Or will you travel?"

He said, "Dr. Chowdhury . . . I did not ask for a sabbatical. I am not prepared for a sabbatical. I do not *want* a sabbatical." She lowered her voice even as she continued to hold his eyes. She was showing the tips of her teeth.

"Vincent, she said. "We very much appreciate you. You are unique around here; we have no one else like you. In fact, I would be willing to bet that no one *anywhere* has anyone like you. In your own unusual way, you are almost irreplaceable. However, over the course of the semester, we've gotten some comments concerning your classroom demeanor. A *number* of comments, in fact. The consensus seems to be that your teaching style has become a bit more *energetic* than is comfortable for a lot of our students." Vincent widened his eyes.

"Oh," he said.

"So, we think—the administration thinks—that it's better if you take some time. Channel that remarkable energy into some new and rewarding project."

"Uh-huh," Vincent said.

"We'll need a proposal by next week. Nothing elaborate; just a page or two we can drop into your file to make everything official. Then, just go on ahead and do something worthwhile. Come back in the fall and tell us all about it. Come back reenergized and less . . . energetic."

"Oh, yeah," Vincent said. "Now that you put it that way."

"How does that all sound?"

"Sounds, um . . . yeah."

"So. Just out of personal curiosity . . . what do you suppose you'll do?"

In the late afternoon on the final day of classes, just after he had arrived at his car with a box of belongings from his office, a student called to him from across the parking lot. She began walking toward him as he set the box on the passenger seat. He didn't know her. Couldn't remember seeing her before.

She stopped on a patch of sand-covered ice beside his front bumper. "Aren't you Vincent Mapp?"

"I am." He'd had enough surprises recently. What fresh hell would this turn out to be?

"I heard you fought a bear." His mouth came open.

"A bear? *I* fought a bear? And I'm here talking to *you*?"

"That's what some of your students told me."

"*What* students?"

"From your Spanish class, I think." He thought for a moment.

"*Oh*," he said. It came to him, and he laughed. In playing Two Truths and a Lie with them, one of his truths had been a story about a black bear. But, as he'd told it to them in Spanish, they'd obviously misinterpreted part of what he said.

"Shit. I didn't *fight* a bear. Who the hell fights a *bear*? I *ran* from a bear. It was *chasing* me. I was *screaming* like a little girl, to tell you the truth. I made it to my truck just in time." The young woman stood blinking at him, and her face fell.

"Oh," she said. Then, after a moment, "You should have just told me that you did."

"Anyway," she said. "Merry Christmas. Happy New Year." She turned and walked back to her car.

On the drive to his house, where he would spend the night for the first time in a month, Vincent thought about that. About the young woman's disappointment. The world was hungry for people who fought bears. The world *needed* people who fought bears and had far too few of them—and fewer all the time.

It made him wish that he had lived a more courageous life. That he could do over some of the things he'd done but not done well or, at least, not done thoroughly. Not done with sufficient passion. Not tried to absolutely *destroy* for fear that he himself would be destroyed. Or at least damaged—which, come to think of it, was the way he'd ended up regardless.

Aloud, he said to himself, "Always fight the bear."

Chapter Four

Sancho

On the plane between Buenos Aires and Bariloche, in Rio Negro, Patagonia, Vincent nodded off watching a documentary on African wildlife. He dreamed that, while standing at the top of the stairs that led down to the lightless basement of his childhood home, he experienced a sudden weakness, a collapse of his legs, and began to fall, the edges of the wooden treads paddling him as he tumbled into that yawning darkness. He jerked awake to find his seatmate, an older woman, staring at him, wide-eyed.

"I'm sorry," he said. "Did I snore?" The woman did not answer but continued to stare.

The plane landed. Vincent dragged his angling duffel and his suitcase from the luggage carousel, passed through a screening area, and emerged into the public space of the small airport. He'd been told his fishing guide would be there to meet him, but as he looked around, he saw no one holding a sign bearing his name. Two men loitering by the glass exit doors asked him if he needed a taxi. He shook his head and pushed his way through the swinging doors and onto a sidewalk that overlooked the parking lot. Pleasant autumn temperature. A hint of rain. Forested mountains all around. No one waiting for him. He stepped off the sidewalk, looked around again, set down his luggage, and dug into his front pocket for his cell phone. The phone had worked well in Buenos Aires; he hoped his service would be good down here as well. If not, and if nobody showed up for him, he was screwed. Around him, people were filtering out of the building and heading to their cars.

A Toyota pickup truck moving too fast rounded the closest row of parked cars and screeched to a stop. The windows were open, and as the driver threw open his door and stepped out, Vincent heard a woman, in urgent Spanish, crying, "Wait! Wait! Stop!"

The man came around the front of his truck, and Vincent immediately saw that he was armed. There were two huge revolvers in holsters hanging from his hips. Spare .45-caliber ammunition gleamed in the loops of his gun belt. Vincent shivered and felt faint. Through vision that had suddenly gone hazy, he noted that, apart from his firearms and their accouterments, the man was dressed strangely. Lanky, all in black, with a leather vest, chaps, and a black, American-style cowboy hat. He wore a black patch over one eye. His single eye locked on Vincent, and he began striding in his direction. Vincent released his breath and didn't draw in another one.

The young woman in the pickup hopped out of the passenger side. Hair done up in a bun. Billowy, rustling dress that reached the pavement. The gunman's hostage, perhaps? She yelled, "*Las pistolas! Es un aeropuerto!*" She seemed to be addressing Vincent. Clearly, he was being called on to do something. To take action. To stop this deranged gunman headed into the airport to commit some horrible crime.

"*Te van a matar!*" screamed the woman. "They're going to kill you."

Vincent, head swirling, chest tight and airless, set himself for action. He would tackle the man around the legs. Pull him to the ground. Try to wrestle away one of the guns. He'd likely be killed but . . . he might save some people. Delay the terrorist until security could get there. Maybe in death he'd finally be something like a hero.

Just before Vincent lurched out after him, the man wheeled and sprinted back to the truck. He pivoted behind the open driver's-side door and went through a series of jerking motions. When he returned, the guns and gun belt were gone.

"Vincent?" the man said. A diagonal pain flashed through Vincent's chest. He had to consciously pull breath into his body. After a moment, he sat down on his fishing duffel.

"Yeah?" Vincent finally said.

"I'm so sorry," the man said in English. Slight British accent. Concern in his voice. "I'm Sancho. We had planned to be here sooner, but we were delayed. Are you all right?"

Vincent looked up at him. "Got any water, Sancho?"

"Clara," Sancho called back at the woman. "*Agua. Por favor.*"

Clara brought a bottle of water. Vincent opened it. Took a drink. Then there were two blue-uniformed cops standing there, a man and a woman. The woman, in a flat tone, said, "*Todo bien acá?*"

"*Sí*," said Sancho. But the two cops continued staring down at Vincent.

Vincent said, "I'm fine, thank you. Just dizzy for a moment, is all."

The cops followed Sancho to the truck and spent a few minutes examining the twin pistols and the spare ammunition, which turned out to be made of shiny plastic, and then crawling all through the double cab. After some further conversation, the two of them walked away. By then, Vincent was standing. He felt pretty good. Sancho put Vincent's gear into the bed of the pickup. Clara tucked herself and her voluminous dress into the back seat. Vincent took her spot in front, and Sancho, his face still bearing a stricken expression, got behind the wheel. They headed out of the parking lot.

"*Boludo*," Clara said, after seeming to think about it for a moment. Asshole.

"*Sí*," Sancho agreed.

"*Pelotudo.*"

"Yes. But you could have reminded me earlier. That I still had the guns."

"My skirt was covering the only pistol I could have seen. Not only that, but it wasn't my responsibility." Sancho looked at Vincent and spoke in English again.

"Are you sure you're all right, Vincent?"

"Yeah, I'm okay."

"Do you have any health problems? Also, there's a hospital in town here, if you want to get checked out, whereas there are no medical facilities near the lodge."

"Nope. I'm as healthy as a horse. You just sort of took me by surprise. The guns, and all."

"I am sorry. I hope you can forgive me. And for being late as well. We were at a dress rehearsal for a play, and it ran late. When I realized how late it was, I didn't even take my costume off; we just jumped into the truck to head down here and get you. Clara is the chef at the lodge; I had planned to drop her off there before I came into Bariloche, but there just was no time. That's why she's here with us. Now lunch will be late. You can be sure we will be spoken to."

Vincent glanced back at Clara. "*Tenés algo de inglés?*"

She smiled. "Not a word," she said.

"Well, we can talk in Spanish then. *Entonces*, you both are actors as well as . . ."

"Just this one time," Clara said. She laughed. "Though of course, we can dream that some important friend of *los* Allman will see us and want to take us away to Hollywood." Vincent turned completely around in his seat to look at her.

"Friends of the Allmans? What do you mean?"

"Angela Allman is a *dramaturga*. She wrote it. The title is *Etta*. A short play. We'll be performing it at a party over there in a couple of nights."

"At Allman's ranch?"

"*Sí.*"

"Angela Allman would be . . . I don't think J. T. Allman has kids."

"*Una sobrina*," said Clara. "A niece."

Sancho said, "The lovely Clara is starring as Etta Place, the lover of the Sundance Kid and Butch Cassidy. I am the Sundance Kid."

"I saw the movie. *Hace mucho tiempo.* I didn't know the Sundance Kid wore an eye patch."

After a long moment, Sancho said, "I wear an eye patch in real life." Vincent briefly went back to English.

"Oh. Ah . . ."

"It's all right," Sancho said. "How could you know?"

They were on the highway now and headed north into the mountains. After a minute, Vincent again turned to Clara. "So, it's set in Bolivia, then?"

"The *obra?*"

"*Sí.*"

"Oh. Because of the movie? No, no. They only *died* in Bolivia. They weren't even there very long. Before then, they were in Argentina for many years, where they continued to rob banks. Most of the time, they were south of here, in Chubut Province. But when the law began to close in down there, they came north of Bariloche. The three of them actually lived for a few months in a cabin on the ranch before they fled over the border into Chile and finally to Bolivia."

"Which ranch? Río Perca—or Allman's ranch?"

Sancho laughed. "That is a matter of some dispute. They used to be the same gigantic ranch until two former co-owners, brothers who had inherited the place, went to war with one another over the affections of a lovely shepherdess and ended up splitting the estate in half, with the thread of the river as the dividing line. Now the Allmans say the hideout was on their side of the river, and the Dodier family say it was on *their* side of the river."

"Who's right?"

"They both are," Sancho said after a moment.

Clara said, "When we're on the Allmans' side of the river, the Allmans are right. When we're on the Dodier side . . ."

"Then *los* Dodier are right," Sancho said, finishing her sentence.

After a moment, Vincent said, "Which guy ended up with the lovely shepherdess, way back when?"

Clara laughed. "Neither one. She married a cousin of theirs and moved to Montevideo."

"And how about the current families? Los Dodier and Los Allman? Apart from the Butch Cassidy controversy, do they get along?"

Clara made a little snorting sound but said nothing. After a long moment, Sancho, in English, said, "Sure. Mostly. It's a bit complicated sometimes." Then he said, "Listen, are you still feeling well?"

"I'm fine. That never happened before, whatever it was. I never expect it to happen again. Just don't come at me with a couple of handguns."

After about an hour and a half, just before a bridge, Sancho turned off the highway and onto a gravel road. They soon came to a locked gate over which hung a wooden sign that read *Río Perca Lodge*. Sancho got out, unlocked and swung open the groaning steel gate, and drove the truck through. He locked the gate behind them, and they rolled on, dust boiling in their wake. They drove through beech woods and open, arid grassland. On the opposite side of the river—Allman's side—open land swept upward toward a ridgeline where a million years of Patagonian wind had sculpted the bare rock into a line of discrete abstract shapes. Some sculptures reminded Vincent of chess pieces; others, the heads of giants and monsters. Clara pointed out one pillar-like structure and told him it was called the Finger of God.

The sinuous Río Perca, whenever Vincent got a glimpse of it below the road, was so clear that he could see the individual stones at its very bottom. The river looked low; its bed was bony with boulders. An angler likely could easily wade right across it in many places.

Vincent said to Sancho, "I don't know if anybody told you. But I've got a specific goal here. While we're fishing."

"Yes? What is that?"

"I need to catch a *salmón encerrado*. You know, if possible." Sancho remained quiet.

"Just one would be okay," Vincent continued. "As long as it's a good one. It's for an article I'm writing. Or maybe it's some kind of video I'm making; something. Something like one of those. It's kind of why the editor sent me here. He's very interested in the salmon, and he wants me to catch one. Catch it and talk about it. Capture its image, I guess. If possible, that is. Of course, I realize a fishing guide can't make guarantees. I do understand that." Vincent felt embarrassed to be talking like this. Bargaining over something that would largely be a matter of luck. The whole thing was ridiculous. Undignified, in fact. Lately, the world seemed determined to diminish him.

Sancho abruptly braked to a halt. Seven swine, all of them cloaked in dark bristles, were crossing the road in front of them. The backs of the two largest beasts would have reached to Vincent's waist. Tusks curved up from their lower jaws.

"Wild boar," Sancho said in English. "Originally from Europe. They're all over the place in Patagonia."

"They're hunted, aren't they?" Vincent asked.

"Yes. But not enough. They're very destructive of the environment." After a moment, he added, "That's the most I've seen together in a while. They've been rather scarce around here recently."

After the pigs had cleared the road and were moving through the woods toward the river, the truck began rolling again. Sancho said, "I'm certain we'll catch some nice rainbow trout and brown trout while you're here. They attain a nice size. As for a *salmón* . . . there is always the possibility. But it's not like it used to be, in the old days. There are fewer of them all the time. And they seem to be getting smaller. And while this is the time of year they normally come into the river from the lake . . . they always wait for the water level to rise a bit . . . and we haven't had any rain recently. The last few autumns have been very dry. Climate change, of course. It's been hitting us very hard here in Patagonia. Many forest fires, among other things. I fear it's not going to get better."

"Like everywhere," said Vincent.

"Well. What I can promise you is that we will do what we can. About the salmon, I mean."

"*Miren!*" said Clara. Ahead of them, a flock of plump birds scurried from one side of the road to the other. A couple of them took brief flight as the truck approached, but the rest just broke into a bobbing run.

"Quail!" Vincent said.

"California quail," Sancho confirmed.

Clara said, "They got their start here on this ranch. They were brought here a long time ago to be raised for food in captivity—but they refused to breed in a cage. So they were turned loose, with the idea that they would survive for a while and then die out, but there's been more and more of them ever since."

They rounded a curve, and Sancho braked for three mounted gauchos riding up the road. "Why aren't these guys with the cows?" Clara asked.

Each gaucho wore a large, knitted beret of the type the Argentines called a *boina*. Loose-fitting canvas pants and calf-high leather boots heeled into steel stirrups set far forward on their sheepskin-covered saddles. Vincent remembered from his previous visits that their horses were of a sturdy South American breed called a *criollo*. The mane of each animal was clipped to a stiff ridge that ran down its spine. Their forelocks were long and pointed and swept to one side, giving each horse a rakish or maybe a punkish appearance. On the approach of Sancho's truck, one gaucho had pulled his horse to the edge of the road on the driver's side; the other two were on the passenger side. Sancho stopped and lowered the window.

"*Qué tal? Qué pasa?*"

"We're looking for the dog. The dog is missing," said the gaucho on Sancho's side.

"*Cuál perro?*" Clara called from over Vincent's shoulder.

"Boris. The señora said she let him out very early this morning and he never came back."

"*Ay*, Boris," Clara said. She said to Vincent, "He's pretty old. Eleven, I think. I hope he didn't get lost."

"Well, good luck," Sancho said. "We hope you find him." The gaucho nodded. The truck rolled on.

About twenty minutes from the highway, they finally pulled into the U-shaped gravel drive in front of the lodge—a modern, sprawling ranch house that stood on the edge of a meadow. The stone stairs leading up to the double front doors were set to one end of the building, with a broad, blue-slate patio, sheltered by a tiled roof, reaching out beyond them to the bottom edge of the driveway. To one side of the doorway Vincent saw a long wooden bench and, above it, a set of wooden pegs that he immediately knew were for hanging anglers' wading gear. *Fishing. There would be fishing here.*

Vincent and Sancho were lifting Vincent's luggage from the back of Sancho's Toyota when a horsewoman on a *criollo* horse turned into the drive and rode down to them. Riding boots. A brimmed felt hat with a flat, shallow crown, a drawstring running beneath her chin. Vincent's age perhaps; perhaps a bit older.

"You must be Mr. Mapp," she said in English.

"I am."

"I'm Marta Dodier. I'm the owner. One of them, anyway."

"*Mucho gusto, señora.*"

"I'd get down and greet you properly, but I'm worried sick about my old wolfhound. I need to keep looking for him. He disappeared last night, which is not like him at all."

"He must just be a little lost, don't you think? There are no animals here that could do him any harm. No predators."

"The occasional puma," she said. "But we haven't seen one here in a long time. With my own eyes, I've only seen two in my life, and I've lived here since I was born. So, yes, we're hopeful of finding him." Then Marta turned her attention to Sancho and Clara. She glared down at them, while they visibly struggled not to drop their eyes to the ground. In Spanish, she said, "You two look absolutely ridiculous."

"We were at a play rehearsal," Sancho explained. He paused to swallow. "Across the river."

"We didn't have time to change before we needed to go to the airport to look for the gentleman," Clara said, her voice a note higher than Vincent had heard it before. "Sancho had to take me with him because he didn't want to arrive late and leave the gentleman waiting." After a pause, she continued, "I left Lulu instructions for setting out lunch. I hope that went well for everyone."

"You must both change immediately," Marta said.

"*Sí, por supuesto,*" the two of them said at once.

"Sancho, you need to take our guest fishing."

"Right away. As soon as . . ."

"Clara, show him to his room. Make sure he gets something to eat and drink."

"*Sí, señora.*"

"Vincent . . . if I may call you that. I look forward to talking with you tonight."

In Spanish, Vincent said, "I look forward to it as well. And to giving Boris a scratch under the chin after you find him and bring him back." She gave him a distracted twitch of a smile, aimed her horse toward the road, and began to trot. Once she had turned onto the gravel road, the horse broke into a gallop. "*Boris!*" she called.

Vincent asked, "How do you speak such good English? Where did you get that accent?"

Sancho answered, "My family are British."

"So, your parents are immigrants? From where in Britain, exactly?"

"No. My great-grandparents. I believe they came in 1915."

"*What?*" Vincent laughed.

"It's not unusual in this country. For a group from Europe to maintain its language and its cultural identity. My mother's never been to England, but if we visited her tomorrow afternoon—in Bariloche—we'd have teatime with her."

They put on their waders at the lodge, and Vincent strung up two rods: a five-weight with a floating line and a six-weight with an eighteen-foot sinking tip. Sancho said, "There are thirty-three named pools on this river; I think this afternoon I'll give you a partial overview of them. We'll probably have time to visit about ten spots and fish the ones that look most promising to us."

Before they left the lodge, Sancho examined Vincent's fly boxes. He pronounced Vincent's entire fly collection "Lovely, but unsuitable for this river." He clipped some length from the leader attached to Vincent's floating line, and then onto each leader he knotted one of his own flies—small bucktail streamers of different colors. He fastened both rods into the rod rack that ran between the hood and the roof of his Toyota HiLux, and then they were off.

First, they went to the Boca—the "Mouth"—a deep, back-eddying pool immediately below the brief set of rapids through which the big lake, Lago Perca, spilled out, giving birth to the river. They waded the shallow tailout of the Boca to a gravel beach on Allman's side—Sancho assured Vincent that they were allowed to do this—and hiked to the head of the pool, where Vincent began casting his sinking line back across the river toward a dark cliff that rose a hundred feet straight up from the swirling water.

Sancho said, "At the top of the cliff—we can't see it from here—there's a cabin where some of Marta's guests sometimes go to spend a couple of nights. It's very nice, with a great view of the lake, but everyone who stays there has to do their own cooking."

Vincent was a right-handed caster. Sancho stood to his left, watching as he stepped his way downstream, casting the line as he went. After a while, Sancho said, "Vincent. Don't go quite so far back on your backcast. Raise your elbow and go up with your arm a little more, instead."

"*Gracias.*"

"That's it. Now wait just one more beat before coming forward. That's a fine rod; let her do her job."

"Got it."

"*Bien.* Good, now. Good."

A few casts later, Vincent felt a thump, and he set the hook. A good rainbow trout rocketed out of the water and crashed back in. He fought the fish until Sancho was able to scoop it into his net. Eighteen inches, at least.

Vincent remembered Dunlevy. He juggled the cell phone from the hand-warmer pocket of his waders, took a few still shots of Sancho holding the rainbow with just its dorsal fin above the water, then switched the camera to video. He said, "This is Vincent Mapp at La Boca pool on the Río Perca in Patagonia, Argentina. We are watching as my guide, Sancho Nelson, releases a really nice rainbow we caught on one of the beautiful bucktail streamers Sancho ties during the long Patagonian winter. There he goes now . . . the trout I mean . . . yes . . . good-bye, fish, and thank you for coming.

"Now as we look around the Boca, here we see the powerful rapids coming out of Lago Perca, along with this really impressive cliff, rising straight up into the sky and . . . *la-deedee, la-deedah*, and whatever the fuck else you want me to say."

A few minutes later, they hooked a fat, butter-colored brown trout of about the same length as the rainbow. In spite of the fact that browns did not usually leap when hooked, this one gave them a couple of low jumps, which Sancho was able to record using Vincent's phone. On Vincent's instructions, Sancho kept the camera running as Vincent knelt at the edge of the pool and expounded professorially on the jumping habits of various salmonid species while he waited for the trout to gather its strength and swim out of his hands. After the fish was gone, Vincent stood up, looked into the lenses of his cell phone, and said, "Of course, while it's always nice to catch browns and rainbows . . . on this trip, we've been assigned to harpoon something of a great white whale—by which I mean catching, photographing, and releasing a landlocked Atlantic salmon of respectable size. A hundred or so years ago, they were brought here to Patagonia from my home state of Maine, from Sebago Lake, specifically, and at one point—for a few decades—there were some very large specimens of landlockeds here in the Río Perca, with all of the world's most famous fly anglers beating their way down to this very spot to cast for them. Now, while this remains a superb brown and rainbow trout river, landlocked salmon numbers have dwindled significantly, especially the numbers of very large fish, which have become incredibly scarce, if not almost nonexistent . . . but nonetheless over the course of the next six days, Sancho and I are going to see what we can do to punch our big salmon card. We're going to do our very best, aren't we, Sancho? Of course, there's no pressure on us at all—is there Sancho? You can't see it, of course, because he's holding the camera, but Sancho at this moment is shaking his head no. *Aaaa*nd . . . fuck *you*, Dunlevy."

Sancho lowered the phone. "Is that a wrap?"

Later that afternoon, they fished several blue pools farther downstream, Vincent casting the floating line now in these shallower places and picking up a fish here and there—always a brown or a rainbow, all of them smaller than the two they'd gotten at the Boca. At one point, Vincent heard an aerial drone buzz by high above them on Allman's side of the river.

"They're always flying drones over there," Sancho said as Vincent squinted up at it. "For various purposes, I suppose. The agreement is, they never fly them over here—and if anyone on our side is using a drone, they're not supposed to cross them beyond the middle of the river."

They continued moving downriver, sometimes walking a trail, sometimes traveling in Sancho's truck, stopping at various stretches of water along the way, and at one spot, Sancho pointed out several wooded plateaus below the sculpted ridgeline on Allman's side. "You will notice that there is nothing but southern beech trees over there," he said. Beneath the blue sky, the beech plateaus were pockets of gold from the color of their autumnal leaves.

Sancho said, "There once were dense spruce forests on that side as well, but Allman had them cut down and their stumps uprooted because they're not native."

"That's admirable," Vincent said. "Must have been quite an effort."

"We've still got plenty of spruces on our side. A number of times, Allman has offered to send people over to remove them, but the Dodiers have always declined. I think perhaps not because they love spruce trees particularly but largely because they don't want an American newcomer telling them what to do."

Over the course of the afternoon, they observed several helicopters following the ridgeline toward the lake.

"They're headed to Allman's palace as they gather for the last big *asado* of the season the night after tomorrow. That's what you would call a barbecue—but the Allmans do it on a grand scale. Their aircraft always stay to the far side of the ridge, which is also part of the agreement."

"Did you say place or palace?"

"More like a castle, actually. My understanding is that Allman would have been happy with the wooden lodge that came with the property when he bought it—it was quite large and made of entire, huge logs—but his wife—ex-wife now, for a long time—wanted to live in a pink castle, and so, there it is."

"*Pink?*"

"*Granito rosa.* Quite costly to haul it all in, I'm told."

"Is that where your play will debut? And during the *asado?*"

"Yes. There will also be *musica altiplánica*—an Andean indigenous band. Fireworks at night. Plenty of entertainment. An obscene amount of food and wine, of course."

"And how about *los* Dodier? Will they be attending, do you think?"

Sancho gave him a wry smile. "It's not likely," he said.

Walking on the path along the bank, they came to a fine-looking pool. Vincent started to pull line off his reel, but Sancho said, "This is one we're not allowed to fish."

"Because of the agreement?"

"Yes. This pool and the next two downriver. And there's another set of three like this about two kilometers down. Everything else, we can fish both sides if we want."

"This agreement. Is it written?"

"It's a handshake. Which is all that is needed here."

They rounded a bend, and there Vincent saw a second pool even larger and better-looking than the one they had just bypassed. So deep that, despite the clarity of the water, the bottom was indistinct. Vincent thought it almost heartbreaking not to be able to fish this spot. Then he noticed something that was jarringly out of place in this otherwise pristine setting: a green, metallic cuboid that stood perched on the opposite bank—a refrigerator-sized machine of some sort or perhaps a reinforced storage shed. After a moment, even as Vincent stood studying it, a red light on the roof of the structure began to strobe with an intensity that struck to the backs of his eyes. From within there came a sound like that of a rumbling stomach, which was followed by a visible vibration that increased in both tempo and volume over the course of half a minute until it reached a thumping crescendo, at which point, from a broad slot near its top, the green device ejaculated a blast of brown pellets that arced through the air and pattered like rain onto every part of the pool. The water immediately came alive with a frenzy of huge fish—browns and rainbows—that appeared as if from nowhere and began slashing at the surface as they fed. Gauging them from dorsal fin to tail, Vincent guessed that some of those trout approached thirty inches in length. After a minute, the fish and the food were gone, and all was quiet again. Vincent looked at Sancho.

"What the fuck?" he said. Sancho shrugged and looked away.

"Sancho, how long has this been going on?"

"For as long as I've been working here. So, ten years at least. Probably longer."

"I mean, J. T. Allman is one of the world's foremost wildlife conservationists. What the hell is he doing feeding dog chow to wild trout?"

"I have never had the opportunity to ask him. In fact, I've never spoken to him at all in spite of seeing him often on the river. However, at the very least, he never fishes this pool or the one farther down, which also has a machine. He'll fish the pool above and the pool below each of them but never the feeder pools themselves."

"I guess that's how he rationalizes it, from the view of sportsman-ship and conservation? That he doesn't *directly* fish to trout he feeds with pellets?"

"Let's move along, Vincent. It's getting late, but we have time to fish one more run."

Vincent followed Sancho around another river bend, and there, on a patch of sand across the river, sitting in what looked to be a leather reclin-ing chair—almost as if they had conjured him with their words—was J. T. Allman himself. No mistaking him. He was close; Vincent could have hooked him with a long cast across the river. Sancho slid a quick glance in Allman's direction, then kept walking; Vincent stopped and stared.

Allman was observing as a young man in waders repeatedly casted an orange fly line over the water. Vincent could hear the swishing of the line above the gurgle of the river. Farther up the bank behind Allman and the angler stood a fit-looking gaucho in a black *boina* and dark glasses who was cradling a military-style rifle.

Allman, looking both older and smaller than Vincent would have expected, also wore sunglasses—gold-rimmed aviators—along with a wide-brimmed white cowboy hat and a tan leather jacket with a sheep-skin collar. The hat seemed too big for his head, and the jacket fit him loosely; rather than wearing them, he appeared to be sheltering inside of them. Tooled cowboy boots crossed at the ankle, the bottom heel press-ing into the sand. Vincent was reminded that Allman had been wearing sunglasses on that long-ago day when he'd arranged for a photographer to visit him at his Montana ranch. The assignment had been for a few fishing photos to run with his magazine's conservation-award write-up, along with a vertical shot for the cover. Although the photographer had been one of the best in the outdoor field, the entire complement of images he captured had turned out less than completely satisfactory because, in every one of them, Allman was scowling back at the camera through those dark lenses. The photographer swore that he had repeat-edly pleaded for and that his subject had repeatedly—and with mounting impatience—refused to remove the glasses and at least pretend to smile. In any case, in all those photos that Vincent had little choice but to publish, Allman came out looking far less like a benevolent environmental angel—a white-knight savior of an endangered species—than an arrogant billionaire land baron who might very well have poisoned an entire stream and thousands of trout on nothing more than a cruel whim, and Vincent had always suspected that this was a major reason for the avalanche of hate mail that ensued.

Now, though it was likely that Allman would have neither a memory nor an idea of who he was, Vincent lifted a hand toward him. Allman's chin may have risen slightly, but otherwise he did not react. Then, just as Vincent was beginning to feel awkward concerning his unacknowledged hand hanging in the air like that, the young man who had been casting lifted the rod sharply and was into a heavy fish.

The fly reel screamed, the taut orange line thrumming against the blue sky. By the way the trout fought, Vincent knew it was a sizable brown. The angler walked backward as the fish peeled off line, and when he reached Allman in the reclining chair, he said, "Here you go, sir," and placed the rod in his hands.

Vincent watched as Allman, even as he remained seated, expertly played the fish, applying just enough pressure from several angles to discourage it from leaving the pool and heading into the short rapids below, where, being unable to follow it on foot, he most certainly would lose it. The young angler produced a long-handled net from behind Allman's chair and carried it down to the edge of the water. He stood facing Vincent with one hand on his hip until the brown was finally thrashing near his feet, then he scooped it into the net. Vincent could see that the fish was well over two feet long, with substantial shoulders. A river monster.

"Whoa-ho," shouted the young angler. "Good job, sir!" As the man carried the bulging net back to Allman so that the old fisher could count coup on his catch, Vincent turned and followed Sancho down the shoreline.

He found Sancho waiting beside a long, blue run that was just below the pool where Allman was fishing. Vincent said, "That was an interesting thing to see." Sancho grunted.

"Good fish," Vincent said. "Brownie."

Sancho nodded.

"It would seem Allman doesn't cast or wade or even walk very well anymore."

"He's quite old."

"The bro with the black rifle, up on the bank. Why would Allman need a bodyguard here? On a river. *His* river. On his own extremely remote property."

"I don't know. I've never seen that before."

"You've never seen a guy with a gun watching over him before?"

"No. Not in all the years and the dozens of times I've come across him on this river. It is a bit interesting. But now, you and I no longer have time to fish this afternoon. We must return to the lodge."

Chapter Five

Merlin

Sancho parked in front of the lodge. A wiry, red-haired young woman stood on the island of grass and fallen beech leaves that was surrounded by the horseshoe of the gravel drive. She was speaking as she faced a young man, likely her boyfriend or husband, who held up a cell phone. Both of them were dressed in pastel-colored fishing clothes, and after Vincent had stepped from the truck, he could hear that the woman was American and that she was addressing the cell phone on the topic of her shirt.

She said, "...autumn here in Patagonia, but the ozone layer is incredibly thin this far south in the Southern Hemisphere, and you can still get a terrible sunburn. And with my complexion, almost any burn is a bad one. I'm talking pain and peeling—even the possibility of skin cancer. Not fun at all. That's why I'm glad to have a good assortment of Over-Cast technical fishing clothes in my angling duffel. When I'm wearing one of my OverCast lightweight hoodies, not only am I always cool and comfortable regardless of the air temperature or the humidity, but I never get a burn. The only places where I ever have to apply sunscreen on are on my face and on the backs of my hands. And when I'm wearing my very comfortable OverCast fingerless angling gloves, I have no need even to worry about my hands."

Vincent and Sancho went into the lodge, where, before the bar at one end of the dining room, Marta and a small gathering of lodge guests were socializing as Clara, looking delicious in a frilled apron, mixed and distributed drinks. "*Qué te sirvo, señor?*" Clara said when she saw Vincent.

"Gin and tonic?"

"*Gin-tonic? Muy bien.*" Sancho asked her for a Scotch. Vincent hovered nearby, waiting for his drink and observing for clues as to whether Clara and Sancho might be a couple. He remembered the casual familiarity of her insults toward him earlier in the day: *Boludo. Pelotudo.* Clara was less than half Vincent's age, and he wasn't sure from what dark source his interest was arising, but arise it did, nonetheless. Instinct, he supposed. The dying twitches of reproductive reflex, like those of an emaciated buck salmon struggling upriver following his final winter at sea. In any case, if she and Sancho were actually together, they were being very discreet about it. She handed Vincent his drink, and he carried it over to where Marta was standing.

Marta introduced him to the other guests: two Englishwomen of about Vincent's age who had come for the horseback riding. He shook their hands. A middle-aged man from southern Brazil, who was there to hunt European red deer. The Brazilian man's local hunting guide. Marta said, "And the two young people out front are also American. They also are fishing. Stevie and Stephen; you'll meet them when they come in."

Vincent asked Marta, "What about Boris? Did he turn up?"

"I'm afraid not. We looked everywhere we could think of. I'm very worried about him."

"I'm sorry. We'll keep our eyes open while we're on the river tomorrow." She nodded, touched the corner of her eye with a finger, and turned to speak to one of the equestrian Englishwomen.

Vincent started talking to the hunter, who spoke good Spanish, and his hunting guide. "How was it today?"

"Not good so far," said the Brazilian. "I've been here three days, and we haven't seen a single one. Not even a female, never mind a bull with a good rack."

The guide said, "It's very unusual. We're not even hearing them. Usually the place is lousy with them. This time of year, it's not uncommon to have your pick of two good males who are fighting each other."

"Could they all be on the other side of the river?"

"Usually, we see plenty on the hillsides over there, but so far this season—not even one," the guide said. "We've seen pigs, but they've seemed somewhat fewer as well. *Muy raro. Muy extraño.*"

"Well," said Vincent. "*Mañana es otro día.*" The three of them toasted to tomorrow.

After a couple of drinks, Sancho and the hunting guide departed for their own quarters, Stevie and Stephen came into the lodge, and Clara and her kitchen understudy, Lulu, served dinner at the long dining room table: seared filets of beef, whole steamed green beans, clouds of whipped potatoes. A full glass of Malbec at each place setting. Marta sat to Vincent's right, at the head of the table. Stevie sat to Vincent's left. Stephen was across the table, between the two equestrian women. The Brazilian sat to Stevie's left.

"How was your fishing today?" Vincent asked Stevie. Her red hair was pulled back tightly now, and she was wearing glasses with huge, round lenses that magnified her moss-colored eyes. Her skin *was* extremely white, nearly to the point of phosphorescence. She looked almost like a different person than the one who had stood in front of the lodge, performing before a cell phone. A bit older. Much more worldly.

"Spectacular," she said. "How about yours?"

"The same. Browns and rainbows. Up to maybe twenty inches. What about you?"

"Some nice browns and rainbows. Didn't really give thought to the inches."

"Uh-huh. So . . . what was going on there, in front of the lodge?"

"Oh, just part of a thing to upload to our YouTube channel. About the wonderful fishing down here and the wonderful accommodations."

"Wonderful. I heard you talking to the camera about your shirt. And your gloves."

"Something to keep one of our sponsors happy. OverCast is a sponsor."

"Oh," said Vincent. "So . . ."

"Marta told me you were a writer. Who are *your* sponsors?"

"*My* sponsors? Don't have them. Just the publication that assigned me to come here. I'm a journalist."

"Hmm," she said and picked up her knife to cut a piece of steak.

"So, you and Stephen would be influencers, then?"

"Why, yes," Stevie said. "Fly-fishing social media influencers. I guess that's what we are. Except that we work at a somewhat higher level than that, so it's probably more accurate to call us brand ambassadors."

"Well. Brave new world," said Vincent. Stevie gave him a thin smile.

"This steak is very good," she said.

Bending forward to look across Stevie's plate, Vincent said "*Opa*" to the Brazilian hunter, and once he had the man's attention, he began unleashing some of his rusty Portuguese. The man, who had been somber up to that point, smiled, then began to laugh. To everything Vincent said to him in his own language, the Brazilian hunter nodded and laughed and occasionally volleyed back a few words of affirmation. Vincent couldn't tell whether the man really understood all of it, but at least he was amused. Meanwhile, caught between them and likely not understanding any of the mostly one-sided conversation, Stevie concentrated on her dinner.

Toward the end of the main course, before dessert, Marta proposed a toast "to friends, new and old." Vincent imagined that she said the same thing to a group of strangers at least once a week. They all clinked glasses.

Everyone moved to the living room after the meal. Through the sliding glass doors at the back of the living room, Vincent could see it was now fully dark outside. Lulu brought tea for the two Englishwomen. Marta asked for another bottle of Malbec to be opened, and both she and Vincent topped off their glasses and toasted.

One of the Englishwomen pulled up some photos—her grandchildren, fishing, riding ponies, blowing out birthday candles—and passed her phone around the room. The influencers, meanwhile, huddled at one end of a couch, in a murmur of intimate conversation. The Brazilian hunter sipped a whiskey and told them about the apartment he owned, up in San Martín. He stored all of his firearms there because it was a bureaucratic hassle taking them back and forth across the border.

In less than an hour, the party began to break up. First the Englishwomen retired to their room. Then the influencers said goodnight and went away. After the Brazilian hunter stood up and said *boa noite*, Marta and Vincent were alone with their wine.

Marta said, "Come with me. I have some exhibits that I think you might appreciate." She led him back through the dining room, past the door to the kitchen, where they could hear the bustle and clink of Clara and Lulu continuing to clean up, and across the entry hall into a library. She directed him to the stone fireplace above which hung a life-size pencil drawing of a huge male salmon. Above it, the artist had written, *April 1991 Río Perca 19 lb 3 oz.* Underneath it was written *Ernest Schwiebert.*

"Always rare, that size of fish," Marta said. "Even rarer now."

Vincent said, "That borders on the unbelievable for a landlocked salmon. I did read that Schwiebert fished the Perca way back when. I didn't know him. I did have a rather unpleasant phone conversation with him one time."

Marta then directed his attention to a coin trapped behind glass in a small wooden frame that was fastened against the wall—an American 1899 twenty-dollar Liberty Head gold piece. She said, "My father, while he was digging a flower bed, found this in the ground on the cliff up above the Boca, where we have our outpost cabin. It's how we know Butch Cassidy's cabin was on our side of the river."

They moved to a black-and-white photo of a bearded man smiling at the camera as he fished in the river. "Mel Krieger!" said Vincent. "He was a friend. Then he got angry at me about something, and we quit talking. But he was always a good guy, and now he's gone."

"Mel was the best caster," Marta said. "But Ernie caught most of the fish."

"I think Joe Brooks was the first *yanqui* angler to come to Argentina, back in the 1950s. Did you know him, too?"

"I was a tiny child, but yes. And when Eisenhower was president, he came here one time as well, to fish for salmon. I've been told that I sat in his lap."

They spent a few minutes looking at books signed by all the well-known angling writers who had made their way to the lodge over the course of decades. Then they returned to the living room, where Clara, minus her apron, was sitting with a glass of wine in her hand. Clara and Marta exchanged an enigmatic smile. In English, Marta asked, "Do you get high, Vincent?"

"Do I . . ." Vincent began, then let the question dangle.

"*Que si fumas marijuana,*" Clara clarified, apparently thinking it might be helpful to interpret Marta's English for his benefit. Vincent smiled.

"Not often. *Muy de vez en cuando.* Not that I . . ."

"Well, we're about to step out onto the back patio," Marta said. "Clara and I. You are welcome to join us, if you like."

Vincent followed them out into the darkness and the swirl of unfamiliar constellations. The night air had a bite to it; real autumn was definitely on its way in. The two women fired up a thin *pucho* with a wooden kitchen match that Clara struck against the stone foundation of the house. "We grow this in our greenhouse," Marta told him. "It's good." Vincent took a couple of hits and then waited as the two of them burned it down until it began to scorch their fingers.

After they went back inside, Clara poured another round of Malbec. Marta told him she had decided that his new name was "Vicente." The women began laughing and calling him Vicente. Clara said no Vicente was complete without the appropriate Vicente headwear, and she went away and came back with a peach-colored *boina* that she painstakingly arranged on his head. They showed him the result in a mirror, then Marta said, "Wait, wait; he is not yet fully a Vicente."

Marta dashed away and returned with an eyebrow pencil in her hand, and they made him relocate from his chair to the couch, where they sat on either side of him, each with a thigh pressed against his thigh, each with a hand on his knee.

Vincent, his head buzzing, thought, *This seems like something that really might happen, doesn't it? And so effortlessly.*

Directly after he had arrived, Clara had shown him to a bedroom containing a small single bed. Then a radio transmitter back in the entrance hallway had barked to life with the sound of Marta's voice—*Clara, Clara, Clariii-ta*—and Clara ran to answer it. She returned shortly thereafter to interrupt his unpacking with news that Marta had called in via walkie-talkie with a change in arrangements: Vincent was to be situated in a different bedroom. His new quarters turned out to be twice as large, with the hugest bed Vincent had ever seen—certainly large enough for three Americans or four people of any other nationality. There were fresh, lily-like alstroemeria flowers in a vase on the dresser.

It was suddenly obvious to Vincent that Marta and Clara had colluded on this preparatory adjustment once they'd gotten a look at him. Sized him up, so to speak. Heard him say witty things in two languages. Vincent wasn't going to fool himself: undoubtedly, it was Marta who had the strongest interest in him. For her, he was age-appropriate, after all. But Clara seemed to be enjoying herself as well and was clearly along for the ride. Apparently not so attached to Sancho after all.

Clara and Marta took turns, each of them working with the eyebrow pencil on one side of Vincent's upper lip, soft knuckles brushing against one side of his face and then the other. When they were finished, they brought back the mirror to show him that they'd given him a curly, black, vaguely Parisian-looking moustache.

"*Pues*," Marta said, once they were done laughing. "It is time for bed." Vincent tried to look agile as he struggled to his feet. Clara moved in on him, pursing her lips and standing up on her toes. She made a smooching noise beside his cheek—and then retreated.

"*Buenas noches*, Vicente," Clara said. "*Hasta mañana*. We do breakfast between eight and nine." She turned and headed for the entrance hall. Vincent heard the front door open and close.

Marta said, "Good night, Vicente. Feel free to finish that bottle of wine." Then she too was gone.

Vincent did finish the wine. He took off the ridiculous *boina* and dropped it onto the couch. Then, after he'd visited his bathroom to scrub off what he could of the painted-on moustache, he went out into his bedroom and sat on his oversize bed. The bed was like an island. All it lacked was a palm tree growing out of its center. His island of shipwrecked solitude.

After a minute, he picked up his laptop computer and opened a page of notes. He typed, *The indignities of aging #136: Because he was an old man, they saw him as a safe toy to play with. A big, soft, stuffed animal.*

Fishing the next morning: Vincent and Sancho came around a bend to find Stevie casting from a rock above a transparent pool while their guide stood below her watching, huge net at the ready. Stephen was capturing her image and her actions with his cell phone. Vincent stopped to observe, and after a moment, he understood that she was a beautiful caster. She had a big, fluffy dry fly tied to her tippet, and she was dropping it a foot or so farther down the pool with each successive cast, each time placing it onto the water with hardly a splash before twitching a mend into the line so that her little package of feathers and fur danced on the current with the appearance of being utterly untethered. She continued working the fly downriver, and when it began settling onto the water at too steep of an angle from where she stood to give her the precise drift she wanted, she tipped her rod upriver toward the end of every cast—reaching back with the rod a little farther with each successive cast—so that when the cast was complete and the line lay on the river, there was a bow of upstream slack that prevented it from too quickly pulling tight in the current and causing the fly to drag—to make a visible and unnatural tear—in the skin of the water.

In the far corner of the pool, just before it shallowed out and ran through rocks as it emptied into a rapid, Stevie seemed to see something that Vincent did not. She hunched forward, her body tensed, and with only a single flick of a false cast between each of them, she dropped several casts in the exact same spot. On the third cast, a large snout broke the surface, the fly vanished, and Stevie's rod bent into a horseshoe. The big rainbow jumped and jumped again, and Stevie worked the rod to keep it from running down into the rapids below.

After the guide had netted the fish—a two-foot slab of a trout with a broad and glowing rainbow stripe along each shining flank—Stevie knelt down in the water and revived it by facing it into the current as she cradled it, her thumb gently pressing open its lower jaw so that cold water would pass through and over its gills. Every few seconds she grinned up into the lenses of Stephen's cell phone and made little remarks: "How awesome was that? ... The fish gods were good to us—but they sure made us work for this one! ... I wanna give a shout-out to our guide, Nestor, who brought us to this perfect spot on the Río Perca, here in Patagonia, Argentina."

When the big trout had finally swum from Stevie's arms, she moved from the river and onto the bank, where she knelt again, holding her fly rod before her as if making an offering of it. Stephen, who was kneeling as well, faced her with his cell phone in hand.

She said, "Hi! Stevie the Fish Witch again! Well, you saw the results: I definitely would not have caught that fish without my Kent Model XXO five-weight rod. As I've said before, the Kent XXO always puts the fly right where I want it to go. Sometimes it even seems to compensate for those little errors that seem to creep into my casting arm from time to time. The XXO five-weight is my very fave—unless I happen to be fishing in a high wind on a big river. In that case, I'll probably decide to go for the extra power and backbone of my *six*-weight XXO."

Stevie stood, grabbed her backpack, which had been resting in the grass, and sat down on a boulder. She said to Stephen, "Babe, I think I'm gonna take a little break. Gonna sit here for a while and watch the river." Vincent—who only now was starting to feel an undeniable twinge of envy over that fine fish, over the immaculate way she'd hooked it and played it and landed it—noticed that Sancho was gone. He must have continued down the path to scout a spot for Vincent to fish.

"Sure, babe, whatever you feel like," said Stephen. "Nestor and I will move on downriver a little ways; you come find us whenever you're ready. Hey—what a great job you did. You're terrific." Stevie lifted her fly rod and smiled.

Nestor and Stephen moved on, laughing about something. Stevie looked up at Vincent as if registering his presence for the first time. "Well, it's the journalist," she said.

Vincent drew a breath. "Great fish," he said. "Good job. I do have a quibble, though."

"A quibble. What might that be?"

"You're a good-enough caster that you could have hooked that fish with a line tied to a broken tree branch. Don't you think it's a little misleading to tell people who follow you online, who trust you, that you couldn't have done it without a fly rod that costs twelve hundred bucks?" Her mouth compressed to a line of annoyance. She pulled her sunglasses off to regard him through narrowed eyes.

"Why, no," she said. "It's not misleading because it's true."

"How so?"

"Kent Fly Rods is our major sponsor. Without their support, we would not be down here in the Southern Hemisphere, staying at this amazing lodge, fishing this amazing river for these amazing fish. Ergo . . . which by the way, sounds like a word someone like you might say a few dozen times a day . . . *ergo*, I would not have been able to catch that fish without this particular fly rod."

"What I said. The ethical situation here . . ."

"Who paid for *your* trip, professor?"

"The publication I work for."

"They shelled out cash to buy the tickets and pay for the lodge and the guide?"

"I don't know what they did," Vincent said—and felt an immediate burn of shame because he really did know. "I don't concern myself with the business side of things."

"And now you're gonna tell me that, no matter who paid for it all, whatever content you create as a result of your experience here is going to be entirely objective. Not at all influenced by the fact that the very thing you're reviewing is basically a payoff that magically became legitimized by being laundered through the publication that sent you here."

"I don't agree with that characterization. But, yes; it'll be objective."

"Because you're a journalist and not some whore of an influencer who takes her kickbacks directly?"

"I never even implied that anybody was a whore. But . . . I do take it seriously that I owe the audience honesty."

"And they should take your word for that?"

"They could base their trust on the full faith and credit of what I've done in the past. Decades of work. I've got some credentials."

Stevie's derisive squint narrowed to an embrasure of unfiltered contempt. "You know, you're smug, on *top* of being a hypocrite." Vincent was knocked back a step by the naked insults. Sure, he was a little smug; he had enough self-awareness to understand that. But her vehemence about it seemed far out of proportion to their disagreement.

"Well, okay," he said. He tried to smile. "I'm glad we got that settled. You know, I watched you here, and I think you're a very fine caster and a fine angler, and I guess I'll leave you with that."

He had turned to head down the path along the river when she said, "Yeah, that always astonishes the shit out of guys. The older guys, the boomers, guys like yourself? It usually pisses them off a little." Vincent turned back.

"I'm not astonished. I'm not pissed off."

"Sure you are. Yesterday you were. The truth was in your eyes. Old guys see a woman—a woman angler or any woman—and they never really get beyond what she looks like. They don't need her to be anything else. You're no different." Vincent shook his head.

"Listen, do I remind you of somebody who did you a bad turn?"

"What's my name?"

"What? Your name? Stevie. Or at least that's what you go by."

"How about that hot girl in the kitchen at the lodge?"

"Which one? Clara or Lulu?"

"You're right; they're both hot. How about those two English grandmoms—those ladies about your age—who are here riding horses?" Vincent opened, then closed, his mouth. He tried to remember.

"Emily and Eloise," he said.

"No."

"Hazel and Hermione."

"Nope."

"Tinker Bell and Titania." Stevie laughed.

"You're funny. But I still don't like you." Vincent smiled his crooked smile.

"A lot of people don't; I can't really blame them."

Vincent walked past Stephen and his guide. Stephen was wading and stripping a streamer through a deep run in the river. "What a day!" Stephen called to him as he went by.

"Couldn't be better," said Vincent. He caught up with Sancho, who was waiting beside a broad riffle.

"Sometimes salmon are in here," Sancho said. "Not usually the largest ones, but . . ." He looked at Vincent. "Are you all right? Not feeling ill again, are you?"

"No. I've just been through a thing."

"With Stevie, you mean?"

"She's very nice. Hey, remind me again: What are the names of those two English ladies who are staying at the lodge?"

"I don't remember," Sancho said.

"Yeah, that's what I thought."

As Vincent was readying to make a cast, they heard the frenzied barking of dogs, and they both stood listening. While on Río Perca Lodge property the dirt road that followed the river was set back from the bank by a good fifty yards, on Allman's side, the road ran hard by the edge of the riverbed. After a moment, on the opposite shore, four dogs burst from among yellow trees, hurling themselves upriver along the road. The leading pair were huge, brown-and-white foxhounds; close behind them ran a couple of even larger canines—pure white, block-headed, muscular, and murderous-looking—that Vincent recognized as being of a breed known as the dogo Argentino. Although the dogos were barking furiously, from the foxhounds there issued no sound at all—and this was especially strange because, as they ran, they kept lifting their heads toward the sky as if they were attempting to howl. Both hounds wheeled to a stop directly across the river from Vincent and Sancho and stood for a moment on restless legs, looking over the water at them as the other two animals charged on ahead. Facing them, their heads tipped back, the hounds kept opening their mouths in that unnatural, unsettling pantomime of baying. Vincent was certain that the gurgle and swish of the river must have drowned out some actual sound that the dogs produced; he imagined that from each one there would come a repeated wheeze or a huff or a gasp. But from where he stood, there was nothing. It was eerie, that mute, ghostly, hunting-hound recital, and it sent a chill through him. Then the hounds scrambled away to catch up with the dogos, and in seconds, all four dogs were out of sight.

"What the hell was that?"

"Some dogs," said Sancho.

"Yes, but two were hounds. Hounds are loud by design; they give voice when they're chasing something. They invariably do. Those two were chasing, but they didn't sing. They only looked like they were *trying* to sing, but they couldn't produce any sound at all. Is that the way they always are?"

"I don't know. Though I sometimes see dog tracks along the river, I've never seen any dogs in the flesh before, and so I have never heard them howl or fail to howl." Vincent looked at him.

"I haven't been with you for even two full days, and already you've seen several things that you never saw before."

"I suppose that is strange." Sancho smiled. "Did you bring all this strangeness with you, from Maine? I'm beginning to think it must be a very strange place."

"And what do you think they were chasing? I assume the two white ones were along to take on an animal that was likely to put up a fight. In the South—the southern U.S.—they used to send Airedales with the hounds to protect them after they caught up with whatever it was they were trailing."

"Boars, perhaps. They get very large. They can be aggressive. There are also some pumas, although we don't see them frequently. And I don't think a puma would fight with several dogs unless it was cornered; it would just go up a tree."

A few minutes later, a man on a mountain bicycle appeared on Allman's road, headed upriver. When he was directly opposite of where they stood, he smiled and waved and called, "*Hola.*" Unlike the mute hounds, Vincent could hear him perfectly well above the sound of the riffle. After the man had vanished, Vincent remembered where he had seen him before: he was the European wildlife biologist who had appeared in a television documentary about Allman's attempts at tallgrass prairie and bison restoration in the western United States. Come to think of it, perhaps Vincent had also seen him in a different documentary about rhinoceroses in southwestern Africa.

Very soon after the bicycle had gone by, a gaucho appeared riding a horse and leading a mule that was burdened with a pair of bulging saddle packs. The gaucho waved at them, not smiling, and continued trotting upriver as if in pursuit of the bicycle and the bugle-less hounds.

"Busy morning," Vincent said.

"I think it would be a brilliant idea to actually do some fishing," said Sancho. Vincent took the hint and began casting out onto the riffle while Sancho stalked the bank, hands cupped against the sides of his sunglasses as he peered through the shallow water in search of salmon. After ten minutes of Vincent's fruitless casting and Sancho's unsuccessful stalking, Sancho said, "Well, I don't see anything here. Let's cross the river."

They waded the riffle and walked a hundred yards downriver on Allman's road until they came to a broad pool. Vincent began casting a dry fly that Sancho had tied to his tippet, first working the water closest to him and then lengthening his casts. In spite of all the wine he'd drunk the previous night, he felt fine and thought he was casting particularly well. He had apparently loosened up and worked out all his kinks during the previous day's shakedown at the Boca and below, and now everything seemed effortless and smooth. He didn't have to think; he simply did. The line flew, it was pure pleasure making it fly and unfurl, and he knew that if he wanted to, if the situation called for him to do so, he could cast all the way across the river and into his backing. It made him feel competent. Young, even.

"You're something of a different angler today," Sancho said. "You must have rested well last night."

"Yes. I seem to be in the groove, now."

A pair of riders emerged from the golden autumnal forest and stopped their *criollo* horses down the road to watch him work. Until then, casting by itself had been satisfaction enough, but when he saw that both riders were women—late thirties, forty perhaps?—he immediately wished that a big brown trout would rise from the bottom and take his fly. No, not a brown but a rainbow or even his Moby Dick—a big salmon— because then they'd see it jump.

Instead, Sancho told him, "Let's stop casting for a minute and let the ladies pass."

Sancho signaled, and the riders came toward them. Each wore a leather gauntlet on one arm, a small, hooded hawk calmly gripping the glove. Except for their hats—a brimmed, black bolero on the first equestrian, a pink *boina* on the second—the two looked very alike. The first rider nodded at them and kept moving up the road. The second halted when she reached them. She smiled at Vincent and spoke to him in perfect American-accented English: "I see a lot of anglers on this river, and I can say that you do that extremely well." Blood rushed to Vincent's head.

"Well, thank you," he said. "Sometimes it all comes together for me." Then, because he thought it might impress her and also because it was true, "I fly fished for a long time before a woman named Joan Wulff taught me how to really cast."

"Well, she seems to have done an excellent job."

"You also fish, I assume?"

"Me? No. I did when I was a child, but now I'd never consider tormenting a living creature for nothing more than my own amusement."

After a moment, Vincent gestured toward the hawk the woman carried on her wrist and said, "Haven't you been encouraging that bird to murder living creatures on your behalf?"

"That's different," she said. "We eat them. We don't play with them. I'm Angela, by the way. Up ahead is my sister, Gabriela."

"I'm sorry. My name is Vincent."

"*Encantada*, Vincent." Then, switching to Spanish for a moment, she directed her attention at Sancho.

"At sixteen hours tomorrow. *Está bien?*"

"I believe so," Sancho said, also speaking in Spanish. "I have to try to make some arrangements. Clara also needs to arrange. We'll do our best to get there by sixteen or at least a bit later. In any case, we'll be there as soon as we are able."

"*Bien*." Then back to English: "Well, I suppose I should say good luck to you both—though I'm not in favor of what you are doing."

"So, what are you out murdering this morning, with your killer bird?" Vincent asked and smiled. Angela laughed.

"California quail. Uncle Jay has brought in falconers from all over the world for a giant hunt this week. He wants to get rid of as many quail as possible. He says they're invasive and they don't belong here."

"Well I think Uncle Jay may be right. But it doesn't seem like falconry would be the most efficient method."

Angela laughed again. "It's the Allman way of doing almost everything. Organic alternatives, followed by gradual escalation, culminating in total biological and nuclear warfare. Sancho tells me you're a writer?" Vincent was surprised.

"Well. Yes; I'm here working on a . . . on an article."

"Have you published a book?"

"A couple, actually. Novels."

"Really? That's impressive. Anything I would have heard of?"

"Absolutely not."

"Well, as I said, good fishing, gentlemen. Many bites or whatever. Sancho, *hasta mañana*."

"*Mañana*, Angela," Sancho said.

She was a dozen yards up the road when Vincent called, "Angela!" She stopped and turned her head. "What kind of falcons are those?"

"Sister's is a sharp-shinned hawk. Not a falcon. This sweet girl is a merlin."

"Thanks." He watched her continue up the road.

Sancho said, "I'm sorry, Vincent."

"*What?*"

"I told Angela a bit about you. Before you got here. I presumed you wouldn't mind, but I shouldn't have done that."

"Oh. Geez. That's fine. It's nice she sort of knew who I was. So, the two sisters . . ."

"*Mellizas*. Twins. Both divorced at the moment, as it happens."

"No kidding. Do they both live with Uncle Jay in the pink castle?"

"Often they're here in Argentina; mostly they're not. Barcelona. London. New York. Gabriela, when she's around, stays at the main house. The castle, yes. Angela seems to prefer Dulcinea."

"What's Dulcinea?"

"In fact, we can see it from here." Sancho turned and pointed toward the top of the ridge high above the river. "Up there, just above that flat meadow. There is a cabin. Do you see it?" Vincent squinted upward. He saw a small building. A fence, maybe a corral, beside it.

"Yeah, I do."

"That's Dulcinea. It used to be called the Butch Cassidy Camp, and it was quite rustic, but Angela had it rebuilt and redecorated. Then she changed the name."

"So. *Both* of them are divorced, you say."

After a moment, Sancho said, "You haven't caught a fish all morning, and it's getting close to lunchtime. Your mind seems to be someplace else."

Chapter Six

The Play's the Thing

First thing the next morning, he heard voices out on the meadow beyond the curtained picture window in the back wall of his room. Several Spanish speakers were talking at once, and then, above them all, Marta yelled, "*Mierda!* Hold her still!"

Head pulsing from last night's Malbec, Vincent went to the window and parted the curtains. He saw five gauchos and a white horse, two of the men holding either side of the animal's halter. The horse, wearing some kind of blindfold, kept jerking her head and trying to rear back on hind legs that were wet with blood. One of her dancing front legs also was bloody. Marta, in a red *boina*, jeans, and a loose-fitting jacket, kept approaching the horse with something in her hands and then quickly backing away to avoid getting kicked or trampled.

By the time Vincent had dressed and gone out, the horse was more settled. The two gauchos at her head were rubbing her neck and speaking to her soothingly. Two others were pressing their hands against either of her flanks. Marta, seated on a stool, was working with a thick needle that trailed black thread, stitching a vertical wound on one of the mare's back legs. Vincent stood next to the one gaucho who was not occupied but merely observing.

"*Que pasó?*" he asked in a low voice.

"Something attacked her last night."

"What was it?"

"We don't know. The worst is that her little foal is missing."

"Jesus. What could have done all that? A puma?" The gaucho shrugged.

"A puma usually prefers to attack from above. But who knows."

"Boars, maybe?"

"It is not known, *señor*."

Vincent didn't want to gawk, and he returned to the house. As he passed through the dining room, he heard the other guests talking about the injured horse as they sat around the table having breakfast. In his room once again, he checked his e-mails. There was one from Dunlevy that said, *Hope you're having an adventure. Did you get a salmon yet?*

Vincent typed *No* and hit send. After he had shaved and changed into fresh fishing clothes, he went back to the dining room, where the influencers had just finished eating and were rising from the table. Stephen greeted him like an old friend he hadn't seen in a while. Gently clapped him on the back as the couple passed by on the way back to their bedroom. Stevie ignored him. Vincent heard Sancho's voice in the kitchen, where he was talking to Clara. After a minute, he came out and said to Vincent, "I'll be back for you at nine o'clock. I think we should return to the Boca; that's the most promising spot for a good salmon."

"Did you hear about the horse?"

"Yes. A terrible thing. Very upsetting."

Vincent turned to the Brazilian hunter, who was still eating at the table. The Brazilian looked up and said, "*Uma coisa horrivel. Una cosa terrible.* Terrible, terrible thing."

Later, in Sancho's HiLux, as they drove to the Boca, Vincent asked, "What do you think did it?"

"Boars," said Sancho.

"Why do you think that?"

"Because they've done it elsewhere and with some frequency. They can be very aggressive. There have been accounts of wild pigs killing and eating an entire cow. And over the past couple of years, we've noticed our local boars becoming a bit bolder in their behavior toward people and livestock. They have actually attacked some sheep on the two ranches. Killed and devoured some lambs."

"Wow."

"Yes, and something more. I hesitate to mention this, not only because it's somewhat folkloric but also because it sounds rather silly. On the other side of the river, I've heard rumors of a specific beast they've been trying to capture or kill, unsuccessfully so far. A huge animal, supposedly half wild boar, half feral hog, approaching four hundred kilograms in weight, and extraordinarily aggressive. Quite evasive for a boar as well. Crafty or even *intelligent*, one would almost be tempted to say. Their name for him is 'Big Mac.' It's possible there could be a similar and similarly destructive individual on Río Perca Lodge property as well."

"*Big Mac?* And you're not shitting me?"

"I told you it sounded silly. And it *is* silly—inappropriately flippant, in fact, when one thinks about poor, old Boris and that missing little foal."

"So, there still has been no sign at all of Marta's dog?"

"No. And please don't make any Big Mac mentions to anyone at the lodge; at this point, it's basically nothing but a gaucho tale I heard from a couple of *boludos* on the other side while I've been over there rehearsing for the play, and I have seen no evidence that it's true or that it is even anything more than a crazy exaggeration."

Once they were on the bank of the Boca, Sancho remarked on the fact that they'd already seen and heard several helicopters come in just beyond the ridgeline on Allman's side of the river, dropping down and out of sight as they approached the lake. "The final guests are arriving for the *asado*," he said.

"You must be excited. You and Clara."

"And somewhat nervous," Sancho said.

Vincent's first hookup of the day was not with a trout or a salmon. It was a dark fish that on his previous trips to Patagonia had always looked to him to be a cross between a brown trout and a walleye. It was the fish for which the river and the lodge were named. "What do you know? An actual *perca*," Vincent said after Sancho had netted it. "A big one, at that." Sancho laughed.

"This is the best fish you'll ever catch in this river. The only native fish, certainly. This fellow is fortunate; he's managed to grow large enough that now no salmon or brown trout will be able to swallow him." They took the barbless hook from the perca's mouth and watched it swim away.

"So, the landlocked salmon," Vincent said. "Tell me about them. Everybody used to swarm here to this lodge to catch them. All the high rollers. Presidents, even. Now the salmon are few and far between. And, by all accounts, smaller. And we haven't even seen one yet. Could it be they're completely gone, as of now? Or what's going on?"

"I'm certain they're not completely gone," said Sancho. "Or at least I assume they're not. We have caught some this season, in fact. But there have been fewer each year since I've been working here. They have been getting smaller."

"*Y eso, porque?*"

"Well. I am not a biologist. But big salmon are more inclined to eat other fish rather than insects, aren't they, even compared to a brown trout? So, a hundred years ago they stocked them here—a brand-new lake and river where they'd never been before. No predators to prey upon them—you've likely noticed that we have no ospreys or eagles. No pike or other large predatory fish. And an abundance of various native species for the salmon themselves to prey upon. And so, once they were introduced here—from Maine, just like yourself—prey upon them they did. The result, for many decades, was that along with growing more numerous with each passing year, they also grew larger in size until they were almost as big as migratory Atlantic salmon. And, why? Because the bigger they got, the more feeding opportunities they had, always feeding on larger fish and larger species of fish.

"And that worked very well for the salmon—and for the anglers who fished for them—until finally it no longer did. Because the salmon here were so successful that they ended up greatly diminishing their own food supply. Basically, they ate up all the native fish until there were far fewer of them left to eat, and then their population crashed."

Vincent said, "That makes sense. Classic invasive-species story. It's too bad. But then, the populations of browns and rainbows are still in good shape here, and they're not native, either."

"But the trouts tend to do better on a diet mostly of insects, don't they? Particularly the rainbows. Even when they're large. As a result, they're able to outreproduce and outcompete the salmon. Meanwhile, with the salmon not as big or as plentiful and salmon anglers now fewer as a result, Río Perca Lodge has had to do a bit of adapting itself. That's why, along with anglers, we have hunters coming here. That's why the horseback riding."

"Well," Vincent said. "*Maybe* we'll get a good salmon then. But I'm not going to get all stressed out about it."

"I am always hopeful," Sancho said. "I believe there are still some huge salmon remaining out in the depths of the lake. Perhaps one will make its way into the river in time for you to catch it."

During the rest of the morning, fishing the Boca with streamer flies on a sinking-tip line, they caught and released a half dozen brown and rainbow trout—all respectable though none of exceptional size. Toward the end, when it was almost noon, Sancho said, "Vincent. I have a favor to ask you."

"What's that?"

"Yesterday, you heard Angela Allman say she'd like Clara and me to help her this afternoon? To help get ready for the play this evening?"

"I understood that, yeah."

"So, I'm wondering if you would not mind joining Stevie and Stephen when they go out fishing after lunch. I believe they'll be heading quite a distance downriver, to places where you have not yet been. Nestor told me he would be delighted to have you along with him as well. He's an excellent guide; he'll get you into good fishing, if there's some to be had. And it's not like you require a lot of attention from a guide in any case."

"You know, I wouldn't mind at all, Sancho. But the problem with your plan is Stevie the Fish Witch. She does not seem to care for me. Seems rather intense about it, in fact. So I don't think she's going to be happy sharing her guide with me—or even having me within a hundred yards of her while she's fishing."

"I've already talked to them. This morning, while they were having breakfast. Stevie and Stephen. They're both fine with the idea."

"You did? They are? *She* is?"

"I can accurately quote Stevie as saying she'd be thrilled to have you along. That she is looking forward to it." Vincent shook his head as if to clear it.

"Thrilled. No *shit*," he said. "Maybe she's planning to murder me."

Sancho said, "You don't even have to tip me for today. You may give it all to Nestor."

Vincent said, "What makes you think I was going to tip you, anyway?"

In the lodge, at lunchtime, Vincent noticed that the alstroemeria flowers in his room had been replaced with fresh ones in yellow, pale pink, and purple. It was definitely a nice touch on the part of the lodge staff. Later, as Vincent and Stephen sat pressed against one another in the tight rear seat of Nestor's pickup truck while Stevie rode shotgun, Nestor drove the three of them to a pullout overlooking the second, farther downriver pool, where Allman maintained a machine for burping out the brown pellets on which he fattened the river fish. They left the truck and walked to the water.

Nestor gestured toward the green box on the opposite bank. "We're not allowed to fish this pool or the one above it. Or the one below it."

"We wouldn't want to, anyway," Vincent said. Just the same, he was secretly hoping to see the feeder vibrate itself to a climax and spew forth a shower of kibble. It really was quite a spectacle when that happened—dozens of giant trout sharking the surface to feed.

Vincent took a couple of photos of the green machine, then they walked downriver to a long riffle below the final forbidden pool. In English, Nestor said, "Vincent, I will leave you here. Do you need me to tie on a fly for you?"

"No," said Vincent. "I can manage."

"Be careful wading." Vincent made a derisive face.

"Don't you worry your pretty head."

Stevie said, "Tight lines, Grump-pa." She, Stephen, and Nestor moved downriver, around a bend and out of sight. For the first time since he'd arrived, Vincent began to cast one of his own flies—a Green Skating Caddis—on his floating line. Although he enjoyed Sancho, it felt good to finally be fishing by himself. To hear no voice but that of the river. When he had finished prospecting the shallows tight to the water's edge, he waded in at the bottom of the riffle and began working his way upstream, casting toward both banks as well as directly up the middle, dropping his fly behind rocks and above likely pockets in the riverbed and then stripping in the slack line as it floated back toward him. He caught and released a couple of trout—again, respectable but nothing huge. Then he thought, what the hell, he might as well try a flashier fly—a pure attention-getter rather than something that looked anything like a natural bug. He clipped off the caddis and tied on a Royal Trude—a gaudy western pattern with a white calf-tail downwing and a red floss body dressed up with ruffs of iridescent peacock herl at either end. Casted it and caught a couple more trout. Finally, after about an hour, when he was satisfied that he had covered all the water well, he reeled up and walked the bank downriver.

As soon as he rounded the downriver bend, he found Stevie sitting by herself on the bank with her feet in the water, her wader-clad calves breaking the current. Just taking in the scenery; Vincent figured she must have recently released a nice fish.

"Well," said Vincent. "Stevie the Fish Witch."

"Well," said Stevie. "Ersatz Hemingway." Vincent laughed.

"Not bad," he said. "Quick wit, no doubt."

He was about to continue onward when Stevie said, "Hey, Vincent."

"What's that?" She pulled off her sunglasses and squinted those amazing eyes at him.

"Remember back when you weren't so fucking old . . . and you used to go on fishing trips with a bunch of other dudes—some you knew, and some you didn't know so well?"

"In fact, I do remember group fishing trips, yes. But I always knew most of the other guys pretty well. What about them?"

"And there would always be this one bro—at first the two of you would lock eyes like lovers. And then from that point, it would be game on. You both would call it 'ball busting,' but it was something a lot deeper, a lot more primal, than that. It kept all the other bros amused all weekend or all week—kept everybody laughing for however long you were out there, in your secluded little clubhouse on the lake or along the river—but there was always an edge like a piece of broken glass in every so-called joke. In spite of all the laughing everybody did, every word you spoke to that one special guy was really meant to draw a little blood."

"Wow," said Vincent. "Look at the imagination on you." But she wasn't finished. Wouldn't let him interrupt. Left him with his mouth hanging partway open.

"*Pickpickpickpickpickpickpick* at every opportunity, both of you, each of you trying to defeat the other dude in some fundamental way. To psychologically break that other man-child so completely that everyone else could see it and would have to acknowledge it."

Vincent smiled with half of his mouth, and when she finally paused, he said, "I don't remember anything quite as dark or as sustained as all that. It was always a fishing trip, not *Lord of the Flies*. We were young or young-ish guys, or at least younger than I am now; we did do some drinking and some good-natured arguing. Sure, ball busting, if you want to put it that way."

"And *then*, when the week or the weekend was finally over, while you all were packing your shit back into somebody's minivan—some mom's minivan or some wife's—the two of you would exchange that smoldering look again, and you'd give each other that big, old, not-at-all-homoerotic bear hug, and you'd both agree about what a lot of fun you'd had. And that was when the spell would be broken."

After a moment, Vincent said, "Stevie, I have to compliment you here; you are an astute observer of young-male-group, alpha-dog dynamics. On the other hand, I think you're just fishing the surface—and not reading the water exactly right. I guess there probably were a couple of times when it might have looked just like that from the outside, to be honest. Just as you describe it. But the way it really was: often one of those guys, even when he was a friend, would turn into kind of a bully on an outing like that. Decide he wanted to be the Big Bad Wolf of the weekend or some fucking thing. The Lord of Misrule. And a psychological bully can be hard to deal with when you're on a trip, you're in close quarters, and you can't get away from him. So, what I'd sometimes do is, I'd run interference for everyone else. I'd serve as a lightning rod by making sure that one guy, that would-be bully, focused all his negative attention on me. That way, he'd be too busy to go after the guys who couldn't take it as well—the guy with the temper he struggled to control, or the one who didn't have a quick wit, or the one who was nursing a broken heart and just wasn't up for hearing any shit. The guys whose weekend he otherwise might completely ruin."

Stevie said, "*That* dude? The one you're calling a would-be bully? If I were talking to him right now, I bet he'd say the same thing about you. That the bully was you. That he was protecting everybody from you."

Vincent paused again before saying, "So, I tried to ask you yesterday, but you didn't answer me: Who is it I remind you of? I'm gonna guess, your dad?"

He didn't expect her to respond, but after he had turned to continue on his way downriver, she said, "My uncle, actually."

Surprised, he turned back. "I'm still here."

"He taught me how to fly fish. Taught me everything about it, just like I was the son he never had because his actual son, my cousin, didn't like to fish. But he was an asshole. I mean like, a *total* asshole. You couldn't *find* a bigger asshole on the face of the planet than my uncle if you tried. He was okay with me, of course; I was his stellar protégé, the living proof of his prowess. But he treated my aunt terribly. Neglected her mostly, said mean things, but . . . some other stuff, too. And the way he talked to my cousin, the complete contempt and rage he had for that poor, sensitive kid—oh my god. And then, whenever he got around a bunch of people who fished—mostly guys, of course—he always had to know more than they did. Had to *be* more than they were. Always had to be the farthest caster, the guy who caught the biggest fish, the most fish, the guy who tied the most effective flies, the one who was never afraid to wade the tailwater no matter how much water was coming through the dam. He was a piece of fucking work."

"And now he's dead."

"Yes. He's dead."

"Well. It's obvious that, at the very least, he taught you well, as far as fishing goes. You're a good one. Just make sure you don't become too much like him yourself. That can happen, you know." She sat blinking at him, and after a moment, she smiled.

Vincent added, "But . . . I'll tell you what." He spread his arms, fly rod gripped vertically in one fist. "For the time being, any time you need a target, I'm right here. I was a magazine editor, so I've got the hide of a rhino. Go ahead and fire away."

"Nah," she said after seeming to think about it. "You just ruined it for me."

They got back to the lodge in the late afternoon. He saw Marta as he passed by the dining room; her subdued expression when she said hello told him that he need not ask whether the injured mare's foal had been found. He took a quick shower, changed his clothes, and went back to the dining room, where Lulu was tending bar. He asked the two English equestrians how their day had gone, and they told him about their spectacular ride up to the cabin on the cliff above the Boca.

He could tell by the Brazilian hunter's demeanor that his day had yet again been disappointing, but Vincent asked him anyway.

"*Nada*," he said. "Didn't see or hear one. Even the tracks we've seen, in the sand down by the river, are old. You know, I've hunted here before, and it's never been like this. This is very strange; it's almost as if something has chased them all away."

To make him feel better, Vincent told him, "I haven't yet seen a *salmón encerrado*. It's the main reason I came. Anyway, once again, to tomorrow." They touched glasses.

Nestor entered the dining room and came up to Vincent. "There's someone outside for you," he said.

"For me? Who is it?"

"I don't know his name. Someone from across the river."

Outside the front door stood a gaucho with two saddled horses. "*Señor* Mapp?" he said.

"*Soy yo.*" The man handed him an envelope. Inside it was a handwritten note, in English:

Hello, Mr. Mapp,
It occurred to me—at the very last minute, I must confess, as I've been quite busy and distracted—that, as a writer, you might enjoy seeing my new play, Etta, which will be premiering tonight during an asado at my uncle's home, here on the north side of the river. And of course, I'd be delighted and honored if you attended. After the play, we can

perhaps share a bit of fine Argentine barbecue; I'm guessing you'll especially enjoy the roasted quail. If you'd like to come, Eduardo will conduct you on one of our very gentle and sure-footed riding horses. You'll actually get here more quickly by horseback than if we sent a car, because of having to drive all the way out to the highway bridge, as well as up and down both very long driveways. I hope to see you . . . Angela Allman

Vincent looked at the gaucho. "Hot dog!" he said.

"*Como?*"

"*Vámanos.*"

Once on the horse, Vincent realized there were no reins. A lead rope was clipped to his horse's halter, and the end of it was in the gaucho's hand.

"*Che,*" he said. "*Quiero las riendas. Yo se montar.*" The gaucho turned to wag a finger at him.

"*No,*" he said. "*Muy peligroso.*" Dangerous. Vincent submitted to the indignity; he was excited to get there, and arguing about it would just waste time.

They rode out onto the dirt road and descended through forest to the river. They crossed at the shallow riffle where Vincent and Sancho had fished the day before and began ascending toward Angela's mountain-side cabin through sloping grassland and stands of beech trees that were shedding their yellow leaves. The trail remained steep, with several long switchbacks, until they arrived at the wooded plateau below the cabin. The plateau provided them with a hundred yards of flat riding, then they were climbing again. At one point, Vincent turned to look back down at the river. He'd never cared much for heights, and when he saw how far below them the river now ran, a current of fear rose through him from his groin to his heart. He returned his eyes to the rump of Eduardo's horse and did not look back again.

As they were passing the log cabin, Vincent saw that it was entirely dark inside—likely no one home. Above the door that overlooked the river hung a weathered plank with the word *Dulcinea* carved along its length, black stain accenting each letter. Below the doorway was an open porch, and on the porch stood several wooden chairs for taking in the view of the river valley. There were three horses in the corral on the other side of the house.

When they reached the summit of the ridge, a second valley opened before them on the other side. This valley was broad and flat at the bottom, its shrubs and grasses golden in the slanting light of late afternoon. A blue thread of a stream divided the valley, the long gravel road from the highway running alongside of it. On either side of the stream and the road milled herds of cattle and flocks of sheep. A scattering of gauchos on horseback moved among the livestock, and thin columns of gray smoke from a half dozen gaucho campfires rose straight into the air. Above them—but not very far above—and making shallow dips of its wings to carve broad circles in the sky flew a small aircraft of an Andean condor, the long feathers at its wing tips fluttering like fingers as they stroked the wind. On the slope at the opposite side of the valley, Vincent could see a grazing herd of wild guanacos, looking very much like humpless camels.

He pulled out his phone, took a few snaps of the valley and the animals, almost half a minute of condor video, and gave thought to the fact that, with the exception of the *perca* he'd caught, the guanacos and the condor were the first creatures he had seen since he arrived that actually belonged on the landscape.

They were headed sharply downward again, angling across the north face of the slope in the direction of the lake. The path was narrow, and Vincent used both hands to grip the pommel of the hornless saddle. "This is pretty steep," he called.

Without turning his head, Eduardo answered, "Trust him, *señor*. He knows where to put his hooves."

As they descended farther and got closer to the lake, Vincent began to see buildings. There were houses, an expanse of tarmac covered with perhaps twenty private helicopters, and an open hangar at one end in which he could see a few fixed-wing aircraft. Then they rounded an outcropping, and there below was J. T. Allman's pink granite castle glowing in the light of the setting sun, with the blue of Lago Perca shimmering behind it.

Sprawling out across the grounds of the castle was what looked to be a carnival or a medieval fair. There were a couple hundred people moving among tents, wooden booths, smoking *asado* pits, croquet and badminton courts, and a huge platform—a stage, no doubt—before which were arranged row after row of wooden chairs.

Eduardo guided their horses beneath a ramada that stood beside Allman's huge confection of a home, and she came over, smiling, just as Vincent's feet hit the ground.

"Vincent," she said.

"Hi, Angela. Thank you for the invitation."

"Actually, I'm Gabriela." She touched his arms and did the Argentine kissy thing beside his face. Vincent never quite knew how to react to that other than to feel awkward. "Sister asked me to come over and meet you. She's talking to some theater people."

"Ah. Theater people," Vincent said.

"Come on. You should say hi before the show."

There were perhaps eight people in the group, and they were speaking Spanish. All of them, including Angela, speaking it with the Iberian—Bar*th*elona—accent.

"Here's Vincent," Gabriela said after waiting a couple of minutes for a pause in the chatter.

"Vincent!" Angela said as if she actually knew him. Did the kissy-kissy beside his cheek. In Spanish, introduced him all around as "my writer friend from New York." Then she said, "I have to go get ready to present my play." In English she said, "I'll see you afterward, Vincent?"

As she walked away, all the theater people yelled, "*Mucha mierda*" and laughed. It was their way to say "*break a leg!*"

Vincent assumed that Gabriela, having carried out her assignment, would make good her escape. Move on to join the company of more interesting, younger people. But she continued to stand at his elbow.

"You may sit with me during the play, if you like," she offered. "I would like that very much."

"You're very nice," he said. "To be honest, I have no idea what I'm doing here."

"Angela thought you were interesting, after talking to you on the river yesterday. So, when we were done hunting last night, she downloaded one of your books. Read a chapter and thought it was interesting. She likes the company of other writers—we both do, actually—so she thought it would be nice for you to come. And, of course, we're very glad you're here."

"Which book?"

"She told me the title, but I've forgotten. Sorry."

"That's all right. So, are you a writer as well, then?"

"I am. But Angela's ahead of me; she's had a couple of her plays produced in Spain. I haven't managed to publish anything but a few poems and exactly three short stories. I've got a novel, in English, that I've been trying to do something with, but that hasn't gone anywhere." Vincent looked at her.

He said, "You know, I hesitate to speak here. I'm afraid of sounding like a resentful asshole. But . . . publishing a book shouldn't be a problem for you. I'm sure your family's got the connections and the influence. And the media attention. For publishing, for blurbs, for reviews. For every damn thing you need. Plus—and, again, I'm not trying to be an ass—but you're young and pretty. That should help."

"Well, thank you. Maybe not so young anymore? In any case, I don't want to do it that way. In fact, I use a pseudonym."

"Wow. You're a rare person. And by that, I don't mean strange." Gabriela laughed.

"Well who knows? Maybe after enough failure, I'll break down and surrender to the opportunities of nepotism. Maybe even while I'm still as young as you seem to think. Are your novels still in print?"

"No. They barely exist anymore. If you looked online, I'm sure you could find someone willing to dig a couple of copies out of a bin in a basement."

"Ah. That's too bad."

"Happens to 95 percent of everybody. I'm not special. I've had a great life."

The people all around them were from everywhere. Vincent heard different accents of Spanish, different accents of English. Some French and some Arabic. Italian. German. An Asian language spoken among a group of perhaps a dozen people wearing long, loose tunics. "Tibetans?" Vincent guessed after he and Gabriela had gone by them.

"Mongolians. Nine of them. And three Kazakhs. Uncle Jay flew them here to give a workshop on hunting with central Asian and west Asian birds of prey. Their falconry culture goes back three thousand years—longer than anybody's—and from my experience with them so far, they are . . . some very intense falconers."

Gabriela said, "Let's get a couple of those quail sister and I caught. And a glass of wine. We can get more to eat after the play."

In the area where gauchos were roasting entire animals over piles of glowing coals—the split and splayed carcasses of calves, lambs, and pigs—they found a pit in which quail, skewered in tandem by the dozen, were browning above a bed of embers. A gaucho used a long knife to push two birds off the end of a steel spit and into a cardboard basket, which he then handed to Vincent, followed by another basket of french fries and a handful of paper napkins. He and Gabriela each took a glass of Malbec from a table attended by a woman in an apron and a *boina*. In the orchestra pit below the stage, a string quartet was beginning to warm up.

"Is your uncle around? I'd like to meet him. He and I had a brief connection way back, and I'd like to remind him of it."

"Unfortunately, we won't see him," Gabriela said. "Ever since he lost his ability to walk, he hasn't wanted to attend any celebrations. He still likes to host them, but he won't put himself in situations where he can't stand up to meet people eye to eye. He doesn't like it when people are literally looking down on him."

"How long has it been like that for him? The walking problem?"

"About four years, now."

"What happened to him?"

"He doesn't talk about it, and so I think neither should I."

"Yes. Of course." After a pause, he said, "He's not going to see Angela's play?"

"I'm sure they're setting him up with a video feed. He won't miss it."

"Ah. Sure. So, am I right to assume that you and Angela were brought up in different places?"

"Why, no. Why do you say that?"

"Accents. When you speak Spanish, you sound Argentinian. But she has a Spanish accent." Gabriela laughed.

"Sister has a Spanish accent because she *wants* to have a Spanish accent."

The sun went down. Twilight deepened. Lights around and above the stage came on and then flashed. The audience began filling their seats. Gabriela led him to chairs in the front row that had been reserved for them. She introduced him to several people beside and around them. One man a row behind she presented as "Otto," and Vincent immediately recognized him as Allman's young wildlife biologist, whom he'd seen on a bicycle by the river.

"Otto *Kruger*," the man said as he shook Vincent's hand. Strong grip. Wide smile. Angular build. Clean-shaven, with round, wire-rimmed glasses. Seated beside a pretty Argentinian woman.

Vincent had a couple of questions for Otto, but the string quartet began to play softly, now in earnest. Several children came along, handing stacks of programs down the rows of chairs. Vincent opened his program:

ETTA: Clara Beltrán
BUTCH CASSIDY: Oscar O'Neil
THE SUNDANCE KID: Sancho Nelson
PINKERTON AGENTS: Federico Cabrera, Guillermo Durán, Carlos Guerrero, Pedro Goinski, Francisco Palacios, Luis Rivera, Pablo Roberts
THE WOLF: Tomás Cisneros

Once it was dark, the lighting changed and, to an explosion of applause and shouts of appreciation, Angela emerged from behind the curtain. In English she said, "Hello, everyone—and welcome to the world premiere of my new play, *Etta*. On behalf of the entire Allman family, thank you all for coming so very far to see our performance—you have come, many of you, almost literally to the end of the earth, and we very much appreciate your time, your effort, and your attendance. Also, thank you for joining us in the final Allman family *asado* before winter descends on us here in Patagonia. If anyone is still hungry, by the way, please do us the great favor of making your way back over to our *asado* pits. There remain literally piles of anything you could possibly want—beef, pork, lamb, chicken, duck—even quail, which some of you were nice enough to help us harvest yesterday—and *las sobras*—the leftovers—will not all fit into our tiny refrigerator." Laughter surged through the crowd. "So, please, by all means, if you possibly can, help us out by taking another plate."

She continued, "I won't go on and on about our play, which after all will speak for itself. I will just tell you that it is an unusual love story and that it's based on events that occurred right here on this ranch almost one hundred and twenty years ago, involving legendary North American bank robbers Butch Cassidy, the Sundance Kid, and Etta Place, the three of whom fled from the United States to Argentina at the very dawn of the twentieth century and were eventually pursued down here by American agents of the notorious Pinkerton Agency.

"Two further notes before I sit down and leave the stage to our fine actors: the first is that, among other things, *Etta* is an experiment in multilingual theater. You'll hear Butch Cassidy and the Sundance Kid speaking in English, while Etta's lines will be delivered entirely in Spanish. And that's rather appropriate, don't you think, as men and women do so often seem to be speaking different languages." The crowd laughed in appreciation, and many began clapping.

"From the Pinkerton agents—the few lines they have—you'll hear a mixture of Spanish, English, Polish, and Welsh. The wolf . . . will speak in howls." After the audience had finished laughing, she said, "The second important note is that you will hear some gunfire toward the end of the play. Please be assured that it's all very safe; there are no live rounds, and even though we're using blanks, the actors have rehearsed this very carefully, and they will not actually be aiming their firearms directly at anyone—nor into the audience, you'll be happy to hear. All that said, please enjoy." Angela repeated all of her remarks in Spanish before she left the stage.

Act 1

The curtain parted to reveal a simple household stage set: downstage right, a round table with three wooden chairs; center stage, a braided throw rug on which stood a pair of upholstered chairs; upstage left and somewhat in shadow, a double bed with a wooden frame and headboard, a wooden chair to either side of the bed. On the round table, in addition to cards and gold coins, an oil lamp glowed with a flickering flame. Sancho—dressed in the Sundance Kid costume that had almost gotten him arrested at the airport—sat at the table playing cards with Butch Cassidy, who was dressed in a similar way. Clara, as Etta, sat on one of the upholstered chairs, wiping down a lever-action rifle with a cloth.

Beyond the stage, someone began howling like a wolf, and the three characters stopped what they were doing and lifted their heads. The howling continued; it took Vincent a moment to spot the source: a gaucho in dark clothing, crouching in the darkness below and to the right of the stage:

BUTCH CASSIDY: Them Argentine wolves. There's just something extra spooky about 'em. It always rattles me some to hear 'em.

SUNDANCE: A lot of things seem to rattle you these days, Butch. Maybe you're gettin' too old for this line of work. Maybe you're gettin' soft. (*The two men glare at each other across the table.*)

ETTA: (*Standing up, rifle in hand, and speaking in Spanish*) Sundance, we talked about this. Butch is only one year older than you are. And nobody is too old for anything. *Anything*, I'm telling you.

SUNDANCE: (*Looks at Etta, then looks down*) Well. Anyway, them wolves ain't nothin' to be rattled about. They're just tellin' us there ain't no Pinkertons around. If there was men with guns creeping around outside, them wolves woulda run off. They'd be ten miles from here by now. But they ain't.

BUTCH: Them damn Pinkertons. Why'd they have to follow us all the way down here to Argentina? Why can't they just let us be? It's costin' them more to chase us all around the world than it would be if they just let us keep all the loot.

SUNDANCE: (*Laughing*) Now, Butch, don't get rattled again.

ETTA: Sundance! You stop that. (*The wolf howls again, and they all freeze for a moment.*)

BUTCH: (*Sweeps gold coins from the table into his hand*) Sundance, if you played poker as good as you talk, you'd have all my share of our loot by now. But you don't. In fact, I reckon I have just about half of all yours along with my own. Maybe a little more.

SUNDANCE: (*Stands up and glares down at Butch*) I'm startin' to think that the way you play ain't got much to do with actual skill. It's you always runnin' your mouth and confusin' everybody, and while you've got 'em confused—

BUTCH: (*Stands up and glares across the table at Sundance. He puts his hand on the handle of the revolver in a holster on his hip.*)

ETTA: You two! You're both equally skilled. Sometimes one takes the pot. Other times the other does. Sometimes you split it. Now, we have things to do tomorrow, and it's time for sleeping. (*Etta leans the rifle against her chair, walks to the table, fiddles with the wick on the lamp, and then blows it out. Stage lights dim. Music from the string quartet grows even softer. As Butch and Sundance continue to glare at one another, Etta goes to the back of the stage, removes her dress (which she folds carefully and places on a chair), and then, still wearing a petticoat, slips into bed. A moment later, Butch leaves the table and goes to the back of the stage, where he undresses, draping his gun belt across the back of a chair. Then, still wearing long underwear, he climbs into bed next to Etta. Sundance walks to the front of the stage and peers out over the audience. He appears to be searching for something in the darkness. The wolf howls again, and Sundance turns and walks to the back of the stage. On the opposite side of the bed from Butch, he strips down to his long underwear and drapes his gun belt over the back of a chair. He gets into bed, and the entire stage goes completely dark. All is quiet for a long minute, after which rustling is heard. The rustling continues for perhaps two minutes, rising in tempo, and then Etta begins to moan. Her moans increase and culminate in a sharp cry—not unlike that of a wolf.*)

Act 2

The stage lights rise to a scene of Butch and Sundance sitting at the table, cleaning their revolvers. Etta is not in the cabin. After many minutes of silence, Sundance, haltingly, painfully, and with some bitterness, confesses that he thinks the relationship among the three of them is getting claustrophobic and that he would like more time alone with Etta. Butch informs him that he also would like some time alone with her. The two of them argue about which of them should take his share of the loot and move out of the cabin. They almost come to blows until Butch suggests that they just take turns, one or the other of them sleeping in the stable at night while the other remains in the cabin with Etta. When Sundance points out that Etta would never agree to such an arrangement, Butch suggests that they tell her they've decided to sleep in the stable by turns in order to better keep an eye out for wolves and Pinkertons. He also suggests that they either cut cards or flip a gold coin to determine who takes the first turn in the stable. He tells Sundance to choose. Sundance remarks that Butch cheats at cards, and he opts for a coin flip—which, to his visible chagrin, he loses. He picks the gold coin off the floor, walks to the front of the stage with it, and flings it off into the darkness. Etta enters from upstage right with a wicker basket full of eggs and reports that she saw wolf prints in the sand by the stable.

Act 3

Scene 1

Nighttime in the cabin. The lamp on the table is burning. Outside, the wolf howls. Sundance reluctantly gathers up a bedroll and walks to the front of the stage. Butch taunts him, saying, "You better hurry up. That she-wolf sounds like she's waitin' on you." Sundance goes to the edge of the stage, jumps to the ground, and heads off into the darkness. Butch undresses, climbs into bed, and watches with his hands behind his head as Etta slowly undresses down to her petticoat, carefully draping her dress over a chair by the bed. She goes to the table and blows out the kerosene lamp, and the stage lights dim. She walks to the bed and gets in next to Butch, and the stage goes dark. There is some rustling in the bed. Moaning. Then Etta cries out, again sounding somewhat like a wolf.

Scene 2

The stage is dimly lit. There is a spotlight front and center on the stage. Behind it, Butch and Etta are sleeping. Sundance's bedroll flies up onto the stage and lands in the spotlight. Sundance himself vaults up onto the stage and stands in the spotlight next to his bedroll, breathing hard, his fists bunched. He stalks over to the table and lights the kerosene lamp; lights come up onstage. He glares back at the sleeping couple, and when they don't awaken, he grabs a wooden chair and smashes it against the floor. Both Butch and Etta leap out of bed and stand staring at him. Butch's hand is resting on his gun belt.

Sundance begins yelling that Butch has tricked and cheated him once again and that he is no longer going to share Etta's affections. Butch calmly answers that if Etta's affections are not to be shared, then Sundance will be the man doing without. Before Sundance can react, Etta interrupts them by launching into a series of sharp questions that eventually reveal the men's shared deception concerning Sundance's reason for sleeping in the stable. She then begins a long and angry denunciation of what they've done, assuring them in no uncertain terms that she is not property to be divided, that she will be the one to decide who is with her and who is not, and that if she chooses to be with both of them, then they each have no choice other than to accept what she has decided—or go to hell.

At this, the audience breaks into wild applause and cheering, many of them standing. When everyone is seated again and quiet, Butch and Sundance resume talking to each other almost as if Etta isn't there. They agree that a duel is the only way to settle their dispute, even as Etta repeatedly interrupts to warn them that rather than remaining with the survivor of any shootout, she will head directly back to New York via Buenos Aires.

Sundance stands with his arms at his sides, ready to draw one or both of his revolvers on Butch. Butch, still in his underwear, lifts his gun belt from the back of the chair and slowly moves his gun hand over one of the revolvers. The two men lock eyes, continuing to ignore Etta, until a sudden shift enters her tone.

"*Esperen, chicos!*" she yells. "Wait! Wait! Wait! *Escuchen!*" They look at her.

Etta says, "Listen, I say to you! For God's sake! The wolves! They're not howling anymore!" The three of them freeze, looking at one another with widened eyes.

Scene 3

Butch, Sundance, and Etta scramble around the cabin gathering weapons and ammunition and piling them on the table. Four Pinkerton agents, dressed in long, black coats and American cowboy hats, begin walking down the aisle between the rows of chairs. A spotlight follows them. One of them yells something in Polish, another yells something in Welsh, and Butch, Sundance, and Etta respond by grabbing guns and then kneeling together at the front of the stage, the men with their revolvers, Etta with her rifle:

> ETTA: (*Yelling*) We are not coming out, *pelotudos de mierda*, so you'll have to come for us, if you dare! (*A gunfight ensues, the Pinkertons firing from the aisle, the outlaws firing from the edge of the stage. One by one, the Pinkertons fall dead in the aisle.*)
>
> ETTA: There will be more of them coming right behind—and our luck here is not going to hold. One of us is bound to stop a slug. We must work together here. Butch, Sundance—get all those bags of gold out from under the bed and strap them to a couple of mules. Then get three horses saddled for us. We're going over the mountains to Chile.
>
> SUNDANCE: You saddle up a horse for yourself, Etta. I'll do the coverin'.
>
> ETTA: Those bags of coins are too heavy for me. But this rifle is good and light. Get moving; we are losing time. (*Butch and Sundance drag four heavy canvas bags from under the bed and exit with them upstage right. Etta remains vigilant at the edge of the stage.*)
>
> BUTCH: (*Calls from the wings*) Etta, we're ready! Let's go. (*Etta stands and runs out through stage right.*)

ETTA: (*Calling from the wings*) *Esperen!* No, wait; *don't* wait! I forgot something. You two, go. Leave my horse tied to the post. I'll catch up in a minute.

SUNDANCE: (*Calls from the wings*) Hurry up! We'll wait.

ETTA: (*Calls from the wings*) Are you deaf, Sundance? I said, *don't* wait! Get gone with all that gold. Head northwest. Don't worry; I'll be right behind you. (*Horses neigh. After a few moments, the sound of galloping. Etta runs back onto the stage with her rifle and crouches at the edge of the stage overlooking the audience. Just as she seems ready to stand and run to her horse, three more Pinkertons start down the aisle. Instead of walking directly in like the last group, they're crouching, trying to be stealthy. Etta aims the rifle and fires.*)

FIRST PINKERTON: (*In English*) Shit! I'm hit! (*Crumples to the ground*)

SECOND PINKERTON: (*Reacting to a fatal shot*) *Mierda!* (*Crumples to the ground*). (*The third Pinkerton shrieks wordlessly, turns around, and goes running back up the aisle.*)

ETTA: (*Standing*) I knew there were more of the bastards. Now we'll be safe—at least for a little while. (*Exits stage right. A moment later, a horse neighs, and there is the receding sound of hoofbeats. Lights fade slowly to black, and then there is heard the howl of a wolf.*)

There was, of course, a standing ovation. The actors came out before the closed curtain and took bow after bow. Sancho, his face flushed, looked almost delirious with happiness. Clara was radiant. "Bravo!" Vincent yelled, pounding his hands together.

Angela appeared onstage, and the applause grew deafening. One by one, she hugged all the actors.

"You liked it, then?" Gabriela asked him once the noise had finally begun to fade.

"I did," Vincent said, trying to sound convincing. "With just one major reservation I just can't get past."

"Oh? What's that?"

"There are no wolves in Patagonia. In fact, there are no wolves in all of Argentina. In all of South America, for that matter. Unless maybe in a zoo."

"But there used to be. Before the south was completely settled. By Argentinians, I mean."

"Nope."

"The wolves were all exterminated at one point."

"They were not exterminated because they were never here in the first place."

"*No?*"

"Never. Ever. You could look it up. Since before the First people arrived, the only large carnivore this far south has been the puma."

"Wow." After a moment, Gabriela said, "Don't tell my sister that."

"Noooooo . . ." Vincent said.

Gabriela said, "Vincent, I've got to go feed the monkey. Perhaps I'll see you afterward."

"You have to . . ." Vincent began. But she was already moving away from him through the departing crowd.

Vincent turned around. Otto was still there, standing and talking to the woman he'd been sitting with. "Otto," Vincent said. Otto looked at him. "What are your thoughts on the wolf element?" Otto at first looked startled, then he just stared at Vincent for a moment.

Finally, Otto said, "The wolf element?"

"Of the play, I mean." Otto gave him a wolfish smile.

"You know, Mr. Mapp, I would love to discuss Angela's wonderful play with you. Unfortunately, we'll have to wait for another opportunity because it is now time for me to go to work. I've got some night tracking to do."

"I'm envious. What are you tracking?"

After a heartbeat of hesitation, Otto said, "Wild boar. They're most active at night."

Vincent said, "Pigs seem to have attacked some livestock across the river. Have you noticed them doing that over here as well?"

"Absolutely. They're a very destructive invasive species. And for some reason, recently many of them seem to be getting more aggressive toward humans as well. We've been looking for ways to bring them under control, if not eliminate them entirely." Vincent decided to take a gamble.

"So . . . this singular animal the gauchos call Big Mac. What can you tell me about him?" Otto again looked startled, but only briefly.

"Mr. Mapp, we'll have to continue this conversation another time. I really do need to get going."

"Okay, then," said Vincent. He watched as Otto and the woman began working their way out of their seating row and through the crowd. Then he was alone and thinking about grabbing another glass of Malbec. Maybe a huge hunk of roasted pork as well. Just stand there in the middle of everything and bite gobbets out of it like a caveman. It would be interesting to see if anyone even noticed. But before he could take a step, Angela Allman had him by the arm.

"What did you think?" she asked.

Vincent said, "Just indescribably amazing."

CHAPTER SEVEN

The Hall of Wands

ANGELA SAID, "WE'VE GOT SOME THINGS HERE THAT MIGHT INTEREST you. But perhaps you're hungry. Perhaps we should eat." The two tiny quails he and Gabriela had picked at had not filled him, and he was hungry.

Vincent said, "Your sister and I ate earlier. You Allmans definitely throw the *asado* of all *asados*."

"Come with me, then." She led him through the crowds of people socializing among the *asado* tables and beneath the array of floodlights that shined down on them from the battlements of the pink castle. Along the way, people snatched at Angela's arm and said, "Wonderful play" and "Congratulations." She smiled and gave a little bow each time. An indigenous Andean musical group, the six of them in woolen ponchos and straw hats, began making melancholy music with bamboo pipes, wooden flutes, and drums skinned with mottled cowhide that still bore the animal's hair. One musician strummed a type of guitar that Vincent knew was called a *charango*, its sound box crafted from the shell of an armadillo.

"Any notes for me?" Angela asked.

"Notes?"

"The play?"

"Ah. So entertaining—yet also full of meaning. The shifting dynamics in a complex romantic relationship. And Etta is such a powerful character. Where do you go with it from here?"

"I may try to do it in Spain. Would have to find a new cast over there, of course. We'll see how all that goes."

"Well, the play certainly deserves to be appreciated elsewhere."

"Thank you. You know . . . I'm just so chuffed, as my British friends like to say. Please don't mind anything I may say or do; I'm"—her hands spun in the air as she searched for the word—"*overloaded* right now. Circuits completely blown. In a good way, I mean. It's almost an out-of-body experience." Vincent smiled at her.

"You should enjoy it. Ride it like a wave. That feeling doesn't come very often to most people."

"The actors were just so terrific, weren't they?"

"You couldn't have asked for a better effort."

"Here. This way." He followed her around a corner and into the darkness on the lake side of the castle, where there were no people and no artificial lights. They went up a narrow stairway to an entrance that was guarded by a gaucho. As soon as he recognized Angela, the gaucho opened the door for them, and they entered a hallway that led onto a vast and echoing central chamber. Vincent looked straight up and saw balconies and winding stairways that continued skyward for five or six stories. On the walls all around the chamber there hung the mounted heads of animals, mostly African antelope of various species sporting impressive horns that curved or twisted. Vincent also spotted a cape buffalo, a zebra, a couple of American bison, a bull moose, a mountain goat, and the head, torso, and forelegs of a very large lion that appeared to be leaping through the wall. In the center of the room, where Vincent might have expected some kind of elaborate fountain, there was instead the huge cube of a black steel cage; Vincent could see some creature flinging itself around inside of it.

"You're sure you don't have a more detailed note or two for me?" Angela asked. "I understand that nothing's perfect, especially the first time around."

"My note for you," Vincent said, "is to follow your instincts. You've got good ones, and so . . . follow them."

"That's so nice to hear. Thank you. I'm just really floating. It's all overwhelming. But, here; let me introduce you to Monty." She led him over to the cage, which was large enough to accommodate a miniature grove of tropical trees, along with a gibbon that was using its set of grotesquely long arms to swing itself among the branches. The animal, as soon as it saw Angela and Vincent, launched itself in their direction, seizing and clinging to the bars with all four of its hands and staring down at them with a sad, almost human, face. Very obviously male, this animal, with its naked, pink finger of a pecker dangling. His fur was mostly black, with a narrow white ring around his face and big, cottony handlebars of white hair that curved out and upward from the sides of his head, giving him the countenance of a mad professor. Sad and mad at once—which Vincent thought was appropriate given the circumstances of the creature's life.

"Definitely not an Argentinian critter here," Vincent said.

"This poor fellow," said Angela, "is a refugee from a lost world. The entire native range for his subspecies is now an endless palm oil plantation in Malaysia. All survivors of his kind are scattered among captive collections on four continents. Without luck, we've been trying to find poor Monty a mate for the past several years. But now we're thinking he's probably too old for all of that. Any female still in her breeding years deserves a younger gentleman." Vincent tried not to take the remark personally.

"Well, I hope you find him one anyway," Vincent said. "Maybe an old grandma gibbon. They could hold hands in front of the TV at night." Angela laughed.

"By the way," Vincent said. "Gabriela told me earlier that she had to go feed the monkey. Is this who she was talking about?"

"Yes. Whenever she's here at the ranch, Gabriela takes charge of caring for Monty. Monkey Montgomery, she calls him. They have a special bond."

"Well, I hope she knows that Monty is not monkey. He's an ape. You see that he doesn't have a tail. It's an important distinction." Angela laughed.

"So, it's very wrong to call him a monkey, then."

"It's close to unforgivably wrong. If he could talk, he'd tell you it's an insult. He's actually got more in common with us than he does with any monkey, which in reality is little more than a rat with hands. I bet your uncle doesn't refer to him as that. I'm sure Otto wouldn't."

"You're just full of all kinds of things, aren't you?"

"Good things mostly, I hope."

"Well, let me show you a few more items of interest." She conducted him away from the cage and over to one of the walls of the central room, against which was fastened a small, square frame that encased a gleaming golden coin. The coin was an American 1899 Liberty Head twenty-dollar gold piece—a twin of the one Marta had shown him a few days before.

"This is one of the foundational relics of our ranch," Angela said. "Obviously a stray from Butch Cassidy's stash of booty and, since it was discovered near my cabin up on the ridge, undeniable proof that their hideout was on our side of the river."

"Well then, I would say that between the two ranches, yours has the winning argument," said Vincent.

"Something else I'm certain you'll like. Come in here." She conducted him into a deep alcove that was lined all around with split-cane fly rods attached vertically to the walls. There must have been a couple of hundred painstakingly crafted bamboo casting instruments on display, from dainty six-foot-long one-weights all the way up to stout, fifteen-foot English dapping rods, the entire collection lighted in such a way that the varnished rods shone as if illuminated from within.

"Uncle Jay calls this the 'Hall of Wands.'"

Vincent could think of no words. The rods were positioned so that the maker's inscription on each faced outward; Vincent stepped into the alcove and began to read them. After a minute, as he moved slowly along one wall, taking in the inscriptions and resisting the impulse to touch, he said, "This has got to be one of the finest collections of bamboo fly-rod craftsmanship in the world."

"Uncle Jay says it *is* the finest," Angela said. "But, come with me now. We can look at all of these later."

Almost reluctantly, Vincent withdrew from the alcove. Angela said, "We're going up a couple of floors. Usually we use the stairs—but there's also an elevator." There seemed to be a question in her voice.

"You're really asking me if I'm able to climb stairs?" Angela laughed. Then his hand was in hers, and she was leading him. They went up two flights of carpeted stairs, around a corner, and into a room with a canopied bed. The soulful music from the Andean band came floating through the open window. He felt the thunder of that hide drum in the pit of his stomach, the mountain wind of the bamboo pipes in his chest. Angela closed the door, turned, hooked her arms around the back of his neck. She rose up on her toes to kiss him. Vincent was surprised by her suddenness, but his hands instinctively went to her waist. Then her tongue was in his mouth, the first tongue aside from his own that had been behind his lips for well over a year, and he thought that this alone was worth the harrowing pony ride across the river and over the ridge.

She stepped back down and stood assessing him, a half smile on her face and her arms still loose around him. "Are you okay?" she asked.

"I'm fine," he said, wondering how he could possibly be otherwise. His heart was gliding like a condor.

"I mean, are you okay with this? I know it's a little abrupt. Perhaps I assume too much. You could be trying to be faithful to someone, for all I know. Or very religious. Or you could have some health issue—"

"Jesus Christ," he said. He kissed her to reassure her and to get her to stop talking.

She took him by both hands and drew him back to the bed. She sat down and quickly unfastened his belt and shoved his pants down to his knees. When she took him in her mouth, he thought that this alone would have been worth every bit of the airfare from Boston to Patagonia, if he had paid for it himself.

He had to stop her after a few minutes. He was more than ready to reciprocate, but instead, after they had finished tearing their way out of their clothing, she shoved him back on the bed, told him to "slide up," and then she herself slid up onto the bed and over him. After a long kiss, she took him in hand and worked him up inside of her—there was a crackling sound from her wetness—and in that first moment when he felt himself fully and warmly engulfed, Vincent thought that this was worth every bit of pain he had ever endured in his entire life, for any reason.

Angela at first squatted above him on the balls of her feet, and on her hard, equestrian thighs, her fingertips pressed against his chest, and she began posting as if on the back of a trotting horse. Her breasts rose and fell, and his hands went to them. In Spanish she told him, *yes, love; squeeze*. Some moments later, her eyes pressed shut, her lips pursed, a rhythmic hum coming from her throat, she moved her hands to either side of his shoulders, lowered herself toward him, and began to gallop. Vincent's hands, now dispossessed and displaced from her breasts, reached back to hold her from behind—where he found her rounded flesh to be so firm it almost startled him. He doubled his knees behind her and began to arch his back; the slapping sound they made kept time with the music from below.

Almost as soon as Vincent had finished, she rolled off of him, their damp skins softly peeling apart. She said, "Would you please hand me that box of tissues on the nightstand beside you?" He did as she asked, then he lay back, glowing and pleasantly stunned.

Internally, he felt himself beginning to unspool into helpless laughter. But just then she rested her hand on his arm and said, "When I saw you casting on the river the other day, I thought it was one of the most graceful things I'd ever seen a man do." Vincent's head spun. In his entire life, he couldn't remember anyone referring to anything he'd ever done as "graceful." Just the opposite, in most cases. Suddenly, rather than laughing, he could imagine himself in tears.

He said, "I thought it might have been because you read part of one of my books."

"No. I did download one of your books, but I haven't gotten the chance to read any of it yet."

"Which one?"

She thought for a moment. Finally, she said, "You know, I can't remember the title. I'm sorry."

"Ah." That made him begin to wonder whether, in recalling his physical prowess as a fly caster, she might not have meant to compare it to his performance during the past fifteen minutes. Compare it unfavorably, perhaps? He longed for her to say something clarifying. He was fairly certain the earth had moved for her, but the signs had been subtle, and he wasn't sure. Of course, he couldn't ask; that would make him sound insecure. And, while it was bad enough for a young man to be insecure in that way, for a man at his stage of the game . . . it would be pretty close to fatal.

Below them, the music had paused. In the room with them some-one's cell phone buzzed. Angela hopped out of bed, ran her hands across their clothing that lay scattered together on the floor, came up with her device. She leaped to a chest of drawers, yanked out a flannel shirt as the phone continued to summon her, jammed her arms into the sleeves, buttoned the top three buttons.

"*Hola, mi vida!*" she said as she answered the phone. "*Como estás?* I was just getting ready to watch the fireworks through my window. How wonderful to see you!"

Vincent was concerned that she might be talking to a lover—some handsome young Spanish guy with a lot of black hair swept back in a rak-ish wave against the side of his muscular brown head. But in a moment it became clear that she was speaking to a child, and he released the breath he had been holding. He waved to get her attention, then pantomimed going out the door to give her some privacy for her conversation. She nodded and lifted a hand at him, then returned to smiling down at her phone, and as quietly as he could, he gathered up his clothing.

He stuck his head through the doorway and looked up and down the empty hallway. Then he stepped out of the room, eased the door closed, and rapidly covered his nakedness. After zipping his fly and lacing his shoes, he decided he would use this intermission to more closely inspect Allman's remarkable bamboo rod collection. He'd never seen anything like it. He descended the carpeted stone stairs, and as he reached the ground floor, he at once felt drawn to the black cube to get another look at the critically endangered primate—its kind, by Angela's account, now extinct in the wild. When he reached the cage, the white-tufted old gib-bon swung its way over to Vincent's side and dangled by its arms from a branch. They locked eyes for a long moment, and Vincent imagined that they were connecting in some profound way—communicating word-lessly across the fathomless and ever-widening gulf that had separated them ever since their ancestral species first diverged, some 10 million years now in the past.

Continuing to hold Vincent's gaze, Monty dropped one hand from the branch and reached down to grasp his swinging man part. That shocking pinkness began playing rapid peekaboo through the tunnel of

Monty's too-long fingers as he stimulated himself, all the while—or at least for as long as Vincent could stand to watch—the morose expression remaining unchanged on the face of the elderly ape. As his surprise wore off, Vincent felt his own face go wry with disgust. He made a wordless noise. Not wanting to witness the earth move for Monty, he turned from the cage and walked to the Hall of Wands.

The fly rods that stood along the wall in J. T. Allman's collection all were of varying shades of radiant amber. Vincent imagined that if he touched them one by one with the tip of his tongue, each would taste like honey from a different variety of flower. He made his way down the left side of the alcove, reading the makers' inscriptions as he moved. All the rods displayed on this one wall were the work of some of the finest current or recent bamboo rod builders, most of whose names Vincent was familiar with. He also knew that of the craftsmen and -women represented here who still took orders for custom fly rods, most maintained waiting lists that extended for years, even for as long as a decade.

Any one of the sublime casting tools on this contemporary side of the collection Vincent would have gladly taken down from the wall and carried down to the Río Perca for a full day of fishing, if he had permission to do so. But the rods on the opposite side, beginning about halfway through the back wall of the alcove, were of a different stature entirely. Every rod from this point onward was a piece created by one of the long-gone classical masters of rod making who had practiced their craft during the first half of the twentieth century. These rare pieces, enchanted objects of veneration that had been conjured into existence by druids with calloused hands, might perhaps properly be fished in a ceremonial fashion once or twice a year—on the solstices, maybe, or during the equinoxes—but otherwise, they belonged in a museum or in a temple, such as the one in which Vincent now found himself standing.

As he moved along those walls, Vincent saw a display of seven trout and salmon rods by F. E. Thomas, who had done his work in Vincent's home state of Maine; the Thomas selection included a twin of the seven-and-a-half-footer he and Sean used once a year on their once-sacred, until recently nameless, and now irredeemably profaned brook trout stream. There were a dozen pieces by West Coast rod maker

E. C. Powell, seven or eight rods by E. F. Payne, and a more or less equal number by Pinky Gillum—all of whose work Vincent knew commanded small fortunes on those rare occasions when pieces came onto the market. Vincent viewed several rods by Goodwin Granger. He saw works by Everett Garrison, who built only six hundred and fifty rods in his entire lifetime—and yet, here were nine of them gracing Allman's alcove. There were examples from many other exalted rod makers as well.

Altogether, the brilliance represented by this collection was almost overwhelming—and it also caused Vincent some confusion. While J. T. Allman seemed to have created the Louvre or the Hermitage of the bamboo fly-rod maker's art, at the same time and with the same mind, he maintained and operated machinery that fed pellets of hatchery chow to otherwise wild trout and salmon, with the apparent dual intention of making them grow large and fat and also keeping them stacked on top of one another in a handful of pools rather than spread out along the course of the river as nature had planned for them, all of them competing and the fittest among them divvying up the prime places from which to glean their natural provisions. It was difficult for Vincent to reconcile, this dissonance of sensitivity and exalted values on the one hand—art and ecology—and vulgarity on the other. If he ever got the opportunity—and although he was in the man's home, the odds of that seemed remote—he would have to question Allman about it. In any case, it would make for a juicy tidbit to feed to Dunlevy and his readers—or his audience, or his followers, or whatever it was they were supposed to be called.

Just as Vincent had finished taking some video of the rods, he heard the thump of the first celebratory rocket exploding over the grounds of the castle, and he thought he should probably head back to the room where he had left Angela. By now, she would likely be done with her call, and together, they could watch the fireworks through her window, and afterward—

Stepping from the Hall of Wands, he felt himself seized by either arm. "Here you are," one of them said. English, an American accent. Huge guys—one Black, one White; crew cuts and polo shirts on both; very obviously *yanquis*.

"Let go of me," said Vincent. With little effort, they hauled him to a wide elevator and dragged him inside. Up they went, four floors, not a word from either henchman. Then out, down a hallway, and onto a balcony where sat J. T. Allman in his sunglasses, his cowboy hat, and an elaborate electronic wheelchair, a cigar burning in his hand. Three rockets burst and flashed before them not far above the level of the granite window ledge, and Vincent thought that the sunglasses must serve to protect Allman's aged eyes from the pyrotechnical brilliance—but then again, perhaps he wore them every moment of the day regardless of lighting, indoors as well as out. A handsome German pointer rose from the carpet beside Allman's chair and turned to face Vincent. Clearly a trained gundog, it was unfazed by the percussion of the fireworks. After a moment, the dog came toward him and, curling one front leg against its body, poked an accusatory nose into Vincent's crotch.

"Who are you?" Allman asked as he continued to look out over the balcony railing. He still had that Texas accent even after so many decades away. A couple of whistling projectiles shot crackling cartwheels of burning magnesium through the sky before them. Vincent thought of responding with his question about the fish-pellet machines, then quickly pushed the idea from his mind.

"My name is Vincent Mapp. Can you have these fucking guys let go of me?"

"Where did you come from?"

"I'm a guest at Río Perca Lodge. I'm actually writing an article."

"And what are you doing here? On my land? In my house?" There were five big explosions in succession, and Vincent waited for their reverberations to fade.

"Your niece invited me."

"Which niece?"

"Angela." The grip from the two men at once became slightly uncertain. Vincent sensed it and shook them off. He stepped back from the prodding muzzle of the pointing dog. After a moment, Allman sighed.

"How do you know Angela?"

"We had a very pleasant conversation down by the river yesterday." Vincent drew Angela's handwritten invitation from his pocket and sidestepped the dog to hand it to Allman. One of the two security men twitched as if about to stop him but changed his mind. Allman opened the letter and peered down at it.

Speaking now to the two big men, Allman said, "See that Mr. Mapp gets back to Marta's place safely."

"May I have my letter, please?" Allman didn't respond. The men had their hands on him again.

"Wait a minute," Vincent said. "Mr. Allman. It's no surprise that you don't remember my name. But the magazine I used to edit gave you an award about twenty years ago. For your conservation work with cutthroat trout in Montana."

After a moment: "Doesn't ring a bell."

"Oh, come on. We got a ton of hate mail over that—and we decided we needed to publish all of the letters. Ten pages of letters, most of them attacking you and attacking me. I always wanted to ask you what you thought of that. Of the fact that we decided to do that. Publish them, I mean. You must have some memory of it."

Waiting for another series of rockets to finish exploding, Allman continued to stare out over the balcony. In the ensuing interlude of relative quiet, he said, "I do have a very vague memory of some pissant publication giving me an award. But that's it. Obviously, it would have been a much more important event to you than to me. As for a few letters from the unwashed rabble, which I'll have to take your word for . . ." He lifted a dismissive hand in the air. "In any case, so long, Mr. Mapp. If you ever come back here again, invitation or no, you're likely to fall out a window."

The goons gripped him once more and hauled him away from the balcony. As the three of them were getting into the elevator, one of the men murmured into a small radio transmitter he had taken from his pocket. Watching him, hearing him, Vincent was struck by a realization.

"Did you guys see Angela's play?" he asked. When neither man responded, he continued, "Because I'm thinking, you two are probably honest-to-God Pinkertons. Tell me I'm wrong."

"Shut the fuck up," the White one answered.

They descended to the ground floor and went out a side door, and there, beneath the ramada where they'd left the horses, was the gaucho,

Eduardo, standing beside a blue Land Cruiser. Eduardo opened the rear door, and the two probable Pinkertons stuffed Vincent inside.

Eduardo shut him in, then slid behind the wheel and closed his own door. Vincent said to him, "We're not going to ride the horses back across the river?"

"*No, señor. Muy peligroso por la noche.*" It's very dangerous at night.

Vincent and Eduardo didn't speak again until they were halfway back to the highway, and three phantasmal forms drifted onto the gravel road ahead of them and stood challenging them with glowing green eyes, forcing Eduardo to brake to a stop. Dogo Argentinos. No way of telling whether two of them were the same ones Vincent had seen the day before.

"What are they doing running around loose?" Vincent wanted to know.

"Protecting."

"Protecting what?"

"Cows. Sheep. People."

"Protecting them *from* what?"

Eduardo did not answer for a moment. Finally, he said, "Anything. Everything." It did make sense; Vincent remembered meeting a Montana rancher who at night would turn loose a few big dogs of a similar breed in order to protect his cattle from wolves. Here, there were pumas and pigs. And possibly, as he thought about it, rustlers. Perhaps Marta could do with a few rugged dogs on her side of the river.

Vincent said, "That breed is considered to be so aggressive that it's illegal to own one in many countries."

Eduardo again took his time in responding. By the time he spoke, the dogs had lost interest in them and had moved off the road, heading north. Vincent could still see their ghostly shapes bobbing through the dry grass. "*Señor,*" Eduardo said, "This is Patagonia."

CHAPTER EIGHT

Green Light

IN THE MORNING, VINCENT AWOKE FEELING EUPHORIC. THE NIGHT HAD been one of unexpected and extraordinary delights and accomplishments. There was Angela—who, less than twenty-four hours earlier, he never would have imagined he'd speak to again (much less . . .). And on a lesser plane of accomplishment and pleasure, he'd gotten a horseback tour that gave him a good overview of Allman's estate, with the opportunity to capture some video for Dunlevy—as well as an unscheduled meeting with the aged lion himself in his own den. True, it had not exactly been a formal interview, and he hadn't had the nerve to try to photograph him; likely the goons would have smashed his phone and maybe his fingers if he had. Also true: Allman had promised to have Vincent murdered Russian-mobster style if he ever saw him again. Nonetheless, he'd seen him, exchanged some interesting words with him, and could speak about him on Dunlevy's . . . whatever it was. Podcast? Twitter feed? YouTube channel? Internet fly-fishing masturbatorium?

Speaking of Dunlevy: Vincent checked his e-mail and found one from him, sent the day before. *Hi, Chief. Having fun? How's the fishing? Catching any landlockeds?*

Vincent responded, *Yes. Good. No. More tk.*

He opened the door to his bedroom to find Lulu coming down the hallway with a fistful of fresh alstroemerias for the vase on his dresser. They both said *buen dia* as they passed, and Vincent moved on into the dining room, where the two English equestrians were saying good-bye to everyone, as they were leaving for Bariloche that morning once they had finished packing. They told Vincent with seeming sincerity that they were delighted to have met him and that they hoped to see him again sometime; Vincent himself struggled to recall their names, which he'd thought he had finally committed to memory. In that moment, he did feel a pinch of poignance, however. Every ship passed was one ship closer to never passing another.

The Brazilian hunter reported that just this one day remained to him to find his stag and that he would be leaving the lodge on the following morning. "*Boa sorte*," Vincent told him. Vincent once again reminded the man that he himself was on the hunt for a specific creature that so far had eluded him—and possibly no longer existed.

The two influencers also were on their last day at Río Perca, and they said that they intended to gather supplies and then ride horses to the Butch Cassidy cabin above the Boca, where they would prepare their own final dinner and spend their final night.

Vincent, the most recent arrival among them, was only halfway through his stay, with three nights remaining to him—three more days of fishing, including the current one, and he felt fortunate. Still, he was acutely aware of how quickly fishing time invariably passed and that very soon his sojourn here, like all others before it, would be nothing more than a shifting, dreamlike memory and some images stored on his cell phone.

Lulu returned from down the hall to ask him what he wanted for breakfast. He had a good appetite, and he requested steak and poached eggs—*huevos pasados por agua*. Then he asked her where Clara was.

"In the kitchen," Lulu answered with a humorous twist of her mouth that told him Clara was hoping not to have to come out into the dining room that morning.

Sancho, looking worse for the wear, came in while he was eating. "Nine-thirty?" Sancho suggested.

"Sounds good." Vincent smiled at him. "Big cast party last night, I imagine."

"Yes. Angela left us very early, but we all carried on the best we could. Didn't I see you in the audience?"

"I was there. Last-minute invitation. Wonderful play; you were great. You and Clara both. Did you get any sleep?"

"Some."

"Hung over, maybe?"

"*Es obvio, no?* Still, one must earn a living. I will work hard to get us into some fish today."

Later, in Sancho's HiLux as they headed for the river, Vincent said, "There were some theater people at the *asado*. All Europeans, I think, but still. Did you and Clara make a professional connection or two?"

"A couple of those Spanish people took down our contact information. They did seem a bit more interested in Clara than in me. One of them was talking about a role in some kind of *telenovela* that called for a scheming and sexy South American housemaid. And if I'm being perfectly honest with myself . . . there is little reason for anyone to be searching for a one-eyed actor, no matter how devilishly handsome he might be." Sancho turned to give Vincent a wry smile before returning his monocular gaze to the road ahead of them.

"Do you mind my asking what happened to your eye?"

"A famous American angler—I won't tell you who he was, but his fame actually stems from something other than angling—he caught me on his backcast with a conehead Woolly Bugger. Chartreuse, I believe it was. My entire world went greenish-yellow for an instant. Then half of it went black."

"What? That's awful."

"Partly my fault, for not having my sunglasses on."

"Jesus. I'm sorry." Sancho shrugged.

"As a result, as compensation, my remaining eye has been endowed with supernatural abilities. It can divine salmon in locations and situations in which neither I nor my client would otherwise anticipate finding them. And at the moment, my eye is feeling particularly active and prognosticative in spite of also being somewhat bloodshot. That's how I can be confident that you and I will see a salmon today. A very good one, in fact."

"Well, we can try, amigo. That's all we can do. No need to make promises."

"Mark what I told you," the guide assured him. "Trust the enchanted eye of Sancho."

They returned to the Boca, which Sancho insisted was the most likely place to find a landlocked salmon when the river flowed at this low a level. While they were fishing, they heard several drones whine past in the air above them. The drones seemed to be following the thread of the river, holding just slightly to Allman's side. After twenty minutes of slinging streamers, Vincent caught a very nice brown trout. He and Sancho spent some time taking video of it and each other as they revived it in the cold current prior to its release. Once the brown had swum back to the depths, Vincent said, "You know, deep down, Sancho, I don't really care whether I catch a salmon on this trip or not. They may or may not be here; they may be here but scarce as unicorns. It doesn't really matter. The fishing has been fine otherwise, and I'll have plenty of good things to say about this place, in whatever medium I'm compelled to say them in. It'll be okay, however it unfolds. No reason for us to put pressure on ourselves."

Sancho said, "Ordinarily that might make me feel a bit better. A bit relieved, anyway. So, thank you for saying that. But, I do remain confident, just as long as we don't stop looking." He pointed to his eye, which, if anything, was redder and more sore-looking than it had been before. Vincent laughed.

"No," he said. "We won't stop looking, then."

They caught another good brown, not quite as large, after which they drove a half mile downriver and hiked to where a riffle turned a crooked corner, jumped down a low fall, and broadened into a pool. Vincent could not remember whether they had fished this spot before. But on the opposite side of the river, a taut white tent now stood pitched on a narrow plain of sand. From behind it somewhere came the monotonous purr of an electrical generator. Above the generator's noise, they heard the buzz of yet another drone that was following the course of the river. As Vincent stood above the head of the pool, preparing to make a cast—floating line, one of Sancho's effective little hair-wing streamers—the tent flap was unzipped from within, and a man wearing a white laboratory jacket ducked through it to step out onto the beach.

"Otto!" Vincent called. Otto lifted his face toward them and froze. Vincent handed his rod to Sancho.

"Go ahead and make a few casts," Vincent said. "I want to talk to this guy. I'll be back in a minute." He moved above the waterfall and splashed across the riffle while Otto stood waiting with a smile locked onto his face. When Vincent reached the sand in front of him, Otto widened his mouth a bit more.

"Vincent, isn't it?"

"Yes. Great meeting you last night. How are you?" Otto slowly accepted the hand Vincent stretched toward him. A surgeon's gripless handshake.

"Very well, thank you. Welcome to our new field laboratory. I'd offer you a tour of the interior, but I'm afraid I'm not in circumstances to be able to do that at the moment." As if to emphasize his words, he pivoted and rezipped the tent flap.

"That's all right," said Vincent. "I just have a question for you." Otto straightened and stood blinking at him through the round lenses of his glasses. Vincent noticed then that there were a few pinhead spots of blood on the lapels of the lab coat.

"The day before yesterday," Vincent said, "a pack of dogs came tearing along on this side of the river. Two were bully dogs—barking, as one would expect. The other two were hounds, and they all were chasing something together. But the hounds—they didn't bay the way hounds do when they're on a trail. We could see that they were *trying* to bay, going through the motions. Lifting their heads toward the sky with their mouths wide open, but no sound came out, and it was apparent they just did not have the ability. It struck me as extremely strange, bordering on the surreal. They were your dogs, weren't they? Running down some critter—because you came along following them on a bicycle. What was wrong with them? Are they sick . . . or something?"

Otto laughed. He almost seemed relieved, for some reason. "Of course they're our dogs—and nothing is *wrong* with them," he said. "They've just been devocalized."

"Devocalized?"

"Surgically silenced."

It took Vincent a moment to react. "Surgically . . . you mean you cut . . ." Otto clucked his tongue and shook his head.

"Brand-new, state-of-the-art procedure that we've developed right here in Argentina over the past couple of years. Much less invasive, much less of a chance of complications than the older, cruder methods, plus a 99.5 percent success rate. In addition, it's practically painless for the animal. Much less uncomfortable than neutering, I can assure you. And we did it entirely for you. For your benefit."

"You did it for *me*?"

"For all the sportsmen on your side who are trying to enjoy the peace and quiet of this pristine river valley. Of this bit of invaluable wilderness. For which you've paid Señora Dodier so much hard-earned money to enjoy. We use hounds quite a bit for various tracking purposes, and we certainly wouldn't want them and their discordant swamp music disturbing the harmony over there."

After a moment, Vincent—wide-eyed, tongue pushing against the inside of his cheek—nodded. "All right. Well. Thanks for explaining that."

"Yes, and now I must get back to my work."

"Okay. Otto." After he'd stepped back into the water, Vincent turned again. Otto was unzipping the tent flap. "Hey, Otto."

"Yes, Vincent?"

"I'm trying to remember. I think they said on that tallgrass prairie television documentary that you're German, originally?"

"I was born in Austria." He vanished into his tent.

Vincent got two strikes on Sancho's streamer as he fished the pool, and both times he failed to set the hook. He was no longer fishing very well; his mind kept drifting elsewhere. The conversation with Otto—that bit of darkness—illustrated as it was with the traces of blood on the white lab coat, had turned something in him, and it didn't only involve the disturbing information about the surgical silencing of the dogs. It now concerned his whole experience of last evening, the fact that he and Angela Allman had come to some sort of mysterious understanding—along with Vincent's growing realization that their connection would forever remain incomplete and almost completely unexplored. It would fade quickly and as quickly be forgotten. It wasn't that he imagined they had formed some magical emotional attachment in their short time together; that sort of thing didn't happen in real life—or if it did, it happened only to kids. Not to old men. Not to divorced single mothers moving on into middle age. But he did feel a strong yearning to talk to her once more; that was all. Just thinking about their conversation, reliving the sight of her smile and hearing her voice in his head, soothed him inside. Afterward, he would be able to tell himself that he actually knew her, and forever after, there would always be the possibility, however remote, of further conversation. They'd each be a part, though undoubtedly, almost assuredly, a tiny one, of one another's lives. As it currently stood, however, and likely as far as Angela was concerned, as far as she knew or *could* know, he was a man who was there for part of an evening and then vanished without saying good-bye, and she was left with no clue as to what had happened to him. Even at this moment, he imagined she was telling herself that their incident was of no importance. On to the next, for her.

He began to feel growing desperation over the fact that he had no way of getting in touch with her. Unlike Angela herself, he couldn't just dispatch a gaucho with a letter and an extra horse. He supposed he could ask Sancho for help—but that would put his new friend in an unacceptable position. While Sancho doubtlessly would feel uncomfortable refusing him the favor, by supplying any of a lady's personal information to a client, no matter the reason, he certainly would be falling short of impeccable conduct as a professional fishing guide. And Sancho was nothing if not impeccable in his standards. As for asking Clara or Marta for assistance . . . that also was out of the question. Regardless of whether one or both of them reluctantly agreed to help him, he could envision himself immediately tumbling in their assessment; they would undoubtedly conclude that they'd been wrong about him, that, after all, he was nothing but a dirty old *yanqui* horndog—when, of course, he wasn't really like that at all.

Anyway. There did remain the long-shot hope that sometime during the next three days—two and a half, now, really—he would catch her riding along the river with her tiny falcon on her wrist. He could talk to her then. He could laugh and pretend he hadn't thought about her one time since gathering up his clothes and fleeing from her room.

"Let's move on," said Sancho.

A turn around a bend in the river revealed a tableau composed of the two influencers and their guide. Nestor was standing, one arm propped atop the hoop of his long-handled net. Stevie and Stephen were down in the water, huddled over a fish. Stevie was holding it by the thick wrist of its tail as it faced into the current. She was talking to it in a soft, encouraging voice. She was telling it that it was beautiful; she was assuring it that everything would be all right again in a minute. Stephen was capturing video with his cell phone. As Vincent and Sancho drew closer, Stephen stood and backed away to get a wider view. That was when they saw that it was a salmon she had caught—a good one, perhaps twenty-three inches, and very thick through the middle. Silver flanks and on either side of its dorsal fin black spots like the tips of bullets.

"Stevie," said Stephen. "Look up now, babe." After a moment, she pulled off her sunglasses and grinned in his direction. "Stevie the Fish Witch here with a very nice landlocked salmon on the Río Perca in Patagonia, Argentina. This is the lady we've been hoping to meet all week. And she certainly put the backbone of my six-weight Kent XXO to the test—which it passed with flying colors, I'm happy to say. That's not even to mention the smooth and powerful drag system on my Ribbon River Technocrat Three reel. This silver beauty of a salmon launched herself skyward a good eight times, and she peeled me into my backing twice. But in the end . . . here she is, resting and hanging out with me on the bank of this wonderful Argentinian river. What a team this rod and this reel make; I couldn't ask for better."

Stevie continued after a pause, "Now please take note that I'm *not* lifting her out of the water. This is important because the more time a fish spends out in the air, the less her chances of making a complete recovery from the stress of being caught. And I really want this pretty lady to survive and make lots of babies, this year and next, so that I can keep coming down here year after year and catching these beautiful landlocked salmon on the incredible Río Perca."

Then Stevie blinked and said, "Okay, fuck, I've got sunscreen in my eyes now, and I need to pee. I'm gonna let her go." Unexpectedly, she nodded in Vincent's direction. "Would you like to take a few photos,

Vincent? I know you were looking for one of these guys. She's a money fish, for sure. You can even release her if you want, and I'll take some video for you with your cell phone." Vincent could detect no sign that she might be taunting him. She was trying to be helpful.

After a moment, he said, "I would, but the camera on my phone isn't working for some reason. Thanks, though. And, congratulations, Stevie. That's a great fish."

As Vincent and Sancho continued downstream, it was a while before they spoke or even looked at one another. When they finally resumed speaking, neither of them mentioned Stevie's salmon.

Later in the day as they moved along the river, they came upon a line of fresh dog tracks pressed into damp sand. "I've only ever seen such tracks once or twice on our side of the river," Sancho said in answer to Vincent's question. "Usually, the river is too high for a dog to want to swim across."

"But it's not high now."

"No, it's not high now."

"They let those dogos—those big, white bastards—run loose at night, at least they do on the other side of the ridge. I wonder if dogs could be swimming across to chase deer over here and driving them away. Hence, the scarcity experienced by our Brazilian hunter friend."

"It's a reasonable question."

"Maybe they've been doing some other things as well."

After a pause, Sancho said, "If you don't mind, shall we not bring this up at home, unless we find stronger evidence? Neighborhood relations are rocky enough as it is. In any case, as I've mentioned before, those other things you're talking about seem much more likely to have been the work of boars."

Day's end: Sancho came into the lodge with him for a drink. Clara was out and about, working at the bar, though she was visibly tired. Vincent saw her exchange a brief look with Sancho, and he thought, *Yes, definitely a couple. Good for him.*

The two Englishwomen were gone, and the influencers also were absent. Vincent remembered that Stevie and Stephen had planned to ride up to the cliff cabin to spend the night. In place of the four who were no longer there, four new guests had arrived. Marta introduced Vincent to a late-middle-aged husband and wife who owned a vineyard outside of Mendoza and had come south for the fishing and two fortyish men from Buenos Aires who were keen to shoot a couple of antlered red deer. Following the handshakes and the *mucho gustos*, the two new hunters returned to their conversation with the Brazilian hunter, who was giving them an account of his disappointing week. The new arrivals already were looking discouraged.

As Vincent accepted a whiskey from Clara, he took the opportunity to tell her she'd been wonderful in the play, and that made her smile. He then joined Marta and the Mendoza fishing couple. Marta was telling them that her gauchos were out searching for a yearling bull that had gone missing. The young bull had been selected as a future *semental*—a breeding animal—and unless it was recovered and was still alive, when the time came, she would have to acquire an expensive replacement from another ranch. So far, the only possible sign of it the searchers had found was a broad patch of bloody earth—no other remains and no proof as to what kind of creature had even done the bleeding. Certainly, it was not possible that a nearly mature *semental* could have somehow been sucked up into the sky, and yet . . . if the missing animal had died on that blood-darkened spot, where was it—or any part of it?

"I'm not sure what is going on around here," Marta said. "Upsetting things have suddenly been happening night after night. I might have to distribute firearms to a few of the gauchos and have them patrol from sunset until dawn."

Vincent said, "That's probably not a bad idea."

Lying in his barge of a bed that night, Vincent felt restless. Remaining to him here were two more days and two more nights. Then he was on his way home. Certainly, having seen a salmon caught, he wanted one of his own. But much more than that . . . Angela. To have a conversation with her about what had happened between them and why, exactly, it had happened. What it meant, what it hadn't meant, or whether it had merely been a random occurrence like most occurrences in the universe, with no actual meaning at all. No; that last possibility he could not accept. It had to be something, even if that something was something very small. A thin connection, a spark, at the very least.

Yes; he was being a teenager now. He understood that, and yet he was powerless against it. He had drifted through a placid marriage for so long that he'd lost touch with his own powerful responses to certain natural signals. That teenager had been coiled within him the whole time—and he wasn't such a bad kid. Maybe he even possessed some wordless wisdom that grown-up Vincent, Old Vincent, had lost along the way. The realization was like stirring from a dreamless sleep to the revelation that he'd slept through a good part of his life. Before it was too late, he needed to wake up completely and smell the pheromones.

Abruptly, things began to happen: Vincent was out of bed, dressed, impulsively snatching the flowers from the vase on the chest of drawers and grabbing up his shoes before gliding on stocking feet through the darkened, sleeping lodge. From somewhere—probably from the room of the defeated Brazilian hunter—came the jagged sound of snoring. He heard the ticking of a clock he could not remember ever having seen.

Good chance she was not in her cabin at the top of the ridge. More likely, she'd packed up everything and was down at the castle, on her first stage toward jetting back to Europe. In which case, he was out of luck. Nonetheless, he needed to know. If she was up there, likely there would be a light, and he would be able to see that light or the lack thereof from the bank of the river.

In the entrance hall, a powerful-looking flashlight stood balanced on the radio transmitter table; Vincent borrowed it. Outside the front door, he tied his shoes, gathered his waders and his wading boots, and headed out onto the gravel road. There was a chill in the air, and he hadn't thought to bring a jacket, but he now was an object in motion, and he would not return to the lodge. In the beech woods to one side of the road, he used the flashlight to find a branch that could serve as a walking stick, a wading staff—and also to whack the snout of a frisky pig or a cranky dog if he needed to do so. Then, his hands full with flashlight, waders, wading boots, flowers, and stout stick, he continued along the gravel road until he reached the sloping forest fork that he knew would lead him to the river. Down he went.

The moon was no more than a sliver, and Vincent was glad for the flashlight. When he finally stood on the riverbank, hearing the murmur and hiss of the water as it descended through its timeless gauntlet of rocks, he tipped back his head and began scanning the ridge. After a moment, he did see light, a single glowing green speck much higher in the sky than he had expected, with the blackness of the ridgetop and the gray, starlit shimmer of the horizon just above it. Ambiguous, he would call the message of that light. Could mean she was up there; could just be a light that always remained on regardless of whether Dulcinea was occupied. And why was it *green* in the first place?

"What do you say, old man?" he asked himself aloud, vapor boiling from his mouth. He had a long history of daring himself to do things, and, if he were being honest about it, many of those things had gone badly. The trail seemed steeper than it did during the daytime. Then Vincent thought . . . *what would a salmon do?*

He slipped off his shoes, slid his legs and feet into waders and wading boots. Using the heavy stick to probe the unseen river bottom ahead of him, he carefully shuffled across as the current tugged at him. Once on Allman's side, he peeled off the waders and laid them folded on a rock, boots on top to weigh them down in case of wind. He put his shoes back on, and then, with the wooden staff in one hand, flashlight and flowers in the other, he began to climb the trail.

Yes, it was steeper than it looked in the daylight. And his legs and lungs were unaccustomed to this level of exertion. It soon became clear that this was going to be an arduous ascent. Yet he was prodded on by the knowledge that, compared to other ascents accomplished by other people, by other creatures, this was a small thing; a weakling's conception of a challenge. After all, on the previous evening, those *criollo* horses had made it up this same trail with just a moderate effort. As for the chinook salmon of the Yukon River . . . their migration from the Bering Sea was nineteen hundred miles. Through rapids, up waterfalls, dodging predators, all in order to reach the spawning waters that lay beyond the inland city of Whitehorse. Fighting, pairing up, then mouths gaping as they quivered side by side, spraying eggs and milt onto redds dug with their powerful tails into beds of ancestral gravel.

And then dying. His throat was raw already, and his knees were hurting. In some spots, he had to transfer his staff to his left hand along with the flowers and the flashlight—in one hand, they were difficult to hold all at once—in order to grip a rock or a hank of grass and pull himself up. How had those horses made this seem so relatively effortless?

But, no; this was not an attempt on his part to fulfill a death wish. It was pure Eros; not a speck of Thanatos. True enough that all the Pacific salmon species—chinook, coho, sockeye, humpback, and chum—died after spawning. But not Atlantic salmon. Many Atlantics lived to return to the ocean and to make yet another or even several spawning runs during the course of their lifetimes. If Vincent were a salmon, he'd be an *Atlantic* salmon—exact same species as the landlocked strain and a close cousin of the brown trout—battered, but a survivor.

Brown trout: European, including the British Isles, where among its habitats were gentle rivers full of watercress that wound their quiet way beneath the windows of fairy-tale castles. Browns had been brought to the Americas, where they now were common in many waters clean and cool enough to support them. There also were strains of brown trout on both sides of the Atlantic that spent most of their time in the salt, ascending rivers time and again, but only to spawn before returning to estuaries or all the way out to the ocean. They also were survivors of the spawn, so perhaps rather than an Atlantic salmon, Vincent would be an anadromous brown. They grew large, and they were quite handsome. More silvery than the inland variety. Some of these sea-run brown trout returned to rivers very far to the south of where Vincent was now, in the most extreme parts of Patagonia. Maybe he would make it there to fish for them one day.

Vincent needed to rest. He sat down on a rock, wheezing and staring up at that green fleck of light. Although nearer, it still seemed almost discouragingly distant given the effort he'd already put in to reaching it. Nonetheless, he was now feeling a nascent pride in his effort; after all, unlike Gatsby, a much younger and fitter fellow who had passively mooned at his light from afar, Vincent was actually doing something to close the distance. He heard an unseen drone buzz by high overhead; he wondered who, exactly, had launched it and what its mission might be.

Perhaps it could see him down there, and they'd be sending a reception party soon. He remembered Allman's threat to have him pitched out a window. No windows here; they'd have to hurl him down the mountain instead; that likely would do the trick. He also recalled the chest pain and breathlessness that had nearly overcome him in the airport parking lot a few days before, but he quickly forced that memory from his mind. Better to keep himself busy fantasizing about salmonids.

Perhaps Vincent would be a steelhead—that seagoing strain of rainbow trout that, in spite of belonging to the same genus as the Pacific salmons, also survived having sex. Funny how ideas of what was a salmon and what was a trout were all jumbled together in the popular mind. People thought of trout as one type of fish, salmon another, with trout being creatures of the fresh water and salmon migrating into and out of the ocean. And yet, brown trout and Atlantic salmon shared that tight connection—same genus: *Salmo*—with only a distant familial link to any of the Pacific salmons or any of the North American fish commonly known as trout. Meanwhile, native rainbow trout, including steelhead, as well as cutthroat trout—more than a dozen subspecies of which had been the predominant fish throughout most of the Rocky Mountain West before being largely displaced and replaced by the introduction of alien browns and rainbows—shared close lineage with all of the Pacific salmon. The genus that encompassed them all—Pacific salmon, rainbow trout, cutthroat trout: *Oncorhynchus*. Vincent had absorbed all of this taxological information long ago during several days spent fishing in Colorado with the great salmonid expert Dr. Robert J. Behnke. Prior to that, he'd been as hazy about it as anybody.

Vincent stood up. His thighs were quivering, but he was breathing a little more smoothly; it seemed that he had gotten a second wind. As he began to climb again, he thought, *Of course it's important to remember that the cutthroat trout native to the West Coast also have a seagoing strain.* Then there were the chars to deal with: Arctic char, brook trout, bull trout, Dolly Varden trout—genus *Salvelinus*—all of which had sea-run populations and none of which was ever referred to as a salmon.

Remember all of this, Vincent commanded an imaginary class. *It might be on the test.*

It almost seemed as if trout—or troutness—was an arbitrary, even imaginary, distinction. In any case, only a single species on the entire globe included the Latin word for trout in its scientific name—*Salmo trutta*—the brown trout. And even then ... could a brown trout be a *true* trout, at least in the way people thought of trout, when, in their habit of traveling into and out of oceans, so many of them behaved exactly like the salmon to which they were so closely related, thereby revealing as nothing more than misconception—or fantasy or mythologization—on the part of the original name givers, the entire concept of "trout" as a colorful inland fish that lived exclusively in streams and lakes and rivers that ran above the reach of tides? Perhaps there really was no such thing as a trout ...

Or maybe Vincent's brain was just starved for oxygen. Most likely, he'd been in academia for far too long. In any case, he finally reached the forested plateau that he knew lay directly below Angela's cabin. A hundred yards across it to the final climb, followed by another fifty vertical yards, more or less—and he will have made it. Not bad for an old bastard, actually. And he could see now that, in addition to the green light over the back door, there were other lights, yellow lights, behind the shaded windows—a very good sign. First, though, another little rest.

Something stirred among the trees to his left. "Fuck off," he said in a loud voice, and whatever it was fell silent.

Now, "salmon," by contrast, was a less ambiguous informal classification. Except for the landlocked Atlantic salmon and the landlocked sockeye salmon known as the kokanee, both of them species that had remained trapped in fresh water due to geological circumstances over which they never had a say, all salmons, Pacific or Atlantic, were salmonids that inhabited seas and oceans but made at least one trip back to their natal rivers to spawn. *Salmonids*, of course, being the various fish—trout, salmon, char, grayling—that all traced their common origin to a 50-million-year-old Ur salmonid that went by the scientific name of *Eosalmo driftwoodensis*. *Eosalmo* and its descendants diverged over time in directions that led to all the contemporary species—as well as wandered into a number of evolutionary blind alleys, one of which Vincent knew to be a 6-million-year-old dead end whose six-foot-long fossilized remains had been dubbed the "saber-toothed salmon"—*Oncorhynchus rastrosus*. And, yes, the saber-toothed salmon did have very large and very prominent dentition and was likely a ferocious predator.

One important fact that did not involve any controversy or ambiguity: all salmonids were natives of the Northern Hemisphere. Any salmonids living and reproducing in the Southern Hemisphere—in South America, subequatorial Africa, Australia, New Zealand—were products of introductions made by humans, introductions that in all cases had results both good and bad and likely irreversible.

Remember all of this; it might be on the test.

He was climbing again. He could make out that there were several horses in the paddock next to Dulcinea, another good sign that Angela would be home. He was shaking all over, as much from excitement and nervousness as from the exhaustion of the climb. In just a minute, Angela might open the door to his knock and see him standing there with his bundle of not-too-wilted flowers, and the rest would be up to Vincent. Vincent and his charm—such as it was—and his devilish wit. Of the two—charm and wit—only wit was always with him anymore. But, charm: scrape through the cold coals, and he could occasionally find an ember down there somewhere. Then he was up and over the edge and onto the narrow yard between the bare planks of the back porch and the downward trail. A horse spotted him and nickered.

It wasn't until he had almost reached the porch that he heard the voices. Laughter; she wasn't alone. He felt himself physically deflating. Shriveling, more like. In his imagination, a big fish broke off and the line went slack—that most horrible feeling. Too tired and discouraged to do anything else, Vincent sat on the edge of the porch and listened.

He didn't hear a man's voice—at least, not yet. There were two women in the cabin. They were speaking English. After a minute, he recognized one voice as that of Angela. The other one . . . he couldn't be sure. It might possibly belong to Gabriela, in which case . . . Vincent's hopes began to reconstitute themselves from the ashes. If the other woman was Gabriela and the two of them were alone, it was possible that both of them would be amused to see him. Yes; amused at first and then . . . who knew? Gabriela also had seemed to find him interesting.

Things within Dulcinea grew quiet. Vincent grew impatient. Before he knocked, he needed to know the twins were in there and no one else. If the other woman were anyone but Gabriela, it would mean mission abort, extraction requested. It would be back down the mountain, with his drooping tail tucked between his hairless old man's legs. Although the shades were drawn down over the two rear windows, on the right side, there was a gap between the sash and the bottom of the shade through which shined a horizontal bar of flickering light. Vincent left the walking stick and the flashlight on the edge of the porch. Still clutching the flowers, he crawled across the porch until he reached the window. Slowly, he raised his head and peered through the slit of an opening. Just then, female laughter resumed. One of them murmured something that Vincent couldn't make out.

Dulcinea was lit within by candles that burned on tables and dressers all around. Vincent could see that the interior was a single, large room with a bed at one back corner and a kitchen alcove at the other. In between was a black woodstove with a chimney pipe that rose through the roof. Doors at the back of the kitchen area and beside the headboard of the bed. In the foreground, an oval braided rug on which stood a couple of big, stuffed chairs; Vincent was reminded of the stage set in Angela's play. On one of those chairs sat Stephen, a drink in his hand, completely unclothed. On the rug below the chair, piles of pillows beneath their knees, were . . . one was Stevie, and the other was Angela. Both women wore stringy underpants and nothing else. They were giving Stephen the royal treatment, handing him from one of them to the other, whispering and laughing and touching their foreheads together as he sat above them looking around the cabin, sipping his drink and seeming somewhat detached from it all, almost as if he were accustomed to this sort of event and perhaps even a little bored by it.

Vincent was immediately aware that he didn't belong here. That he had made a mistake. That he was doing something shameful and that he should leave. Yet he also felt powerless to turn his eyes from the dreamlike vision before him. Another minute, and Angela murmured something indistinct that Vincent interpreted as *May I?* Then she ascended to the stuffed chair to kneel astride Stephen's legs, facing him with her shins pressing into the upholstery on either side of him. Stephen's hands went to her hips as she wrapped her arms around the back of his neck and drew him to her, her face tilted toward the ceiling. Soon, Stevie touched Angela from behind, pinched her gently, and said something to her, and Angela, while still pressing Stephen's face against her, obediently rose onto her knees. Stephen slid his hands to her waist, and Stevie hooked her forefingers into the waistband of Angela's thong and began working it down her thighs.

This finally broke the spell for Vincent. *What's wrong with you?* he asked himself. He dropped his head below the level of the window-sill and slid back crab-like until he reached the edge of the porch. He flopped off the porch, grabbed the flashlight and his walking stick, and, moving quickly, retreated downslope toward the river. After a moment, he pitched the ridiculous bundle of flowers out into the darkness. Only when he was a safe distance from Dulcinea did he turn on the flashlight.

He said to himself, *Nothing at all wrong with it; just young people having fun.*

You know what's really wrong? It's you. Stupid old man.

He made up a simple little song that he sang under his breath as he descended:

Stupid old man
Stupid old man
Stupid old man, stupid old man, stupid old man

He fell one time and got right up, still singing. When he reached the plateau below the cabin and was among the autumnal beech trees, he felt it was safe to raise his voice, and he began to sing more loudly: *Stupid old man!* He was heartbroken and at the same time almost exultant; after all, what other man his age would have had the courage to be so stupid? No one. No one at all. He, Vincent Fucking Mapp, was a singular, lonesome hero; he was an Odysseus, a Don Quixote, of astonishing, breathtaking, awe-inspiring stupidity—long may it live. He began laughing out loud.

Then, with the concurrent sensation of time having suddenly slowed, Vincent found himself falling again, this time because he was being dragged from behind. Something had taken him at the cuff of his pants and hauled him down onto his face, driving the breath from his lungs. The heavy stick was beneath him and the flashlight on the ground beyond his reach, shining out into nowhere. He lay stunned until he felt the jaws release his cuff to close again around his foot. Puncture pain and crushing pressure. At the same time, he felt hot breath and wetness against his ear. A rough brush against his cheek. The stench of death in his nose.

Vincent screamed: loud, high-pitched, completely unselfconscious. Instinctively, he twisted onto his back in order to defend himself. He felt his shoe come off. He drew back the still-shod foot and kicked, striking something solid and living with the heel. Heard a grunt. Drew back, kicked again, and struck only air. Made hard contact once more with the third kick and heard a muffled whine. *Fuck off*, he yelled.

Off in the woods to his left, he saw a flash. Heard the crack of a rifle. He kicked and kicked, and there was nothing. Flailed his arms, and there seemed to be nothing to either side of him. He sat up, lifted his body off of the heavy stick, and, still sitting, grabbed up the stick and held it before him. Helicoptered it all around his head, but the creature or creatures seemed to be gone. He peered off in the direction from which the rifle shot had come.

"Hey," Vincent said. No answer. Thought he could make out the silhouette of somebody still standing there, watching him. Using the staff, he pushed himself to his feet. His foot hurt, he felt wetness there, but it supported his weight.

"*Estoy herido*," Vincent yelled. "I'm hurt."

After a moment, a man's voice: "*Podes caminar, pelotudo?*" Vincent took a few steps. It wasn't difficult. He was injured, but not critically. No bones crushed. Not in a great deal of pain.

"I can walk. But I'm bleeding."

"*Si podes caminar, camine entonces.*" If you can walk, start walking.

"*What?* Come here and help me." When the man said nothing more, Vincent limped over to grab the flashlight. Shined it off into the woods, but the man with the gun was gone. He found his shoe, torn but still wearable, and put it on.

"Are you still there, *loco?*" No answer. Vincent waited another minute, then continued down the trail. On the bank of the river, he located his waders and his wading boots and put them on. Carried his shoes across the river, switched back into them on the other side. Ascended to the dirt road along the river, crossed it, and headed up through woods toward the lodge.

Half a mile from the lodge, a bolt of pain shot through his chest. The pain continued; he felt a squeezing, a shortness of breath, a gray veil descending over his eyes, and he sat down to rest with his back against a tree. He thought he heard voices cackling in the forest around him. *The Little People*, he thought. He rested his head against the tree and let the grayness swallow him.

CHAPTER NINE

The Fisher King

HE DREAMED A HUGE SNAKE WAS CONSTRICTING HIM, CRUSHING THE breath out of him. After a while, the snake peered at him through J. T. Allman's aviator sunglasses. "Oh," the dreaming Vincent said. Once more during the night, he either heard or imagined he heard elfin tittering from several different points in the woods around him, and he thought, *There's nothing funny here, fuckers.*

When he fully awoke, he was still in the forest. The sun had not yet risen, but the sky had brightened sufficiently for him to see. He was cold, shivering. His waders, wading boots, flashlight, and wading staff lay beside him in a pile. He could breathe; he actually felt relatively well considering the animal attack and the subsequent pain and tightness and the feeling of weakness, followed by several hours of sleeping slumped against a tree. He pulled off his damaged shoe and the shredded sock and inspected his injured foot. The blood had partly dried, and peeling away the sock made the wounds bleed again. Nonetheless, the foot was in better shape than he expected. There were a couple of gashes above his heel, on either side of the tendon. This was where the animal had first bitten through his jeans to grab him. The cuts were not especially serious. There were another two slices, a little deeper, on either side of the top of his foot. Much of the foot was purple from bruising, but there were no deep punctures, and nothing seemed broken. If his shoe hadn't pulled off . . . Vincent felt sick visualizing it.

No doubt, he should make his way to a hospital. Get his chest checked out and his foot patched up. But down here in Patagonia, that was problematic. For one thing, he didn't know about these Argentine hospitals—at least for the chest question. It's likely the facilities and the doctors were fine, but he just wasn't sure, and, because he was American and in spite of his languages and his travels and the fact that he should know better, he remained viscerally and irrationally skeptical of foreign institutions and aptitudes. As for the foot, the cuts needed a good cleaning out and disinfecting, followed by a professional bandaging, if not also a stitch or two. A rabies shot likely would be advisable—though he wasn't certain that pigs even carried rabies, if it was in fact a pig that had attacked him—and in any case, he'd read that rabies was not endemic to Argentina, so his risk of contracting the disease was low. But his largest reluctance to visiting a hospital stemmed from the fact that the nearest one was nearly two hours away in Bariloche, the services he required would likely be time consuming, and he would lose, at the very least, a whole day at Río Perca, if not the entire remainder of his fishing time at the lodge. No, that wasn't acceptable; he was willing to take a small risk, and he'd probably be just fine if he handled everything himself. What he would do: clean and swaddle his own foot so it was almost as good as new. As for the . . . chest thing, he'd take some aspirin. He understood that if he chewed a few aspirin every day—he'd need to Google how many and how frequently—it would thin his blood and prevent any sort of cardiac inconvenience from occurring; it would tide him over until he could get back to Maine and see his own doctor and get tested at his local hospital. He wasn't going to let what likely had been nothing more than an extreme panic attack ruin his trip.

Vincent reached for the walking stick. Groaning "Heigh-ho, heigh-ho," he pushed against the ground with the stick to propel himself to his feet. He stood taking stock for a minute, enjoying the altitude and pleased to find that his legs were steady, his foot did not hurt too badly, and he did not feel dizzy or faint.

"Fucking indestructible," he said aloud, defiance in his voice. He bent to gather the waders, wading boots, and flashlight and headed up through the woods.

Once he reached the lodge, he hung his waders on a peg and tossed his wading boots onto the flagstones beneath the wooden bench. When he opened the door, Clara was coming down the entry hall with an alarmed expression on her face.

"Vicente!" she said. "What are you doing? This early—were you outside?"

"I went for a little walk," he said. He showed her the flashlight. "I borrowed this. Thank you." He set the light on the table that held the radio transmitter.

"*Estás bien?* You don't look well."

"I have never been better." Telling the truth to anyone at the lodge would be a mistake. Not only would they insist on taking him to get professional medical treatment, but much worse than that, their opinion of him would change with the knowledge that he had gone creeping around at night.

"Wait." Clara lifted a hand toward the side of his head, and when she drew it back, she held a beech leaf scissored between two fingers. She stared at him. After a moment, almost as if struggling to stop herself, she reached toward him again and smoothed his damp hair against his scalp. Vincent visualized his weightless hair sticking out in all directions with yellow leaves all through it, and he laughed.

"You may call me Rip van Winkle," he said. "Which, by the way, was the first short story ever published in the United States. Is breakfast ready?"

"No! Not for another hour."

"Okay. See you then." He headed for his room, trying not to limp. On the way—and looking around to make sure neither Clara nor Lulu was watching him—he snatched a bottle of vodka from the bar.

First thing, he found the aspirin in his kit bag and chewed two of them. The taste was not entirely intolerable; more sour than bitter. Needed a glass of water to wash down all the grit. Then he stripped down and stepped into the shower. Blood from his foot swirled down the drain—but then, a little further bleeding to flush the wounds probably was a good thing.

He dried off, carried the vodka bottle back into the shower, drank a couple of swallows straight from the neck, then doused his foot, wincing and letting out a ragged whine as the liquor seared him. Finally, he gingerly patted his wounds with a towel, took a few photos of his injuries with his phone, and wound the foot in one of a pair of elastic compression stockings he'd bought for the long airline flight to Buenos Aires—and had not worn because just thinking about it made him feel old.

He fell asleep, half dressed, on the bed, arms wide and feet against the floor, and awoke only when Clara knocked on the door. "Vicente?" she called.

"Hah?" He said. "Breakfast?"

"They're looking for you outside."

"Who is?"

"*Dos caballeros*. From across the river."

"Okay," Vincent said after a moment. In his stomach, a drum thud of anxiety. To himself he said, *What fresh hell?*

He finished dressing, put on the sneakers he'd brought as a spare pair of shoes, and went out through the dining room. He said *buen dia* to all the deer hunters, who were sitting down to coffee, and he continued out through the entrance hall and through the front door.

Outside, a blue Land Cruiser idled in the drive, and standing beside it were the two large men who had intercepted him as he emerged from the Hall of Wands on the night of Allman's *asado* and Angela's play. Somehow, it seemed like a long time ago. Both men were clean-shaven, the darker of the two wearing a yellow polo shirt, the pink man in red. Vincent left the door open behind him. He widened his eyes at them. "Oh," he said. "Fuck you. Fuck you *both* with a flagpole." He turned to go back inside.

"Wait. Mr. Mapp," the man in yellow said. Vincent turned back.

"*Mister* Mapp, is it?"

"Mr. Allman would very much like to speak with you."

"You think I'm getting in that car with the two of you, you're out of your fucking minds."

"He asked us to let you know that it would be worth your while."

"He's going to *pay* me to talk to him, now?" Vincent looked from one to the other of them, and they shifted around uncomfortably.

"He's ready with some kind of proposal. We are not privy to the details." Of course, whatever it was, Vincent could not resist hearing what

Allman had to say. Discovering the *why* of this intriguing reversal in attitude toward him. Maybe even asking him a few questions on Dunlevy's behalf. Best of all: it was also apparent that, at the very least, Vincent had a temporary but large advantage in the current negotiation with these two *yanqui* thugs. Which meant there was amusement to be had.

"What's your name?" Vincent said.

"Henry," the man in yellow said, after a pause.

"How about you?"

"I'm Stanley."

"Well, Henry and Stanley, before I get in that car with you, I need to hear from you what a couple of complete Pinkerton dickheads you are." The two of them stiffened; Stanley's ham-like hands opened in the air in front of him, and he looked like he was restraining himself from moving toward Vincent. Neither of them said anything.

"All right," said Vincent. "Well, I've got breakfast and a full day of guided fishing scheduled for today, for which I've paid good money, by the way, so . . ."

"I'm a complete Pinkerton dickhead," Henry said in flat voice. A moment later: "Is that what you're looking for?"

"I need to hear your name in there somewhere."

"I, Henry, am a complete Pinkerton dickhead." Vincent lifted his chin at the other one. The man's eyes were slits.

"I, Stanley, am a complete . . . Pinkerton dickhead."

"All right," Vincent said. He smiled. "Now we're getting somewhere. Let me pay a visit to the little boys' room, and I'll be right out."

When Vincent returned, Stanley held the rear door for him, and he settled himself onto the slippery blue leather of the Land Cruiser's back seat. They drove out to the highway, turned to cross the bridge, then a few minutes later turned again onto the gravel road that wound along the northern base of the ridge toward Allman's castle and Lago Perca. To their immediate north sprawled the flat, golden rangeland, rolling out toward the next, distant line of high hills that Vincent had seen from atop the ridge and from horseback the evening before. Driving out in darkness following his expulsion a few hours later, he'd been able to see very little. Just a few cows that passed through the headlights as they crossed the road . . . and, of course, the troika of dogo Argentinos. Now, in morning daylight, he saw cattle near and far, mounted gauchos moving among them, and small herds of guanacos off in the distance. At one point, they came on four wild boar crashing through the roadside brush and, at another, four ostrich-like rheas that entered the road, sturdy legs churning, rump feathers shaking, and began racing ahead of the Land Cruiser until finally the flock divided, two and two, and ran off into the grassland on either side.

He had been assuming it was an aggressive boar that pulled him down, but now, thinking about those night-roaming dogs, he no longer was as certain. Dogos were famous for the incredible crushing force of their jaws, as well as for their willingness to attack. A pit bull terrier had nothing on a dogo; in fact, dogos were larger and more muscular. And while the Allmans' dogos supposedly were trained to defend rather than to harm ranch animals, Vincent vividly recalled a real-life account by the Canadian author Ernest Thompson Seton of a dog that was a loyal sheep guardian by day and an enthusiastic sheep slayer by night. This same treacherous sheepdog—Vincent believed it was the same dog, although it had been a long time since he'd read the story—also enjoyed murdering smaller dogs that lived nearby and burying their bodies in a gravel pit. Such a dual personality on the part of one or more dogos could account for the disappearances and savagings of animals on Marta's side of the river. And although it seemed logical that he would have seen a flash or two of white fur had his own attacker been one of these white dogs—or more than one, as it had been a very dark night—Vincent had just finished getting the wind knocked out of him and was practically seeing stars . . . and the struggle had lasted for a mere, albeit extremely intense, few seconds during which his mind, rather than filing the memory, was focused entirely on his immediate need to remain alive.

Would Vincent's anonymous rescuer have fired a rifle to scare them off and stop the attack if the attackers had been dogs that were known to him? Likely not; he would have whistled or called them off instead—unless he either did not know them well or had reason to believe that a mere verbal command might not stop them in time.

146

"The hounds of the Baskervilles," Vincent said aloud. Henry glanced at him in the rearview mirror before returning his eyes to the road; Stanley craned his head around the front passenger seat to fix him with a glare. Vincent smiled and said, "Come to think of it, that'd make me Sherlock Holmes, now wouldn't it?"

Almost an hour after leaving Marta's lodge, Henry pulled the Land Cruiser beneath the ramada beside Allman's palace. Stanley stepped out and opened the door for Vincent, and then, as Henry drove off, he and Vincent headed toward the pink building. Vincent heard tango music coming from within. As they entered the vast central room, he saw a band playing just outside the Hall of Wands: a grand piano, an accordion, a violin, a clarinet, a couple of guitars, a double bass. Between the band and Monty's huge cage in the center of the room, a man in a black tuxedo and a woman in a long red dress and heels were dancing. The dancers were precise; they were elegant, they were gorgeous, and around them in a rough semicircle stood an audience consisting of perhaps a dozen Argentine- or European-looking people, also in fine dancing clothes, as well as maybe a dozen of the Mongolian and Kazakh falconers Vincent had seen on the night of the *asado*, all of them in their bright tunic-like dress. Vincent scanned the Europeans among the spectators, hoping to see either Angela or Gabriela, but neither of the sisters was present.

Stanley led him around the opposite side of Monty's cage in order to avoid passing through the tango audience, and Vincent noticed that the steel door to the black cage was yawning, its occupant absent.

"Where's Monty?" Vincent asked, raising his voice to make himself heard above the music.

Stanley said, "The monkey has gone to his winter quarters in Florida. He left yesterday."

After a moment, Vincent said, "He's not a monkey. He's an ape." By then they had reached the elevator. They stepped inside, the doors closed, and Stanley turned to look down at him.

In a quiet voice, Stanley said, "I don't care if you are old. If I ever run into you back in the States, I'm going to pound you to a pulp."

The doors opened, and Stanley led him down a hallway and out onto a balcony on the opposite side of the castle from where Vincent had met

Allman two nights before. Vincent could still hear the tango music from below. Allman relaxed in his wheelchair, drinking coffee and enjoying the music and the view of his vast territory to the north and the east. Cowboy hat, string tie, tooled boots on the footrest of his robotic, rolling machine, trademark aviator sunglasses. One long bay of the shining blue lake was visible from the table before which the mega-billionaire sat. Vincent knew he owned a good portion of that shoreline.

"Mr. Mapp!" Allman said, raising a trembling arm in Vincent's direction. They shook—Allman, despite the tremble and the mysterious weakness in his legs, still had a firm grip. "Please, sit down. Have you had breakfast?"

"I could use some coffee," said Vincent. There was a small table, along with a chair, in front of Allman. Vincent sat down across from him. Allman looked up at Stanley, who turned and stepped back into the building for a moment. Vincent heard him speaking to someone. When he returned, he stood with his back against the wall, huge hands at his waist, one on top of the other.

Allman said, "It's good to see you, Mr. Mapp. How are you, by the way?"

"You can call me Vincent, Mr. Allman. And, I am well."

"Yes? Everything's fine, then? All good?"

"Absolutely." Allman studied him through the dark glasses.

"Because I'm well aware that, men our age, when we're away from home, we sometimes have trouble sleeping."

"Not me. I sleep like a baby."

"Last night, for instance, I was a bit restless. But not you, I take it?"

"Never better." A woman came in with a tray supporting a ceramic pitcher, an empty cup and saucer, a smaller pitcher of cream, a small bowl of sugar cubes. A spoon and silver tweezers for the sugar.

"Well, I'm glad to hear that," Allman said. "Angling is a demanding sport, and we anglers need our rest."

Vincent waited until the woman had unloaded her tray onto his table and left the room. He said, "Excuse me; would this be cream, here, in this little pitcher?"

"I am sure that it is."

"Could I trouble you for some skim milk instead?"

"Why, of course." Allman looked up at Stanley, and Stanley left the room.

Allman said, "Anyway, I believe I owe you something of an apology. I had a lot of things on my mind when we talked the other night. I wasn't in my most hospitable frame of mind. You mentioned my Angling Conservationist of the Year Award . . . and of course I remember it."

Stanley came back into the room with another tiny pitcher, placed it on the tray, and took away the pitcher of cream.

Vincent said, "So, the Angling Conservationist Award."

"Yes. And of course, I was very grateful to receive it."

"You were?" Stanley returned to the room, a big, pink man pressing his back against the pink stone wall. His thin-lipped face and nearly colorless hair and eyebrows matched the granite so closely that Vincent was easily able to imagine him headless. Blue Cheshire-cat eyes hovering above a hulking body.

"Of course. It was an honor. It's just that it was a long time ago, and it didn't quite click in with me the other night. Now that I've thought about it, much of the, um . . . excitement I felt back then has come back to me."

"Excuse me," Vincent said. "But I *did* miss my breakfast. May I reconsider your offer? Have you got any fresh fruit?"

"Stanley," said Allman. Stanley left the room.

Vincent said, "Anyway, I'm glad to hear that, Mr. Allman. Thank you for telling me that. It means a great deal to me. I do remember now that we got a very gracious note from you after we sent you the award. I still have that note somewhere, I believe."

"Like I said, a terrific honor." Stanley came back in with a large bowl of sliced fruit, a small bowl of fine brown sugar, a tiny spoon on a miniature plate. The fruit: sliced peaches and pears, blackberries, raspberries, strawberries. Some walnut halves sprinkled in.

"Well, sir," said Vincent, "I've always been a huge admirer of your conservation work. Not just in fish conservation but globally—North American tallgrass prairie, sub-Saharan Africa, central Asia, the Arctic. You've been an inspiration to me."

"Well, th—"

"By the way, could I get some honey for this delicious fruit? Rather than the brown sugar? Have you got any?"

"Of course we do," Allman said, looking up at Stanley.

Stanley said. "Sure. And, anything else? Mister. Mapp."

"Not that I can think of at the moment," Vincent said. "Thank you, buddy." Vincent smiled. Stanley left the room.

"As I was saying," Allman continued. "What you just said sort of brings me to my point. Why I asked you here."

Vincent said, "You know, I always wondered. All those letters we received after we gave you the award. Some people had some really strong feelings about your Westslope cutthroat trout project—about using rotenone to clear a little habitat for the Westslope cutthroats. Most of those letters weren't very complimentary toward either of us, to say the least. But we thought—at the time, we at the magazine . . . thought—that we needed to publish all the letters. To let the sun shine in, so to speak, on the differences of opinion out there in the trout conservation community. Not everyone appreciates native species in quite the same way you and I do; they just don't have that highly refined taste in natural objects, as Aldo Leopold so aptly put it. They'd just as soon catch rainbow trout and even brown trout in the Rockies, no matter whether they really belong there, ecologically speaking, and regardless of whether those fish are occupying waters in which the native species could relatively easily be restored. And many of those people . . . a bit abusive, *personal*, even, in their messages to us. And I always wondered what you thought about that—all those letters being published—or whether you even gave it any consideration at all."

"Oh," said Allman, with a subtle shift of tone. "I did think about it." Stanley came back in with a bowl of honey and a wooden honey dripper.

Vincent said to Allman, "Excuse me. I'm sorry, but I just thought of something. You know what would go really well with all of this? Some unsweetened yogurt. Would you happen to have some?"

"Stanley—" Allman began—but Stanley was already headed through the doorway.

"I'm sorry," said Vincent. "You were saying?"

"Well," Allman said, an edge to his tone. "Of course, it does sting somewhat, when the rabble comes after you in print with torches and pitchforks. When they say things about you that aren't true. Completely misunderstand your intentions. Call you names. When they go after innocent members of your family with libelous insults. But." He raised his coffee cup with a trembling hand and took a sip, his lips twisted in a grimace. "I'm aware that they did attack you as well. And I would imagine that having the willingness and the fortitude to intentionally sail into such a shitstorm no matter what innocent passengers might have been riding with you on your little boat was perhaps one of your strengths as an editor."

Stanley returned. "Yogurt," he intoned from between his teeth. He placed the bowl on the table. Vincent smiled at him.

"Thank you," Vincent said. "Pal." He thought, *I'm not touching that fucking yogurt.*

Vincent said, "Well, I'm glad you understood it that way. I was never sure. As I said, I always wondered."

"In fact," said Allman. He also was speaking through a tightened jaw. "The reason I asked you here. That editorial courage I just mentioned. And some of your other work. You're a terrific environmental writer as well. We've got all the back issues of your magazine here, and we've just been going through some of them. Your editor's column. Very good."

"That was quite a long time ago."

"Well, you're here, now. You're fishing our fine river. So, you must still be in the game, to some extent. And that's good—because, to lay my cards on the table here, I happen to find myself in need of a writer." It took Vincent a few moments to respond.

"You do?" he finally said.

"Yes. And after much thinking, we've determined that you're the one. If . . . you'll have us."

"You have?" said Vincent. He was both baffled and suspicious. Also intrigued. "What would the project be?"

"A book. A ghostwritten book on all my native-species restoration projects around the world. Fisheries; everything. Two-year deadline, but flexible schedule. You'd need to do some traveling. You'd also get some fishing in, I imagine. You'd get to New Zealand once or twice. Maybe the Seychelles. *Huge* bonefish there, I'm sure you're aware. Best bonefishing on the planet, if you happen to enjoy catching those little speedboats."

"Ghostwriting for you? So, the book—whatever it was—would be published under your name?"

"You'd be working directly for me, yes."

"I already have a job, though."

"We're aware of that. But, you're a professor. You get lots of free time. We'd work around your schedule."

"Well that's . . . interesting. Why me, again? Specifically?"

"We are prepared to offer you four hundred thousand dollars. Cash. Up front." Vincent sat back in his chair. After a long moment, he turned his head to look back at Stanley. Stanley was staring out toward the distant ridge and did not meet his gaze.

Vincent said, "I never take on a project of this duration and complexity for any less than two million." His most recent book advance had been fifteen hundred dollars. Hadn't gotten a penny more in royalties.

Allman stuck a spoon into his nearly empty coffee cup and twirled it, banging it noisily against the sides. Tossed the spoon onto the table. Took a breath and in a sharp voice said, "The very most we could do is six hundred thousand. Take, or leave." Vincent sat blinking at him.

"When would you pay me?" he asked.

"Almost immediately. We could have a contract done up, PDQ. One thing: we really insist on confidentiality around here."

"Uh-huh," said Vincent. "No doubt."

"There would be a nondisclosure agreement. That would mean that anything you learned from us—anything you'd see or *have* seen, involving us or on our property—or anything you've heard or even *sensed*—would be strictly confidential. You couldn't share it with anyone, in either written, verbal, or visual form, until such time as you delivered to us a completed manuscript that we considered to be completely acceptable."

"That sounds . . . frighteningly comprehensive," Vincent said. "Quite the gag order, actually." Allman gave a derisive bark of a laugh.

"Actually, it's pretty standard for a celebrity ghostwriting gig. Nobody shells out the big money just so they can get stabbed in the back at a later date. Am I right, Stanley?"

"Pardon?" said Stanley. Then: "I guess so, Mr. Allman."

"But rest assured," said Allman, "that once we've got that manuscript in hand—well, let's say two years *after* it's been published, anyway—you'll be free to say or write whatever you want. How's that? You'll be able to write your own goddamn book with your own goddamn perspective on things."

"So, two years after the publication of a book that you think will take me two years to write—provided my first version of said book is completely acceptable to you?"

"Why, yes."

"But until then, I couldn't say one word to anyone. Not to my dead mother, or anybody?"

"Like I said, that's pretty standard. For a celebrity ghostwriting gig."

"Okay. Well, I've got to think about it."

"Vincent, we need to get this project underway. You do have a potential competitor who's right here on the premises even as we speak. He flew in from Malta specifically to apply for the job. Now he's just cooling his heels as he waits for my word, the poor bastard. And he *will* work for substantially less than I offered you originally. It's either you or him. We'd rather have you, of course, but the Maltese guy will do in a pinch."

"So, I sign right this very minute, or . . ."

"Take a few hours. We don't have the contracts ready anyway. We'll get them to you over at Marta's place."

"Okay. Well . . ."

"Meanwhile, mum's the word, right? The confidentiality starts as of this moment. Six hundred thousand dollars hanging in the balance." Vincent again glanced at Stanley.

"Well, I look forward to seeing that contract, anyway." Vincent stood. "Thank you for the breakfast." Vincent had not eaten any of it. "Do we have any further business, Mr. Allman?"

"In fact, we do. Leave my niece, Angela, alone. She recently went through a very bad romantic breakup, and the last thing she needs right now is a rebound guy. Beyond that . . . poor men—especially poor *old* men—shouldn't aspire to date wealthy young women. Nothing in it for her but the eventual, inevitable feelings of contempt and loathing she'll develop for you, and nothing in it for you but heartbreak and disillusionment."

Vincent said, "If I sign your contract, I won't be poor anymore." Allman laughed, this time loudly and with authentic mirth—barks of laughter almost immediately cut short by a bout of coughing that caused him to double over. After a moment, he grabbed a napkin from the table and pressed it to his mouth.

When Allman finally was able to speak again, he lowered the napkin, aimed his chin at Vincent, his cowboy-hatted head cocked slightly to the side, and said, "Son, there's no surer indication that you're poor than thinking six hundred thousand dollars makes you rich. Stanley, take Vincent back across the river."

"I've got a question," Vincent said. Having assumed that all matters between them had been wrapped up with a bow on top, Allman stiffened with irritation.

"*One* question. I've said to you everything I needed or wanted to say, and now I need to relax. I will answer just one."

Vincent said, "You're an international wildlife conservation leader. You understand as much as anyone about the need for intact ecosystems and the importance of native species. As I said before, you have a highly refined taste in natural objects. So . . . why do you maintain two machines on the river that burp out pellets to feed wild fish? It seems contradictory to everything else about you."

Allman stared at him. After a moment, he grinned. "Well," he said, "For one thing, and as I am positive you already know, while they are *wild* fish, they're not *native* fish, and there's a huge difference in that. The only reason they're here in the first place is because we like to play with them. Basically, they're toys with fins, so why *not* feed them? And you know what *else* . . . Mapp? I love my ranches. I love my homes. I love pristine wilderness, and I love native wildlife. I love mountains and the ocean. I love having my own airplanes and helicopters and boats to take me wherever I want to go. I love beautiful women. I love having the means to do whatever the hell it occurs to me to do. I even love certain members of my family from time to time. But do you know the one thing I love, far, far above all other things? It's catching great, big, fucking trout and great, big, fucking salmon. Now try to tell me that you're so different and that it isn't the same for you."

"It isn't, really . . ." Vincent began.

"Oh, yeah, you're so holy. Down here at undoubtedly great expense fishing for trout on the Perca River, where, objectively speaking, they have no business being. The *Perca* River. Listen, fellow, I've done enough good for this planet that I'm entitled to a few indulgences."

They dropped Vincent off in front of the lodge and drove away. Sancho was sitting on the bench outside the doorway, looking forlorn. Vincent said, "Did you miss me, Sancho?"

"I was hoping to go fishing with you sometime today. If that's what you mean by missing you—well then, I've missed you."

"*Vámanos, entonces.*"

Sancho said, "They're all eating lunch in there. Have your lunch. Then we'll go."

Vincent realized then that he'd had nothing to eat since last night's dinner. No food. Little sleep. Injury from an animal attack. A possibly life-threatening . . . spell of some sort. Yes, lunch was a good idea. "Okay," Vincent said. "Lunch." He began moving toward the door.

"Why are you limping?" asked Sancho.

"Because I am torn and covered with scars."

Sancho, after a moment, just as Vincent had grasped the door handle, said, "Maestro, the word is *despreciado*. I believe the actual quote in English is, '*scorned* and covered with scars.'"

"That too," said Vincent. He opened the door and went inside.

Chapter Ten

Dulcinea

In the entrance hallway, Vincent encountered a mound of luggage. Brand-new, high-end stuff made by angling-specific companies; he knew it had to belong to the influencers. He found them, along with all the remaining guests, in the dining room, where lunch was wrapping up. The unsuccessful Brazilian hunter was already gone, having headed back to San Martín that morning. Clara and Lulu were beginning to serve coffee and dessert. Marta, sitting at the head of the table, was telling Stevie and Stephen that she had enjoyed having them, that she hoped they had found everything to be satisfactory, and that they were always welcome to visit Río Perca Lodge. When she was done speaking, everyone around the table murmured in agreement, and Stevie thanked them all. Vincent sensed that this was the right moment to step into the room.

"Vincent," Marta said. "I understand you made a somewhat mysterious trip to my neighbor's house."

"So mysterious I can't even tell you about it," Vincent answered.

"So, it *was* mysterious," Marta said.

"Also a little crazy, to be honest."

"Don't say more unless you can tell me all of it, or I will die of curiosity."

Clara touched his arm. "*Vas a comer*, Vicente?"

"*Claro que sí*. Bring me *all* the food."

The influencers, explaining that they had an early evening flight to catch, rose from the table. Stephen shook hands all around. When he reached Vincent, Vincent said, "How was your stay up at the outpost camp?"

"Just spectacular," said Stephen. "What an amazing view."

Vincent said, "I can only imagine."

Stevie surprised him by giving him a tight hug. Vincent, after a moment, put his arms around her. She said, "I'd like to keep in touch with you, if you don't mind, Uncle Vincent."

Vincent laughed. "Of course."

"I'll send you an e-mail. Isn't that how your generation likes to communicate?"

"It's how *I* prefer to communicate. Everyone else in my generation uses the telegraph."

Then they were gone. Feeling a touch of nostalgia, Vincent sat down to his late lunch. The other guests finished their dessert and departed for their rooms; Marta lingered over her coffee to keep him company. She did not return to the topic of his trip to Allman's castle.

After eating, he chewed and swallowed two more aspirin tablets. His foot was aching and stiff, but he decided there was nothing to do but try to ignore it. In Sancho's truck, on the way to the river, Vincent said, "After today, one more day of fishing, you and I."

"Yes."

"Am I your final client for the fall semester?"

"Likely, unless someone appears at the last minute. The river closes to fishing on the first of May."

"Listen, you're going to hate this, but before we start fishing today, I'd like to stop by Little Otto's research tent and see if he's there."

After a moment, Sancho said, "Otto is not so little."

"I like to think of him as little."

"In any case, we can stop wherever you like. It's your money."

After a moment, Vincent said, "Not really."

Once they were on the river opposite the white tent, Vincent waded across. Fifty feet behind the tent, the generator purred monotonously. "Otto!" he yelled. No answer. "Otto!" he yelled, a bit more loudly. A minute later, the tent flap unzipped partway, and Otto poked his head through.

"Vincent," he said. That wide and chilly smile. "How nice to see you."

"I have a few questions."

"Wonderful." Vincent took out his phone and opened one of the photos of his foot. He showed it to Otto.

"What the fuck tried to kill me last night?"

"That's *your* foot?" said Otto. But Vincent got the strong sense that Otto was not surprised.

"It is." Otto unzipped the tent the rest of the way and stepped out onto the sand.

"Where were you when this happened?"

"I was out and about."

"What time was it?"

"It was nighttime, Otto."

"What were you doing when it happened?"

"I was putting one foot in front of the other. Also, singing. Listen, do you have an answer for me?"

"So, you're not being rhetorical. You really did not see what attacked you?"

"Why would I be asking you if I had?"

"Did the—the thing that attacked you make any sort of sound?"

"No." Then he said, "I don't know. Maybe a grunt or a growl; I'm not sure. When I kicked it. I do have an idea though. I'm thinking maybe one or two of your dogos were out wandering at the same time and came after me."

"*Dogos?*" Ottos said. He looked legitimately confused.

"The dogo Argentinos? Those white, nasty, guardian dogs that apparently have free range on this side of the river?"

Otto began to laugh. "That's really something," he said. He continued laughing.

"I don't see what's funny."

"You really have *no* idea."

"I *do* have a couple of ideas. I just told you one of them. Can you deduce anything by looking at a photo of my wounds or not?"

Otto had quit laughing by then, but he was still smiling. "You think one of our dogs did this to you?" Then he surprised Vincent by saying, "Step into my laboratory, why don't you?"

Otto held the tent flap so Vincent could slip inside. The chill of refrigeration. Around the sides, tables with computer screens, miniature refrigerators, arrays of surgical tools, specimen bottles. On a stainless-steel table, a huge wild boar, slit down the middle and propped open with steel rods. Vincent got a good view of the animal's exposed innards. A male pig: softball-size testicles.

"I was just about to slice open the stomach on this fellow. See what he had for dinner last night. It seems that over the past year or so, their diet has been changing. Much more animal protein than previously. They've been cooperating to take down larger prey. That's what we've been investigating. Listen, you don't get squeamish, do you?"

"Usually not."

"All right. Come up here. To the head." Otto was snapping on a pair of blue elastic gloves. The boar's dark eyes were wide open. Its snout stuck out over the end of the table. An impressive pair of yellow tusks curved up from its lower jaw. Otto drew a ballpoint pen from the top pocket of his lab coat, then he spread the animal's jaws and wedged in the pen to hold them open. The pig then looked like it was silently screaming.

Otto said, "Like us, they are omnivores. Twelve incisors, not all that different from ours. Sixteen premolars, twelve molars, also somewhat similar to ours. The main difference, as you can see, is in the four canine teeth, top and bottom, known popularly as tushes, or tusks.

"Now, these bottom tushes—they are not only long but razor sharp. Together, they're a formidable set of weapons, a pair of ivory daggers. Among people who raise domestic swine, those two bottom teeth are referred to as 'cutters.' And how, you might ask, does the animal maintain the sharpness of those teeth?" Otto yanked out the pen, pressed the jaws shut, and opened them again.

"You see, every time the mouth closes, the cutters rasp against those top two canines, don't they? Again, popularly, the upper canines are known as 'whetters' because they act as living, growing whetstones, serving to hone the two cutters every time the animal operates its jaws.

"Now, having seen your unfortunate double set of twin wounds, I can say with some certainty that they are the result of a couple of separate bites from a wild boar—though, fortunately for you, not particularly serious ones. In fact, you are extremely lucky the animal did not excise your entire foot—or even devour a good part of the rest of you. And I'll tell you—as with most predators, once boars have pulled down a prey animal, they are likely to begin eating it alive.

"And one further thing I will tell you? You asked me the other day about a particular specimen the local peasants refer to as 'Big Mac.' Well, an exceptional and exceptionally dangerous animal of the description you've likely heard does in fact exist, unfortunately. It has ambushed, attacked, and seriously injured a number of people, and in spite of the plethora of technology we have at our command, this creature has so far eluded all our attempts to catch it or kill it. It is likely that if it had been this Big Mac creature that you encountered on the mountain and in the dark, you would not now be standing here and talking to me. You were lucky; it must have been a smaller one.

"My advice, my venerable friend? Do not go stumbling around here after sunset."

When they finally started fishing, Vincent found himself casting poorly. Not only was he still shaken by his conversation with Otto, but the pain in his foot, his lack of sleep, the residual stress of . . . whatever had happened in his chest the previous night, all were catching up with him.

Sancho said, "You need to wait a bit longer on your backcast."

"I'm a fucking mess," said Vincent.

They finally caught a decent rainbow, and that made him feel a little better. Not long after they had released the fish, they heard the buzz of a drone overhead. They looked up; it was just a speck in the sky, but then it began to descend. As it dropped closer to the river, Vincent could see that it was blue and that it seemed to have homed in on them.

"It's a blue fairy," Vincent said.

Sancho said, "To me, it seems like something demonic. A flying monkey, perhaps." It came down directly over Vincent. He could see that some kind of flat payload dangled beneath it.

Vincent said, "It's my fairy godmother, come to grant me a wish." Hovering just above his head, the blue fairy released a plastic folder into Vincent's hands. Then it flew to a flat outcropping above the riverbank and settled down to wait. Inside the folder: a sheaf of legal documents, a pen, a check for six hundred thousand dollars, signed by Allman. Little yellow arrows inscribed with the words *Sign Here* pasted in various places throughout the paperwork.

"What is it?" asked Sancho.

"Something from Allman. I can't tell you much more." Sancho grunted.

Vincent said, "I'm sorry, but I have to look this over. Why don't you fish while you wait?"

"I'll just wait," said Sancho.

"Fish, why don't you?"

"Because, what if I were to catch a *big* fish?"

"That wouldn't bother me. Why would it?"

"You say that now. But I know fishing clients quite well. If I caught a bigger fish than any of yours, you would smile, you would congratulate me—but you would resent me for it. You would silently wonder why I hadn't guided you to that fish rather than catching it myself."

"That's not me," Vincent said.

"As I told you, I understand the psychology of fishing clients. And . . . what if I were to catch a large *salmon*? Imagine how you would feel about me then."

"Suit yourself, *loco*," said Vincent.

He sat down with his back against a rock and began shuffling through the paperwork. The NDA—the nondisclosure agreement, the four-year gag requirement—was almost half of it. He tried to read it word for word, but he found the legal language boring, redundant, soporific, even, and in the end, he just skimmed it for its main points.

Of course, a lawyer should look everything over. But Allman was making no allowance for that, which in itself was fishy. As was the entire offer—though he had no doubt the sum and signature on the check were very real.

In the end, Vincent evaluated it this way: signing would open the route to some kind of an adventure, good or bad. For all he knew, it might even bring him into contact with the Allman twins again. Not signing . . . wouldn't open anything. Instead of surging up an unexplored river, he'd remain a spawned-out chum salmon, an ever-thickening shroud of mold overspreading him as he slipped downstream toward an ocean he would never live to see.

Vincent signed his name beside all the yellow arrows. He stuck the pricey-looking pen into one pocket of his fishing shirt, then folded the check and buttoned it into the other. He slid the documents back into the plastic folder, sealed the folder, stood up, and waved the folder in the air above his head. The blue fairy buzzed to life; she lifted from her rocky perch, came forward to clasp the folder beneath her abdomen, and began ascending across the river toward the ridge on Allman's side. A minute later, she cleared the ridge top, turned in the direction of the lake, and continued climbing until Vincent could no longer see her.

Sancho said, "I don't know what you just did, but I take the liberty of telling you I don't have a good feeling about it."

Vincent said, "Well, Sancho. My old man was a gambler, and as he used to say, sometimes you gotta roll the dice. Let's fish now, shall we?"

Two brown trout later, a mounted gaucho appeared on Allman's side of the river. After he had spotted Vincent and Sancho, he steered his horse across a riffle and rode up beside them.

"Señor Mapp?" he said.

"*Soy yo.*" The man handed him a white envelope. Inside was a note from Gabriela Allman:

Hi, Vincent,
I hope you are well, and enjoying your fishing. Sister and I were wondering whether you'd like to come up to our cabin this evening, for a conversation about writing. Either way, you can pen a response on the back of this note and send it back with our messenger. If you would like to visit, we'll send a gaucho with a horse for you sometime after dinner. I do hope to see you! Best regards—Gabriela Allman

"Well, hot dog," Vincent said.

"*Como?*" said the gaucho.

"*Por favor*, wait a minute while I write. *Sí?*" Vincent waded out of the river and sat down on a rock. He took out the pen he'd swiped from the blue fairy and wrote a response on the back of Gabriela's note:

Dear Gabriela,
I'd love to! Please make sure that, 1) My horse has a set of reins, so I don't have to be led on a rope like a little girl, and 2) Your gaucho has a loaded rifle with him. I hear that the wild pigs have been getting quite aggressive recently. I am very much looking forward to seeing you and Angela—and talking about writing.—Vincent

He stuffed the note back into the envelope and handed it to the gaucho. "Thanks for waiting," he said.

Back at the lodge, at cocktail time, the couple from Mendoza told Vincent that they'd had some fine fishing with Nestor. The two hunters from Buenos Aires reported results for the day that were every bit as glum as every daily report from the recently departed Brazilian. Marta introduced Vincent to a middle-aged couple from Vancouver who were there to do some horseback riding. Vincent knew that for his own ride that evening, rather than wearing sneakers, he would need shoes with heels to keep his feet from slipping through the stirrups. He asked Sancho for some duct tape if there happened to be any on the property; Sancho went off and eventually returned with a roll of black electrical tape, which Vincent wound around and around his boar-damaged shoe to hold it together while he rode.

Eduardo the gaucho came for him just as the sun had set. As Vincent had requested, the horse he'd brought was bitted and fitted with reins. Vincent was glad to see that the gaucho also had come equipped with a lever-action rifle in a scabbard that hung from his saddle. But he wasn't carrying any type of light or lantern, so Vincent went back inside to ask Marta if he could borrow the powerful flashlight in the entrance hall. Then he and Eduardo rode down to the river and up the steep trail that Vincent had almost killed himself climbing on foot the night before. As the sky continued to dim, they ascended toward the green light that shone from the back porch of Dulcinea.

By the time they reached the beech plateau below the cabin, they rode through fading twilight. Just as they were approaching the spot where Vincent had been attacked, they saw something white lying across the trail ahead of them, and when they had drawn closer, they saw that it was a dog—a dogo Argentino—stretched out, unmoving on the grass, its white coat matted with blood and torn open on the side to expose a section of its ribs, its jaws gaping in what must have been its final yelp of agony.

"Fuck me," said Vincent.

"*Carajo*," Eduardo said, a shudder in his voice.

They sat staring for a bit longer, neither of them wanting to get down from his horse. In any case, the dog was beyond any help they could give. Vincent finally urged his mount closer and snapped a photograph with his phone. He was shaken by the fact that the white carcass lay on almost the exact spot where he himself had been pulled to the ground. He and Eduardo steered their mounts around it and had resumed moving toward Dulcinea when some creature off in the forest shrieked and then continued to shriek, its cries at once shrill and hoarse and loud enough to hurt Vincent's ears. Rising and falling and rising again with barely a pause for breath, the quavering, unbroken plaint shocked and shook the air with its message of fear and protest and despair and unfathomable physical pain.

Every part of his body clenched, his skin tightening against him, Vincent stopped his horse to listen. Eduardo said, "Just some boars fighting. Let's keep moving."

But after a minute, Vincent shook off his paralysis and turned his trembling horse toward those sounds of murder. He said to Eduardo, "Follow me. Have your rifle ready."

Eduardo said, "*Señor*, it is prohibited to leave the trail."

"Follow me," Vincent repeated. It wasn't so much that he was brave; it wasn't that he was unafraid; it was that he was *curious*. How could he resist finding out what this audible horror was all about and whether it might be connected to the violent death of the white dog and to his own attack during his midnight retreat from Dulcinea? His horse was hesitant, but he was a good, steady, *criollo* mount, and with a bit of coaxing, he did as Vincent asked. Together they wound their way through darkening woods where there was no trail, Eduardo reluctantly riding behind. Meanwhile, the tortured screaming continued unabated.

"*Señor*, this is prohibited," Eduardo called, a shake in his voice. "And I lack the authority to accompany you."

"The rifle," Vincent responded. "Just have the rifle ready."

A minute later they came to a clearing. It was there that his mount dug in and began to twist; Vincent knew he could push the animal no farther. "Easy," Vincent said. "Easy; it's okay, now. It's okay."

In any case, he could already see them, or at least see their darkening, writhing silhouettes. Ahead in the clearing were creatures: the dark mass of what was obviously a colossal boar, perhaps seven feet in length and large enough overall to approach half a ton in weight. The boar was shrieking and straining forward, as four smaller—but not small—slope-backed, four-legged forms gripped it and pulled at it from behind.

"*La puta madre*," Eduardo said as he rode up beside him. "I thought it was just a story. A legend. But that beast. The size of it. That has to be the one they call Big Mac. They say he killed a man." He spoke as if hoping his words would inspire Vincent to turn around and leave with him.

Abruptly, although it remained on its feet, something fundamental broke inside the boar, and it fell disturbingly silent. Vincent heard strange laughter in the sudden silence.

"*Señor*. Look, we lack the authority . . ."

Another cackle out there on the small meadow. Vincent turned on the big flashlight, swept it ahead of them, and let out a grunt of astonishment. He had expected to see dogs—a pack of renegade dogo Argentinos doing what dogos did best. But they were hyenas. Spotted hyenas. *African* spotted hyenas. One, two, three, four. And they weren't just bullying and mauling the boar the way a team of dogs would do; they were *eating* it. Eating it even as it remained standing and breathing.

The hyenas paused to stare into his bright light, their eyes shining yellow. The two largest wore collars with black boxes attached; the two smaller animals were collarless. The smaller hyenas tittered nervously as they gazed into the light; the larger, older assassins made no sound at all. After a moment, all four seemed to collectively conclude that Vincent and Eduardo presented no threat, and they returned to their living meal, the younger ones continuing to giggle even as they filled their jaws with ragged, red gobbets that gleamed wetly in the flashlight beam.

"*Señor*, we must go."

"*Che*, are you going to shoot those fucking things, or what?"

"I must report this. But I lack the authority to shoot."

"Give me the rifle, then. I'll shoot them."

"I lack the authority to give you this rifle."

"Okay," Vincent said after a moment. He took out his cell phone. He aimed both phone and flashlight at the scene ahead and began to record.

"It is prohibited to take photos."

"You lack the authority to stop me."

By then, the four hyenas had widened a breach in the hindquarters of their victim, which now, clearly in shock, seemed almost resigned to its fate. The boar stood unmoving save for wistfully sniffing the air as the hyenas by turns entered it with their snouts, each emerging a moment later with its head from nose tip to shoulders completely painted in blood. One of the two larger ones drew out a length of glistening pink sausage casing, and the rest of them snapped into it and began stretching it among them in every direction until it finally shredded. Seconds thereafter, the monstrous boar gave a final wheeze and settled to its knees.

At that point, Vincent had seen enough. Recorded enough. He allowed the horse to turn, and Eduardo followed him back out to the trail. Vincent said, "Did you know those *bichos* were out here killing things? How many are there altogether?"

Eduardo answered, "I lack the authority."

"*Muy, muy bien*," said Vincent. His chest was suddenly tight; he had to work at breathing. He had aspirin in his pocket, and he took out two and began to chew them. He quickly felt a little better.

At the cabin, buttery light filtered through the window shades. Eduardo was clearly relieved to be out of the trees and away from the scene of the slaughter. He said, "I'll take your horse. I'll wait for you. When you're ready, I'll be right here."

"My fucking hero," Vincent said in English. They both dismounted, and Vincent handed his reins to Eduardo. In Spanish: "Don't pet the stray dogs."

Gabriela came to the door when he knocked. She was immediately concerned. "Are you all right? You don't look well." Gabriela herself looked like an angel.

"Could I trouble you for a glass of water?" The screams of the boar were still ringing in his ears.

When they were sitting on the stuffed chairs—Vincent on the same one Stephen had occupied the night before—Gabriela said, "Angela sends her regrets. A problem came up at home—her teenage son is having some issues. She's on her way to the airport in Buenos Aires."

"Well, of course that's understandable. Kids are the most important thing. They're the reason we're here, isn't it?" A moment later: "Tell me something. Do you know anything about the animals?"

"What animals?"

"The predators."

"Here, do you mean? The only large predator we have is the puma—and we hardly ever see them. They're actually quite shy. I did think we had wolves here decades ago—but you've disabused me of that misconception, haven't you? I looked it up, and you're right—although of course I didn't share that information with Angela. Other than that, the wild boars do steal a lamb or even a small calf from time to time. Uncle Jay is taking some steps to control them, but I don't know much about all that. You remember Otto, don't you? From the play? Our zoologist? You could ask him, if you were curious."

Vincent studied her face. He detected no trace of guile. She likely really did not know. Like Angela, she jetted down here from time to time, flew some hawks, rode some horses, ate some *asado*, perhaps danced a casual tango or two, and then went back to civilization. Didn't know, had no reason to know, what went on when she wasn't here.

He settled back into the comfortable chair. Stephen's throne of ecstasy. Vincent especially envied him for the way he'd seemingly been able to take it all for granted. As if that kind of thing happened to him all the time, no big deal. Hell, maybe it did; there was no way of knowing. As for Vincent himself . . . right now he was feeling his age, a bit. He said, "You're right that I'm a little under the weather. I'm not quite sure what it is but . . . I wonder if it would be okay if we just talked tonight."

Gabriela gave him a look that shifted from uncomprehending to incredulous. After a moment, she began laughing. She wiped her eyes with her fingertips and kept on laughing. When she finally had control of herself, she said, "Of course, we'll talk, Vincent. What did you imagine was going to happen?"

Chapter Eleven

Damned Spots

Vincent's final day of fishing. Clouds assembled in the sky. He felt tired; there was a slight rattle in his chest. Fortunately, his foot, though stiff and painful, still did not seem to be infected. He could walk on it with just a bit of a limp. At breakfast, there was talk of heavy rain, several centimeters of it, which would wash out all outdoor activities in the late afternoon. The hunters from Buenos Aires announced that they would hunt through the morning and then, assuming they were unsuccessful, pack up and head home after lunch, a day and a half earlier than they had planned.

"No sense in staying if there are no deer and it's raining," one of them said. "Save our pesos for another trip."

Vincent was sitting next to Marta, who was in her place at the head of the table. While all the others were distracted with a different topic, in a low voice, she said to Vincent, "For most of the fall, we've badly needed rain for the river, but this now is something of a disaster for us."

"Why is that?"

"Hunting helps us pay the bills around here. This season—as well as most of last season, actually—we've had nothing but groups of hunters returning home to tell all their friends they didn't even *see* a stag on our property. Much more of that, and clients will stop coming. I fear a great deal of damage has already been done."

"Well," Vincent said. "I myself have had a wonderful time here." Marta gave him a tight smile and touched his arm for a moment. He felt guilty for not telling her what he'd seen the previous night . . . but then, he had signed those papers.

Sancho came in. He told Vincent, "We could get an early start this morning. Perhaps find you a salmon before the rain begins."

"I told you, the fishing's been fine here. A salmon doesn't much matter to me. I wish I'd never mentioned it in the first place."

"Well, I feel as though I've failed."

"Jesus Christ," Vincent said.

In the truck, on the way to the river, Vincent said, "Again, you're not going to be happy, but I need to have another short conversation with Little Otto. It won't take long."

After a moment, Sancho said, "It's *your* last day on the river. You may spend it how you like, I suppose."

Sancho remained on Marta's side while Vincent waded across to the white tent. "Oh, Otto!" he called, as he stepped up onto the beach. Otto unzipped the flap and poked his head out.

"Vincent!" For the first time, his smile seemed genuine. "I am delighted to see you, my friend."

"I don't think you'll stay delighted," Vincent said. "Why don't you come out here?" Otto stepped out and rezipped his tent. Vincent handed him his cell phone, on which was playing the video from the night before.

"My question for you is, what the fuck?" But Otto's smile only broadened. He nodded enthusiastically as he stared down at the phone. After he'd finished watching, he looked at Vincent with deep blue eyes that were full of mirth.

"Not much for table manners, are they? Not exactly a scene for the squeamish, is it?"

"As I said—"

"I'm actually delighted you've come," Otto said. "Until now, I've had no one I could really talk to about this project. Well, except for Mr. Allman, of course—but he's not one for much conversation. Not a warm person at all. I'm not even sure he actually likes me. As for my local assistants here . . . they're all so full of fear. None of them has any intellectual curiosity. You, on the other hand, Vincent."

"I'm a very warm person."

"A curious one, at least. And you've got a sense of humor, along with enough amateur background to understand most of what I tell you. And now that you've joined the team, so to speak—now that you are one of us and have agreed to discretion concerning certain matters—I can speak to you freely about our groundbreaking work. About what we've been accomplishing here. In fact, I'm told it's actually your *job* now to listen to me, which I find amusing."

"Yeah. I'm all ears," Vincent said.

"Step into my laboratory." Once they were inside, Otto rezipped the flap. That jolt of refrigerated air. On the table lay a spotted hyena the size of a German shepherd. Glazed eyes; tongue lolling onto the stainless-steel tabletop. The very picture of death.

"Overall, throughout the past six years, it's been an amazingly successful project. But of course, you are most curious about the unexpected challenges we've experienced recently, so let's not beat around the bush.

"The problems," Otto said, "begin with the genitalia." He was snapping on a pair of blue elastic gloves.

Vincent couldn't help himself: "In my experience, most problems do." Otto laughed.

"I *do* so much enjoy talking to you," Otto said. "It is *so* much fun. Here, have a look at this." With the blue-sheathed fingers of his left hand, he lifted the hyena's uppermost rear leg.

"Tell me what you see." Vincent curled his lip.

"Yes, I see his doggie junk. What about it?"

"*His.* You're certain this is a male?"

"Well, obviously. We've got a *pene* and a pair of *pelotas* there. What more needs to be said?"

"If you wish, you may touch them, just to be sure."

"I don't *want* to touch them."

"Very well. But so . . ." Otto startled him by mimicking the sound of a game-show buzzer, then laughing at his own gag. "*Wrrrrong!* What we have here is a young female. Are you more inclined to touch her now?"

"Otto, really. What the fuck is wrong with you?" Otto laughed again and bobbed his head. He released the leg and allowed it to settle, which it did, slowly; when it came to a stop, it wasn't quite touching the other leg.

"What you have mistaken for the penis? This is actually the animal's clitoris. Almost indistinguishable from the penis of the male. A physical anomaly unique to spotted hyenas, among all other mammals that currently exist.

"In fact, the clitoris of the spotted hyena readily becomes quite erect. Female hyenas invariably sprout boners when they greet one another on the savanna."

"Fascinating. Hard to believe, even. And those balls, though, Otto?"

"Pseudo-testes. Also unique to the species. If you had palpated them when I gave you the opportunity, you'd have discovered that there is no actual gland inside the scrotum. It's a different tissue altogether; a fat deposit. You may still . . ."

"No."

"In any case, the upshot is that, unlike virtually any other large mammal on the planet, even at close range it is often difficult to distinguish male from female in the spotted hyena—especially before they've achieved their full adult growth and prior to mammary development in the female."

"And, so, the unexpected 'challenge' you mentioned earlier is what?"

"In the beginning, when we brought the first twenty-four young hyenas here to Patagonia, a mistake was made. But first, I'd like to skip back and tell you about the astonishing successes of our project.

"The spotted hyena, though it has a popular reputation as a scavenger, actually is one of the world's most efficient predators. As cooperative hunters of big game, their success rate is actually much higher than that of the lion—with which they share much of their native range in Africa. In fact, lions are much more inclined to scavenge hyena kills than the other way around.

"Spotted hyenas also are incredibly intelligent. In scientific tests of cooperative achievement—communicating collaboratively and working together toward a common objective, in other words—they score more highly than do chimpanzees. One advantage for us is that this intelligence makes it easy to condition them for certain behaviors. The black boxes that you undoubtedly saw strapped to the necks of the two larger hyenas last night? They do three things: they transmit a constant signal that tells us where the animal is—at least when it is outside of its underground lair and moving about. Two: the box also delivers a painful shock to the animal whenever it starts to stray beyond the territorial boundaries we have assigned to it. That's how we've been able to sleep soundly at night—at least until recently—knowing our animals will never stray across the river and onto our neighbor's property or out onto the pastures where our own livestock grazes. Or approach human dwellings. The hyenas are *so* highly intelligent that we can condition them to memorize and follow an extraordinarily complex map; they are able to recognize and respect the borders of an irregular territory consisting of several widely separated hunting areas, all of which are connected by a network of narrow travel corridors. They learn those boundaries and those routes through conditioning, and they generally do not stray outside of them—and if they happen to forget, the transmitter box each of them wears warns the animal with a sound signal whenever it is about to wander beyond its hunting area or one of the connecting corridors between hunting areas. But remarkably, they almost never forget. In fact, each individual hyena, after a bit of trial and error on its part, becomes so well-conditioned that they rarely ever experience that warning signal.

"And all of this, all of what I've told you, makes the spotted hyena an ideal natural tool for the job we've assigned to them—which is to reduce or even eliminate invasive species on our property."

"Which invasive species?"

"At this point, we're primarily talking about red deer and wild boar, both of which are extremely environmentally destructive here in Patagonia. And we've been *very* successful with the deer; those the hyenas haven't killed they've largely driven from the area, sending them to areas where the deer believe they won't encounter predators. Now, if we had access to all those *other* areas as well and the authority to operate there, we likely could almost entirely eliminate the red deer problem in this corner of the world.

"As for European wild boar . . . on our ranch, we've managed to drive their numbers down substantially—though we haven't been able to completely push them off the range as thoroughly as we have the deer. Boar are more intelligent and somewhat more adaptable than deer. But mink?

You perhaps did not know that invasive mink, escaped from fur farms, comprise a huge problem in Patagonia, but in fact, they do. And our hyenas have done a stellar job of reducing the mink population to almost zero within our research zone. They dig them right out of their dens and devour them in a couple of bites.

"One more amazing virtue of hyenas: anything they consume, they consume completely—bones and all. This makes their work very discrete; not only do they labor only at night, but they leave behind little evidence. Other than their chalky white feces, of course—the whiteness coming from digested bone—which we then send out drones to locate and collect.

"And, one final trait that makes the spotted hyena ideal for invasive-species work in Argentina—or almost anywhere else, for that matter? Even though their current native range is sub-Saharan Africa, they were vastly more widely distributed, geographically speaking, during prehistoric times, roaming as far north as the Ural Mountains in Russia. And we have found that they tolerate the Patagonian winter cold just as blissfully as they do the African heat."

Vincent said, "The thing that attacked me the other night. You lied to me when you said it was a pig. You made a big song and dance of it as well." Otto lifted open hands toward Vincent.

"I very much hope you can forgive me for that. As I said, now that you've become part of our team—"

"Otto, I could have died. If it weren't for whoever was out there with the rifle, I *would* have died—and very fucking painfully, apparently. Disemboweled alive, for fuck's sake. *Watching* as they ate my entrails in front of me. And I have to assume that the trail I was walking on when those things tried to kill me was supposed to be safe—was supposed to be outside of any territory or corridor where your hyenas are allowed to be. And yet, somehow, in spite of all your technological precautions, it was not. Then there's the fact that the Dodier family have been losing livestock and pets, so we have to assume that your hyenas have also been making their way across the river. How long before everyone's luck runs out and they actually kill a person?"

Otto, after a pause, said, "Returning to the subject of genitals. The problem I mentioned earlier? The one for which I said we were quickly course-correcting? It has to do with the fact that, among those original twenty-four young female animals we transported here . . . apparently there was at least one hyena, and probably one or two more, that were not actually females."

"Just under-endowed males, then?"

"Yes. That is, unless some of the females somehow have become able to reproduce asexually—but that sort of phenomenon, while it's been observed in fish and reptiles, has never been known to occur among mammals. Hyenas *are* an extremely anomalous species, but . . . the 99 percent most likely explanation is that a couple of males slipped into the group, unannounced and ready for action."

"You're supposedly the expert. How could you let that happen?"

"Yes. Well. I wasn't the one who trapped them over in Botswana, Vincent. I didn't sort through them over there; that was another team. I didn't crate them up for shipment. My only failure—and I do own up to it—is that when we anesthetized each one for its devocalization, as well as to fit them with their collars, I did not give their genitals a closer inspection. I just assumed that our sub-Saharan team had done its job correctly. And as they say about assumptions . . ."

"That's why they didn't make any noise at all when they were attacking me. You cut their vocal cords."

"Yet again, 'cutting their vocal cords' is not an accurate description of what we do. Ours is an entirely new and more effective procedure. But, yes; we did devocalize the original two dozen animals. The G-Ones. By that I mean the cohort of animals we're now calling Generation One. But I'm quite sure that, since they tackled you beyond the boundaries of a corridor and obviously were not fitted with collars, the animals that came after you were G-Two or G-Three. Possibly even G-Four. I told you they were smart. It's not that they weren't physically and fully capable of making the normal repertoire of hyena hunting-and-feeding vocalizations while they were attacking you; it's that they *chose* not to do so. They had *learned* a certain strategic silence either directly from their devocalized G-One progenitors or through learning that had been passed down to them through the subsequent generations. They must have thought it advantageous in some way *not* to vocalize while they were stalking you. In fact, we've observed that all generations of these Patagonian-born hyenas now tend to communicate mainly through a vocabulary of various gestures and glances and body postures they've developed; a sort of a hyena sign language, if you will."

"Jesus Christ, Otto. So, by now you must know that you need to get rid of them. Quickly. Like I said, it's only been luck that they haven't killed anybody."

"Yes, well. We are working on it. It's not as easy as you might think, given . . . well, some disturbingly unexpected intellectual performance on their part. Until very recently, we thought we had much more time to work. The different generations have always instructed one another about the territories and corridors—all of those restrictions having become part of their culture, part of their belief system, and up until just a couple of weeks ago, all the generations continued to religiously respect the boundaries we had set for them. Our rules were like the word of God to them. There *was* no problem. Everything was under control—going according to plan and going spectacularly well. Now, however—and of course, and as I said, quite unexpectedly—in combination with the drought and low water levels that have allowed them to more easily cross the river, there has been an apostate clique of younger animals who . . ."

"Listen to you. A *belief* system, Otto?"

"I told you, intelligent. They've shown strong indications of abstract thinking. Of a certain level of imagination. They definitely possess some mathematical skills."

"They're animals. You're people. People are the best at killing. Do it, Otto."

"Well, yes, but we're trying to be selective. We don't want to kill *all* of them. I've already explained to you how beneficial they are when they're under appropriate control. How scientifically interesting they are. In any case, one problem we face in trying to work quickly, even if we wanted to: during daylight hours, hyenas spend most of their time in underground dens, where we can't locate them either by drone or by satellite tracking. They bear their uncollared young in those same underground dens, where we can't always find them. Also, ever since they've become aware that we have fatal intentions toward some of them, they've been extremely wary. They also seem to have figured out that we're able to track down the collared individuals at night and also during the dawn and twilight hours when they're active but *not* when they're underground, and they have begun to develop various tactics for evading us. We've seen some evidence of tunneling."

"They have *tactics*? Really, what's going on here is that you've lost control of them. Now, because of you, hyenas themselves are likely to become an invasive species here in Argentina. It seems possible they'll even spread throughout the rest of the country and the rest of the continent from here. And they *will* kill people." Otto's palms were again raised in Vincent's direction.

"No. No. We can't say anything like that just yet. In fact, I'm very confident our current plans will be effective. Two advantages we have: hyenas breed relatively slowly. Two pups at a time, and not very frequently. We're not talking about rodent-like reproductive rates, here. Also, we are confident that the entire population, all generations, remains confined to a relatively small area. Allman ranch property. Mostly. We'll get them, my friend. We'll bring them back under control. It's a challenge—which I relish—but we'll get them. And we will leave just enough of them, the original collared ones, as well as the others that we're able to trap and collar, to continue with our important work."

"How many are there now?"

"We think fewer than seventy."

"You *think*? You do know that when you start talking about an invasive species in terms of a 'population,' you're already in serious trouble? And, what will you do, Otto, when they attack another person while you're dicking around, trying to sort the good ones from the bad ones?"

"We are working as fast as we can, Vincent. We are coming up with a combined strategy for hyena management. A very creative strategy. We are taking all appropriate measures. We've got drones with night-vision and heat-sensing optics patrolling at all times. And you yourself were rescued by one of the many armed guards we have posted at night in strategic places, poised to react at a moment's notice. And you've also seen that we've got a few squads of guardian dogs on the job as well. Other measures are also being developed."

Vincent stood blinking at Otto. He shook his head and was ready to leave, but then he thought of something. He pointed. "This dead one, here. I don't see a bullet wound anywhere. How did you kill it?"

"An eagle dragged her off of a cliff. If you look carefully about her shoulders, you can see the wounds from the talons."

"There are no eagles in Patagonia." Otto smiled.

"Oh. Well then, if there are no eagles, I suppose I must be mistaken. It must have been a condor."

Vincent said, "Enough of this. I'm going fishing." He unzipped the tent flap and stepped outside. The air was warm, but the clouds had thickened and lowered. On the other side, Sancho was standing on the edge of the river, looking forlorn as he stared across at him.

From inside the tent, Otto called, "Remember, Vincent. Mum's the word." Then he zipped the tent flap from within.

Sancho said, "I don't suppose you can tell me what's going on?"

"I cannot, amigo. I'm sorry. Let's fish before the sky starts pissing on us."

Vincent fished poorly. His mind once again was elsewhere. He wrestled with ways to get a message, perhaps anonymously, to the provincial fish and wildlife agency. Then he decided such an action likely would do little good. For one thing, the whole story was so outlandish that his words undoubtedly would be dismissed as the ravings of a crank. A foreign crank, at that. For another—and for all Vincent knew—the provincial people likely had a cozy relationship with Allman's organization. No telling how a message to them might backfire. And if Vincent were discovered to be an informant and in violation of his newly signed NDA . . . there would go his six hundred thousand dollars, his opportunity to travel—Africa, New Zealand, the Seychelles—and his chance to maybe run into one or both of the Allman twins again. It made him grieve a little, just thinking about it.

But by lunchtime back at the lodge, he had it figured out. Exactly what he needed to do regardless of the consequences. He lingered over dessert and coffee until all the other guests had drifted away. Then he said to Marta, "I've got something to show you." He passed her his phone with the video running.

Ten minutes later, after he had told her almost everything, Marta pulled a satellite phone from a cabinet in the entrance hall and called across the river, asking for Allman. She spoke only briefly to someone at the other end, and after hanging up, she fired up the radio transmitter to contact somebody on her own property. She said, "Our neighbor is out fishing on the river. Put up the drone and go find him. He'll be either at nineteen or at twenty-seven; let me know which."

There came a blast of rapid, crackling Spanish from the other end, which Vincent couldn't make out. Marta responded, "Yes, I know there are clouds. Fly as low as you need to. Land it on his head if you must. It's important that I find him. Also, tell Alberto to saddle up el Blanco and one other horse and bring them to the lodge. *Tan pronto como posible.*"

After she had finished marshaling transportation and a drone, Marta said to Vincent, "While we're still in the lodge and have the Wi-Fi available, please send me that video. And then go get your raincoat; you will need it."

As soon as the answer came back that Allman was at twenty-seven, Marta and Vincent went out the front door and mounted the two waiting horses. They rode down the road, then along a trail toward the river.

Vincent said, "Do you know him very well?" Marta laughed.

"Jay? Maybe too well. I dated him for an entire summer a long time ago. The summer after he broke up with his second wife—the one who insisted he build her a pink castle above the lake. I was still in my twenties, and he was a little more than twenty years older. He'd take me to Bariloche or to San Martín in his yellow sports car or in a helicopter. Buenos Aires a couple of times. A weekend once in Montevideo."

"Big age difference," Vincent said for lack of anything better to say. "Though I think sometimes that kind of thing can work. . . ."

"Summer ended, he went back to the States. To New York and to his place in Montana, I suppose he went, and by the time spring rolled around again, we were both with different people. Interesting while it lasted."

"Interesting is an odd word to describe a romance."

"Not a warm person, Jay."

"I heard that from someone else just today."

"Since then, he's continued to make offers on our property. Astronomical sums, really. I and all my family could live lives of leisure for the next ten generations with all those dollars. But you know what? I think Argentina should be owned by Argentines."

"That's what I think as well. But I know firsthand that it's hard to resist someone when they're flapping all that money at you."

After a minute, Marta said, "Jay was very handsome back then. But then, I was very pretty."

"You still are," said Vincent. Marta laughed.

"Not pretty. Something else, maybe. But it's not the same. You likely know that yourself—though it's different for men. An unacquainted head never turns." It was Vincent's turn to laugh.

"It's not so different," he said. A raindrop struck him, and he was glad Marta had reminded him to bring his jacket.

They emerged onto the riverbank, and there was Allman, sitting in his recliner, watching his guide cast over the pool. Allman, in waders and a raincoat, wearing sunglasses in spite of the rain clouds pressing down, giving no indication that he had noticed the two riders on the opposite shore. As before, a gaucho stood thirty yards behind him, cradling a black rifle. Behind the gaucho, a parked Land Cruiser. Marta and Vincent turned their horses and followed the river downstream to cross at a riffle. Then they rode toward where Allman sat.

Allman's guide, in the meantime—a different man than the one Vincent had seen before—had hooked a large fish and was handing Allman the rod. They stopped the horses and watched as Allman played it expertly and brought it to the beach, where the guide scooped it into a net—it was an obese, pellet-fed brown trout of seven or eight pounds—and carried it up for the old man to admire. Then he took it back down to the river for release. Marta and Vincent rode up to Allman then and sat looking down at him.

"Nice fish," said Vincent.

At that, Allman finally acknowledged their presence by turning his face in their direction. "Hello, Marta," he said. Marta herself said nothing.

She sat waiting, staring down—it was a long, strained silence, and Vincent began to feel uncomfortable—but finally Allman lifted a shaking hand and removed his sunglasses to reveal eyes that were pale green and wincing. Eyes that seldom saw direct sunlight.

"Hello, Jay," she said. She called over to the guide, who now stood at the water's edge with an empty net. "*Vos, como te llamas?*"

"*Tomás, señora.*"

"*Por favor, vení acá, Tomás.*" The guide came up beside her horse, and Marta handed him her cell phone. "Give it to him," she said.

The guide took the phone from her and handed it to Allman. Allman didn't bother to watch the entire video; he scowled at the screen for about ten seconds, then returned the phone to Tomás. The guide gave it back to Marta.

"Yes," Allman said. "We've had an unanticipated problem with one of our conservation projects. It's being addressed."

"It's being addressed?" Marta said. "How is it being addressed? They've killed livestock. They killed my dog. Ate him, I assume."

Allman's mouth came open. After a moment, he said, "I knew there was some livestock. I hadn't heard about your dog. I'm very sorry."

"How long until they attack one of my guests? Or the child of one of your gauchos?"

"They almost killed *me*," Vincent volunteered.

"*What?*" Marta said.

"Yes, but you were trespassing," Allman said. "At night."

"*What?*" Marta repeated. "They attacked you?"

"I was on my way to visit one of Mr. Allman's nieces. Hiking up to her cabin. They attacked me. Fortunately, somebody was there with a gun and scared them off."

"Is that why you've been limping?"

"They almost took my foot off."

"Trespassing," Allman repeated. "*Private* land. Marta, I am sorry about your dog. Of course, we will certainly compensate you for your other losses. And we are eliminating all the hyenas that we can't control."

"It doesn't sound to me like you can control any of them. And what's the purpose of this 'project' in the first place? Of having these dangerous animals on the landscape? It sounds completely insane."

"We're actually doing some good science. It's actually been of great environmental benefit. We had some leftover hyenas from one of our African operations, and rather than putting all of them down, we thought it might work well to bring some of them here in order to control destructive invasive species. And it has."

"*Which* destructive invasive species?"

"Mink," Allman said. "They do a hell of a job on the mink. Feral swine. The hyenas have cut their numbers by half around here." Allman looked down at his hands. "And other feral ungulates."

"Other feral what?"

"Cervids."

"Why not speak English or Spanish; I understand both." Allman sighed and looked up. Those washed-out, watery, pea-soup eyes that almost no one ever got to see.

"European red deer," Allman said. "Just on *our* side of the river, of course." Marta's mouth dropped open. She widened her eyes at him and leaned forward in the saddle as if to see him better.

"Could you truly be this crazy?"

"They're very destructive of the native vegetation, Marta. And they compete with guanacos for guanaco habitat. And rheas for rhea habitat."

"Jay, I'm not a scientist, but I've been around deer all my life, and I can guarantee you that you're not eliminating them; you're just killing a very few and scaring the rest off of your property and off of my property and onto someplace where they feel safe. Onto someone *else's* property. Meanwhile . . . were you really unaware that the local deer herds constantly travel back and forth across the river and that I make a good part of my income from hosting deer hunters at my ranch? That I pay my staff of local people—*Argentinian* people—out of income that I receive from hunters?" Allman, his lips tight, nodded his head.

"We have caused you some economic losses; I understand that. We'll compensate you for those. And of course, the offer is still on the table for us to purchase . . ."

"*Jay!*" Marta said, raising her voice for the first time. "My family and I are not interested in selling. We are not interested in your foreign aid. Do you understand?"

"If you just listened . . ."

"*Do you understand?*"

"Okay, Marta. So, what would you like, then?"

"Get rid of them."

"We are getting rid of the troublesome ones. The others . . ."

"All of them."

"There's no need for that, Marta. We have control . . ."

"You *don't* have control. If you had control, we wouldn't be having this conversation in the first place. And with something as dangerous as this, all you need is to lose one tiny bit of control at exactly the wrong time, and someone ends up killed or horribly mutilated. We're all very lucky that hasn't yet happened—unless it actually has happened, and you've covered it up.

"*All* of them, Jay. Every single one of those awful creatures. Remove them. I don't care how you do it. You have two weeks. We're going to be watching. We're going to be monitoring. The minister of the interior is a good friend of mine. She's a former schoolmate. I have her on speed dial. If, after two weeks we see signs that any hyenas are still roaming on either side of the river, I'm giving her a call. She's got the authority to put federal troops on your property. Am I being clear enough for you?" After a moment, Allman nodded.

"All right, Marta. You're right. We'll get it done." Unexpectedly, startlingly, he turned his attention to Vincent.

"As for you, Mapp. I have your signature on some documents."

"That's true enough," Vincent said.

"There will be legal consequences for you back in the U.S. You'll end up ruined—which I frankly look forward to seeing. Not a threat at this point; just a fair warning."

"Maybe. But think of the amazing story I'll have to tell. Soulless American billionaire inflicts man-eating monsters—creatures that eat their prey alive—on the rural inhabitants of a struggling nation, then tries to financially destroy the crusading truth teller who dared expose him to the world. Yes, you'll ruin me—and having been ruined, I'll rise, reborn from the ashes like a Phoenix." Allman stared at him as he slid his sunglasses back over his eyes, then continued to stare.

"But, in all seriousness, Mr. Allman," Vincent said, "I'm not out to harm you. I've actually been an admirer of your work. On the native-species front, I'm a true believer. I just think that in this case, you got carried away, you and Little Otto. A bit toxically ambitious. A bit lost in your own excitement. A bit unheeding of the human equation in all of this. A bit arrogant, I guess. I mean, I don't particularly like you, Mr. Allman, and Otto's not my cup of tea either—but overall, I think you do some fine work. You've made some important differences in the world, and not many people can say that." Vincent turned in his saddle to look at the fishing guide, Tomás, who still stood beside Marta's horse.

"*Tomás, venga acá por favor.*"

"I'm a fishing guide. I'm Mr. *Allman's* fishing guide. I speak English," said Tomás in English.

"Super. Would you come here, please?" He took Allman's check from his pocket and handed it down to Tomás, the fishing guide. "Would you please deliver that back to Mr. Allman?"

Allman took the check. "I don't ever want to see you on my land again, Mapp. Not fishing, even if you're a guest of Marta's; not anything. Two interactions between us, twenty years apart, and in both of them you have caused me heartburn."

Marta said, "Perhaps it's none of my affair, but I think Mr. Mapp is due some compensation for his injured foot. And the trauma that went along with it."

Before Allman could respond, Vincent said, "Oh, really. Thank you, Marta. But, with all respect to you, the hell with my foot. Worse things have happened to better people."

Chapter Twelve

Kilimanjaro

THE RAIN STARTED SLOWLY, EACH DROP MAKING A DISCRETE *PLINK* AS IT hit the river. Marta and Vincent slipped on their raincoats and pulled up their hoods, tightening the drawstrings. Allman's armed gaucho backed the Land Cruiser onto the beach, and both he and Tomás lifted Allman from his easy chair and settled him into the rear seat. The guide came back with a waterproof cover that he fitted over the chair and attached to its legs with elastic cords. He began gathering up all the fishing gear. The rain increased in tempo until it had swelled to a drumming roar. There was no wind, and the water fell straight down in streams. Vincent couldn't help but laugh like a child from the excitement.

"Shall we go?" Marta said.

"Right behind you."

Once they had crossed the river, the trail back to the lodge was wide enough for them to ride side by side. Still, they had to shout to be heard above the rain and the splashing hoofbeats of their mounts.

Marta said, "So, there was *another* night when you crossed the river to visit Jay's niece? Up at the cabin? But on foot and in the dark?"

"The *other* niece, when I went on foot, that first time. As you likely know, they're both writers, those ladies. They like to talk about writing." He decided on a slight revision of the truth: "And I never really made it all the way up there. Because of the hyenas."

"Well, you must be *extremely* interested in talking about writing yourself if you were willing to climb a mountain at night just for a conversation."

Vincent laughed. "I am quite literary," he said.

"That's what I meant earlier about things being different for older men than for older women."

"It's not all that different, believe me," said Vincent. "A bit, I guess. But not that much. We're a lot more willing to act foolishly, I suppose. To risk our dignity. Or to actually humiliate ourselves; take your pick."

"You're not a very experienced rider, Vincent. Do you think you could survive a gallop?"

"I'd probably fall off. Even if I didn't fall off, I'd still scream the whole way."

"Well, I'm tired of being pounded by this cold rain. Try to keep up. Or not." She leaned forward and made a kissing sound, and her horse picked up its pace and quickly shifted into a run. Then Vincent's horse—without his asking it to, without even his permission—bolted after it. Marta and Vincent pounded their way back to the roofed shelter over the entryway to the lodge, and they tied the horses there.

The remaining guests had all returned early to the lodge because of the rain, and they were helping themselves at the bar. Vincent heard Sancho in the kitchen, talking to Clara.

After Vincent had showered, put a fresh dressing on his wounded foot, and changed into dry clothing, he came out of his room carrying a white envelope. He looked for Marta until he found her sitting alone in the living room. The other guests were still making merry in the dining room. Marta also had changed clothes, but her hair was still slightly wet. She had a glass of whiskey in her hand.

"Vincent," she said. "Get yourself a glass of something and come join me."

He went out to the bar and returned with a glass of bourbon. He handed her the envelope and sat down on the couch. "That's something for your staff," he said. "I'll take care of Sancho separately. Thank you for a wonderful stay. After I get back home, I'll be doing a few things that bring you a little publicity."

Marta said, "You returned a check to my neighbor. I assume that was some kind of payment from him to buy your silence?"

"Pretty much. It was a bit more involved than that. A lot of other strings attached. I couldn't have lived up to most of what he wanted, anyway."

"I suppose you won't tell me how much it was for?"

"I don't see a reason to do that."

"Well, it must have been substantial." Vincent shrugged.

"My old man used to say, a fool and his money are soon parted."

"What is your schedule like? The rain is supposed to stop by midnight. Are you flexible enough to be able to spend one more day fishing here?"

"Really?"

"I'd like you to have one more try for that salmon you've been after. If you would like. Compliments of the lodge."

"That salmon. You all keep talking about it, while I myself have nearly forgotten it. It's almost become a curse."

"Nonetheless, you'll stay?"

"Sure. I just have to change my flight to Buenos Aires, but it's flexible. Thank you. What a nice thing."

Marta said, "You're a very good person, Vincent."

Vincent thought, *She has a crush on me now.*

Then he thought, *You're an asshole, Vincent.*

Vincent said, "Oh, you don't know me as well as I do."

"I'm not extremely optimistic," Sancho confessed the following morning as they were headed out to the river in his HiLux. "Of course, the heavy rain we just had will bring fish out of the lake. But the water is too high now, and it needs to drop a bit before the fishing is good. And by that time . . ." Vincent finished the thought for him:

"I'll be in B.A., eating a steak and listening to *cumbia villera* music. Well, we can only do what we can do."

"We can only do what we can do," Sancho agreed.

The sky was now cloudless, but the riverside willows still dripped from the rain; the sand along the banks was saturated and dark. The river itself, though not badly discolored, was running high and pushing hard. All the gentle riffles were gone, having turned into fast-gliding runs.

"It's a completely different river today," Vincent remarked.

"Yes, it is. You wouldn't want to try wading all the way across."

"Looks like streamer fishing for us."

"That is what we must do. Prospect for them with your sinking-tip line. We'll fish different depths; try streamers with different amounts of weight on them."

Sancho still liked the Boca as the most likely place for a salmon, but even if Vincent had not been prohibited from setting foot on Allman's land, there was no way to get across the swollen Río Perca in order to cast toward the cliff. Instead, they started their fishing at the long pool where Stevie the Fish Witch had caught her salmon a couple of days before. The pool was swollen—wider, longer, darker, deeper than it had been the last time they'd seen it. Vincent began casting, but to no effect. Down and across; strip in the line. Vary the length and speed of the strip on several subsequent casts. Take a step downstream and do it all again. Tie on a different streamer. Larger. Smaller. Heavier. Different color. More sparse. More fully dressed. It didn't seem to matter. He quickly began to conclude that this would be a fishless day. He almost wished he had declined Marta's generous offer and instead was on his way back to Buenos Aires. There were things he wanted to do there.

The worst part of it was Sancho. The guide was hovering behind him, and Vincent could sense him radiating helplessness and frustration—almost as if he believed he was being silently blamed for the poor fishing conditions. Almost as if he, too, felt regret that Marta had sent them out for one more day. Sancho was beginning to get on Vincent's nerves.

Vincent said, "You know what I haven't done so far this trip?"

"What is it?"

"Had a streamside sip of *yerba maté*. Every other trip I've taken down here, maté was a part of it."

"Do you *like* maté?" Sancho sounded mildly surprised.

"I think the taste can grow on a person who's not from Argentina. And I certainly enjoy the energy boost it gives me."

"Well of course I've always got some in my truck, along with a small stove to heat water. I could go back and prepare to brew some up, if you'd like."

"I think that's a great idea."

"You're all right by yourself for ten minutes or so?"

"I'm great by myself."

As soon as Sancho was gone, Vincent reeled up and sat down on a rock. Wished he had a cigar. Wished he had a flask of brandy. Wondered whether he should go back to his job at the college in the fall or find something else to do. After some minutes had passed and he began to worry that Sancho could pop back up on the bank above him at any moment, he reluctantly dragged himself to his feet and began casting again.

Sancho returned with a thermos of hot water and a silver maté cup from which rose the *bombillo*, the metal straw, through which they would drink their bitter tea.

Sancho said, "Were you aware that there is a bit of a ceremony surrounding the sharing of maté?"

"I know that you get to drink first since you're the one who made it."

"Yes, I drink first. But it's not out of privilege for having made it. It's actually because the first infusion is always too strong, too bitter, and less than ideal to drink."

"It's bitter anyway," Vincent said. They both laughed.

"I usually spit out the entire first cup. Then it's perfect. Perfect for you, that is." Sancho poured hot water into the cup, let it steep, and then sucked and spat until the cup was empty. He then poured more hot water over the sodden herbs and handed the cup to Vincent.

"It's always passed to the right," Sancho said.

"With only two of us here, that's going to take some shifting around." Sancho laughed again.

"I have enjoyed fishing with you," Sancho said.

"Likewise," Vincent said. "It has been good."

When they'd finished drinking the maté, Sancho said, "I don't like to carry my favorite cup around on the river for fear of forgetting it somewhere. I'm going to take it back to my truck and then find myself a convenient tree for a moment. After that, I'll return, and we'll move downriver."

"Sounds like a plan. I'll be here."

As soon as Sancho was gone again, Vincent reeled in and sat back down. Once more, he began dreaming of cigars and brandy and elegant, tango-dancing women in spike heels, legs flashing through long, slit-up-the-side dresses. The work he needed to do for Dunlevy began trying to arrange itself in his mind—but he had neither inclination nor energy for that, and he pushed it all away. Later on there'd be plenty of time, much too much time, but not now. Back to more pleasant thoughts, endorphin-producing thoughts, his daydreams of Cuban tobacco, fine booze, and elegant, athletic ladies. Then he heard the clatter of stones, and across the river, from around the upstream bend, there came a horse and rider. Although his heart leapt, the answer was no, it was not one of the Allman sisters. A dark person in a fur-fringed leather coat and hat, followed by another and another and another. They were the Mongols and Kazakhs Vincent had seen taking a tango lesson two days before.

There came more than a dozen such riders altogether, with several European-looking people interspersed among them. Each of the Asian falconers bore a huge, hooded bird on their arm—not a falcon at all but an eagle. A *golden* eagle; Vincent counted twelve such birds, each riding regally on the gloved forearm of its handler, so huge and so heavy that in order to support the weight, every handler crutched that arm in the fork of a stout stick whose base was braced against the side of the saddle. Vincent remembered then that mounted falconers in Mongolia hunted wolves with eagles; they deployed teams of several eagles to tackle a running wolf and pin it to the ground, writhing and snapping, until the hunters could ride up and kill it.

As they rode past in single file, the riders one by one briefly turned their eyes toward Vincent, taking Vincent in without acknowledging him, before one by one returning their gaze to the back of the rider ahead. The last hunter in the long column rode with the limp, tawny carcass of a large hyena draped across the withers of his horse. This final falconer gave Vincent a longer look than had all the others; Vincent thought he detected a smirk struggling to break out onto the man's lips. Then he too faced ahead and continued along the river. Within a minute, they all were out of sight.

Sancho returned. "Anything going on?" he asked.

"Not a thing."

"All right. Well, my latest idea is not to bother continuing to walk downstream from here. There's a part of the river where you haven't yet been—the last section before the highway bridge. About two kilometers above the bridge. We don't usually spend a lot of time there because most of it is deep and there are sheer cliffs on either side, which makes it difficult to wade and to cast. But there are a few spots from which we might make a cast—and at the very least, you'll get to see our final beat."

"Sounds fine to me," Vincent said. Secretly, he was looking forward to lunch at the lodge.

Sancho parked the truck, and they hiked down to the stretch above the bridge. Some spots along Allman's side looked okay for fishing, but, at least from what Vincent could see, there was no safe place to wade across to it, and, in any case, it was now off limits. On Marta's bank rose a series of palisades stacked one behind the other like the risers of a broken staircase as they ascended directly from the river, each vertical wall separated from the higher one behind it by a narrow, rugged tread of rock and sand. Vincent stood studying this challenging topography.

Sancho said, "It doesn't look ideal, does it? Not for casting, anyway. But it's deep water, and it holds some good fish—and the level looks like it may have already started dropping since the rain.

"So, my idea is that, as we work our way toward the bridge, we will find a few spots where we won't be too high above the river to roll a streamer out into it with your sinking-tip line; it's even remotely possible we'll be able to land a fish if you happen to hook one."

"Sounds like an adventure," Vincent said. Together, they began creeping along the undulating shelf that divided two sheer rock walls rising from the river. Whenever they reached a position that was close enough to the water, Vincent would make an awkward, backhanded roll cast that landed his streamer about a third of the way across the river. He would then let it sink for a ten-count before stripping it back in.

After an unproductive half an hour, he was starting to think he had probably had about enough of this inelegant style of fishing. Then they reached a wide breach in the ledge along which they were traveling; there would be a rugged climb of about thirty feet down to the river with hands as well as feet employed in the descent, followed by an equally steep ascent up the other side.

Sancho said, "There is some good water just below us here. The best in this section. Hardly ever gets fished. But we'll have to take care in getting across to it."

Vincent's foot was throbbing by then, and he felt like just sitting for a few minutes. Contemplating his trip. All the adventure, with maybe a bit yet to come. Which would be impossible with Sancho hovering around, trying to prod him into trying this or that. He said, "You know what I wish I had right now? A gourd of maté."

"Are you joking?"

"Not at all. Soon I'll be back in the States, and the flavor of maté will be nothing but a memory for me. I mean, I could take some home with me—but it's just not the same unless I'm drinking it on the bank of a river. An Argentine river. As far as I'm concerned, that's the only place to drink it."

"Well, there remains some hot water in the thermos. Enough to brew two cups, I'm sure. I could go back to the truck and get it."

"No. At this point, that's much too far for you, backtracking all that way. It would take you forever. I wouldn't do that to you."

"It would only take me ten minutes."

"You couldn't get there and back in ten minutes."

"Fifteen, at most. I'll be back. Don't wander too close to the edge, here; I've never lost a client, and I'd like to keep my record clean." Then Sancho was gone.

Vincent sat on a rock. He allowed himself a crooked smile. In a minute, he found himself going through the pockets of his fishing vest. Many items in it he hadn't handled in a while, some of them with memories attached. He opened a tiny box of terrestrial flies, and his eye immediately went to the lone grasshopper. Same pattern—hell, the same exact fly—that he'd used back in the fall on the Kennebec to catch a really huge rainbow. The fish hadn't chewed it up too badly during the long fight; it was still in good shape. Of course, that was mostly because he tied them to be durable. This one had wings sculpted from two opposing sections he'd clipped from either side of a turkey feather, a buoyant head of spun deer hair, legs of knotted pheasant-tail fibers, and an indicator post of white calf tail wound parachute-style with a grizzly rooster hackle. While most contemporary tiers would have built the body from foam rubber, Vincent had used tight turns of urine-stained white wool snipped from the scrotum of a ram. He had always preferred to tie with natural materials, excluding even chemical dyes whenever he could, and there was not a single artificial element in the makeup of this hopper fly. It was all organic save for the hook and the nylon thread, and over the years, from time to time, this same pattern tied with those same materials had proven magical.

Truth be told, in all the angling world, Vincent loved nothing more than fishing a well-crafted grasshopper for trout or salmon. Either the fish were in the mood for it or they weren't, but watching a big hopper splash into shallow water and then tickle the bank as it drifted down-river was a pleasure all on its own. Right here, right now, fishing a hopper made little sense because not only was the water deep right up to the edge of the cliff, but in their week on the river, he and Sancho had not seen a single natural grasshopper anywhere near the water. Nonetheless, Vincent found himself digging into his vest for the reel spool that was loaded with his floating line.

He clipped off Sancho's streamer, cranked in all the sinking-tip line until just two inches of tippet stuck from the reel, popped out the sinking-tip spool, and snapped in the floater. He hauled some floating line from the reel, doubled it and ran it up through the line guides, tied his grasshopper to the end of the tippet, and massaged the bug with a generous dollop of floatant.

Vincent pointed his rod tip toward the river that ran nearly ten yards below and began peeling line off the reel and shaking it out through the guides until the grasshopper plopped onto the water, the leader landing and lying loosely coiled behind it. He continued flicking out line with rhythmic twitches of the rod tip, sending the fly drifting downriver and nearly brushing the rock wall as it traveled. When all the line plus a yard or more of thread-like backing was off of both the reel and the rod tip, some of it dangling in the air and the rest lying on the water as it followed the fly, he stripped most of it back in, drawing back the fly until it made a V-wake in the current directly below him. Then he hauled a few more feet of backing from the reel and sent the hopper on another, longer downriver drift. He watched the fly carefully, making frequent adjustments with the rod and the line so that it floated as freely as any natural, untethered terrestrial insect that had suffered the catastrophic misfortune of having been caught by the wind and blown into the river.

Sancho returned. "I have the makings for maté," he said.

"Perfect," said Vincent, not looking at him.

"What are you doing?"

"It's a game I play when I'm bored. I try to see how far I can drift a dry fly without letting it drag. Once I see the tiniest bit of drag, I have to strip it in and start all over."

"That sounds rather pointless. And I assume you realize that if you hooked a fish from here, you couldn't land it? Not unless it was a minnow and you could haul it up the face of the cliff?"

"First you have to hook a fish; only then you can fail at landing it." Vincent saw his fly begin to make a tiny tear in the skin of the water, and he stripped in line to bring it back to him. Once the fly was directly below him, he let the current take it again.

Sancho said, "How do you even mend your line when you've got two meters of backing off the tip?"

"With great difficulty," Vincent admitted. "In any case, my fly's getting a decent drift. Theoretically, if there were any fish in here and if there were any natural hoppers on the water, those hoppers would be drifting close to the cliff, and the fish would all be facing upstream, each one a fin's distance from the rock itself, waiting there to eat them. And the *biggest* brown trout . . . just below the water line they'd be peering out of dark little recesses like underwater trolls lurking in the mouths of caves. . . ."

"Yes? You're just playing then," Sancho said with a tone of impatience. "Shall we climb down and up and head to a place where you might actually catch a fish?"

"Sancho, it's all just play anyway," Vincent said. "And what about that maté?"

Along the cliff, a silver snout broke the surface of the river and made Vincent's grasshopper disappear. Instinctively, he hauled down on the line and lifted the rod; it was a solid feeling, almost as if his fly were caught on the face of the cliff itself. But he also felt the pulse of life.

"Oh, my," said Sancho.

"Maybe a good one."

"As I told you . . ." A silver missile rose from the river. They could hear it throwing water as it shook and twisted in the air. Crashed back into the river and took off downstream. Yards of slack fly line burned through Vincent's fingers until all of it was gone and the reel began to scream.

"Holy shit," said Vincent.

"That's a salmon," Sancho said dejectedly, grieving its loss already. The salmon danced in the air again. It was huge.

Vincent said, "Oh, my God. That's Ernie Fucking Schweibert's salmon. Maybe a little bigger. Could be over twenty pounds." Now *here* was the story that Dunlevy had been fantasizing about. Drooling over. It flashed through his mind just then that Dunlevy might be the only person in the world who actually appreciated Vincent as a writer. And Vincent had never treated the kid all that well.

His reel continued to scream; all his fly line was out in the river, the fish well into the two hundred yards of orange dental floss that was his fly-line backing.

"You'll have to break that fish off, I'm afraid. Otherwise, you'll lose your entire line." Vincent watched—fascinated, horrified—as the backing melted from the arbor of his reel. The fish made two jumps in succession; Vincent dipped the rod both times to put a little slack into the line.

"Always bow to a silver king," Vincent said.

"Just clamp down on the reel. He'll break that fly right off."

Without looking, Vincent sent his left hand to fumble the cell phone from the pocket of his waders. He pushed the phone into Sancho's reluctant fingers. Sancho said, "What are you doing? You have just a few more winds of backing left."

Vincent stepped out into the sky. In Vincent's head, Butch Cassidy said, *The fall probably will kill you*. In Vincent's head, Norman Maclean's father, from *A River Runs Through It*, said *He is beautiful*. From above him, he heard Sancho shrieking wordlessly as he plummeted. *Like a little girl*, Vincent thought. The water smacked him hard and closed around him, and he seemed to go down into it forever. He opened his eyes as he continued to sink; skeins of bubbles from his violent entrance streamed past him on their way to the surface. The river was so deep here that the bottom was shrouded in mysterious darkness. Around him and above him, he imagined he saw faces. Still gripping the rod, he kicked and clawed one-handedly until slowly he began to rise. An eternity later, his head broke the surface, and he made a loud and desperate sound as he heaved in a breath.

"*Viejo de mierda!*" he heard Sancho yell. Then in English: "You crazy old man. What are you doing?"

Vincent kept gasping. He was picking up speed as he headed down-river. He could hear fast water ahead. There was no tension on his fly rod, and he assumed the fish had spat the barbless hook—probably a good thing since that would allow him to concentrate completely on saving himself from drowning. But out of reflex he began hauling in backing, using his forefinger to pinch more of it against his rod with each long draw, and on the third long strip, the line came tight again and the rod tip bent and pulsed. Ahead of him in the river, the big fish jumped, the leader that trailed from its mouth flashing in the sun. Behind him, on the cliff, Sancho was shouting in a high, panicked voice—but his shouts were fading.

The water continued to gain velocity. Vincent could see white waves leaping into the air ahead of him. The darkness of monstrous rocks loom-ing below the surface. His knee banged off of a rock, partially spinning him in the water, the pain immediate and sharp, but he didn't have time to assess the damage. Instead, he lay back in order to ride the river boots first, hopefully to spring off of rocks with his feet rather than crash into any more of them. He felt icy water on the leg that had struck the rock, and he understood that his waders were torn.

He realized that if he continued to strip in his backing by hand as he gained on the salmon, he was likely to end up with a huge tangle that, when the fish made a run, would snag in the line guides and precipitate disaster. Instead, he let all the backing slip back through the tip-top, careful to keep tension on it, and then once the line and backing were tight all the way through to the reel, he was able to maintain pressure on the fish directly from the reel. He was even able to crank in backing until all but twenty or thirty feet had returned to the spool. Ahead of him, the salmon jumped again—a monstrous male. Yes, Ernie Schweibert's salmon, plus a little—and then his hip hit a rock; this one also hurt, but he continued on downriver. Dimly, he wondered where Sancho might be.

When he was finally within a couple of hundred yards of the highway bridge, the river spread and slowed and shallowed out, and the fish was able to gain some distance from him under its own power. It was one hundred and fifty yards downriver from him now, almost beneath the bridge, and Vincent's reel was again close to empty. Vincent could see that, up on the bridge, along the steel railing, eight or ten people were gathered, looking down at him and watching as the fish tail-danced below them. Off to Marta's side of the river, the bank was low and sandy, and Vincent, as the fish took out still more backing and jumped, once, twice, three more times, steered himself bankward until he found that he was finally able to stand. His right hip was throbbing, and his left leg wanted to fold. But he stood nonetheless and was able to recover some backing, letting the fish go when it surged, then reeling again, until slowly the salmon stopped jumping and tired and came in to him, rolling over onto its platter-like silver side. Vincent reached and took it by the tail and knelt in the water beside it, righting the fish so that it faced upriver.

A clamor came from up on the bridge. Vincent turned his eyes upward. Cars had pulled over, and people were standing all along the bridge railing. Some of them were clapping. As Vincent watched, the applause spread all the way down the line of bystanders. Some of the people on the bridge produced rocks and sticks and began banging on the railing. He lifted his rod in the air to acknowledge them, and they began to shout in wordless cheers. It made Vincent laugh and shiver at the same time.

Tears came to his eyes. He would have stood and bowed—but there was the salmon. He needed to tend to his fish.

This was an old salmon, the veteran of many seasons of autumnal combat—but still a warrior. The powerful wrist above its tail bore the dark scars of ancient battles; the tail itself was wider than Vincent's spread fingers. The deepest part of the buck salmon's gleaming fuselage was broader than Vincent's open hand from wrist to fingertips. The fish's long kype—the hooked, sharp-toothed jaw that male salmon developed in the fall for making war on other males—was a fearsome wonder. This studded weapon on a big male salmon had always reminded Vincent of the lower jaw of a sperm whale.

Vincent rested his rod on the gravel of the riverbed in order to free his hand, and then he worked the barbless hook from the side of the fish's mouth before gently, with his thumb, pressing open the jaw so that oxygenated water would run through the mouth and over the gills. The fish was his now to care for, its well-being his responsibility. He felt it beginning to twist against his grip as it regained its strength.

"Old fellow," Vincent said as he held the salmon. "Old man. God bless you. God *bless* you. I think you've got another few fights left in you yet."

The people on the bridge were still shouting and banging when Sancho came running up, gasping for breath. "My God," he said. "I thought you were dead. I truly did. You're an extremely irresponsible person, Vincent. But . . . oh my God, look at that fish!"

"A wonder of the world, no?" said Vincent. "He's almost ready to go. Do you have my phone? Take a few photos. Take a little video. Get some video of those people up on the bridge; my new boss will like that."

A few minutes later, as Sancho continued to record with Vincent's phone, the big salmon gave a strong kick of its tail and rocketed into the depths.

"Truly, Vincent," Sancho said. "That is the largest fish I have ever seen taken from this river."

"You're only saying that because you want a bigger tip." Vincent stood up, shook Sancho's hand, gave him a hug. Then he began to feel dizzy, so he picked his rod off the river bottom and carried it to the beach, where he sat down on a rock.

"Are you all right?"

"Never better." Vincent began patting his sodden vest for the little bottle of aspirin he'd stashed in one of the pockets. It wasn't there; there was nothing at all in the vest. Even the reel spool containing the sinking-tip line was gone. The river had picked him clean.

"Have you got any aspirin on you?" Vincent asked.

"My first aid kit is back in the truck. Are you feeling unwell?"

"As I told you . . ." Vincent felt a lightning bolt go through him. "Uh-oh," he said.

"Is something wrong?" Another sharp pain stiffened him, and he slid off of the rock and onto the sand.

"I shall be pinched to death," said Vincent.

"Is it your chest?"

"It is."

Sancho began digging through his backpack. He came up with a radio and drew out the telescoping antenna. Turned it on and started calling, "Clara, Clara, *me copias?* Clara, Clarita, *me copias?*"

"Ouch," Vincent said. He lay back against the sand. The sun was blinding. The world shrank in around him. He heard Sancho talking, and there was squawking from the radio. Woman's voice. Back and forth like that; Vincent found it annoying. He had a car parked on his chest; why were these two clandestine lovebirds chattering away as if nothing were going on?

Sancho was squatting beside him. Touching the side of his neck. Pulling the wader straps off of his shoulders and unbuttoning his shirt. Vincent managed to wheeze, "Do you know CPR?"

"I do," said Sancho. "I'll use it if I have to. But your heart is still beating. It's weak, it's irregular, but it's still beating, and I wouldn't want to disturb it unless I had to."

Another incomprehensible blast from the radio. A minute later, Sancho said, "Very good news, Vincent. Allman's people are sending a helicopter, along with someone who is a doctor. You just have to hang on for another five minutes. They'll take you all the way in to Bariloche."

"All I need is a couple of fucking aspirins," Vincent said.

A moment later, a shadow fell across his face as Sancho lowered the side of his head toward Vincent's mouth. "What, Vincent? What did you say?"

Vincent said, "The hyena's cry is strangely human." Sancho turned to look at him.

"I suppose so," Sancho said after a moment. "Though I've only seen them on television."

Vincent said, "I am the . . . dried and frozen carcass of a salmon. No one has explained what a salmon is doing at this latitude."

"*Carajo*. I hope you're not also having a stroke as well," he heard Sancho say.

There came a roaring and a ferocious wind that drove needles of sand into Vincent's face and neck. A black shadow fell over them; it made Vincent imagine a golden eagle descending over a wolf running full tilt with its tongue hanging out. People speaking sharply in Spanish. Everything began to dim.

"*Ponle las paletas.*"

"That means put the paddles on him, "Vincent smugly informed his class.

"*Listo. Despejen.*"

"Do you understand? That's 'Ready. Clear.'"

CHAPTER THIRTEEN

One Flies East, One Flies West

"WELL SO, THAT'S EVERYTHING I HAVE TO SAY ON THE SUBJECT OF cocaine hippos," Vincent told the class. "Remember that those research papers are due the next time we meet." Leaving his computer bag and all his belongings behind, he abruptly walked out of the classroom, down a flight of stairs, and out onto an infinite meadow through which flowed a gravel-bottomed brook. Details on each clean stone in the bed of the brook were magnified by a gliding lens of water so immaculately transparent that fly anglers who were dull or unimaginative or at least addicted to regurgitating clichés might have described it as "gin clear." The sky was daylight-bright, although there was no sun to be seen. He could see stars; they were arranged in constellations unfamiliar to him. The meadow went on forever, and nothing stood between Vincent and the horizon. He began to walk, moving upstream like a homebound salmon.

He held a set of keys and the vague aim of arriving at a parking lot and finding his truck. But there was no truck, no parking lot, or anything else; the brook and its meadow continued onward over the curve of the earth for as far as he could see, and the campus receded behind him. A pair of hyenas materialized on either side of the brook and began dogging him from a distance. He kept glancing back at them, but at the moment, they seemed more like an honor guard than a hunting party, and they gave no sign that they were yet ready to team up and surge forward to pull him down. Two boys, each carrying a spinning rod and a coffee can of garden worms, came walking downstream, and as they split up to move past him along the bank, they yelled in Spanish, "Very soon the fireworks will start!" He turned to warn them about the hyenas, but the boys were already gone; he saw only the patient hyenas padding along, each on its own side of the brook.

He came to an escalator, thought nothing strange about encountering an escalator rising from a meadow, and without hesitation began to ascend. He glanced back to see the hyenas staring up at him, apparently trying to decide what to do. Maybe he would lose them now—give the slip to those slippery beasts. When he stepped off at the top, he found himself in some or other iteration of the International Fly Tackle Dealer Show. He wondered what year this might be—but, although there were people all around him now, "what year is this?" was never a question a person could safely ask of anyone. Dividing the huge exhibition hall, endless alleyways of elaborate booths displayed the wares of just about everyone who made or sold anything or provided services in the so-called industry of fly fishing. The aisles were arranged around a pair of casting pools—low, rectangular enclosures nearly half the length of a football field, each of which contained a finger's depth of water. Vincent arrived at the head of the first pool and found himself on the edge of a crowd that was spectating as Lefty Kreh, up on the casting platform and bantering, gave a demonstration. "It's all about timing, not power," Lefty was telling them. "You can make a good cast without ripping your underwear." It was one of his signature lines, and the spectators laughed.

People spotted Vincent and began coming up to him, telling him about this or that new piece of fishing gear—rod, reel, fly line, tool, gadget, wading boot, hat, technical angling shirt, personal water craft, duffel bag, landing net, fly-tying vise—that they thought he needed to review for the magazine. He shook the hand of each person and said, "I'll stop by your booth as soon as I can. Right now, I'm just trying to dodge a pair of hyenas that are coming after me with their androgynous genitalia."

Everyone said they understood completely, that they knew exactly what he was talking about, that they themselves had been in nearly identical situations, and that they looked forward to talking to him later. Soon the only person remaining near him was a persistent man who represented a new lodge in Argentina.

"Unfortunately," Vincent told him, "I just left Patagonia. It'll probably be a while before we can do another Argentina story. There's only so much about one exotic location that our readers want to hear."

At the head of the second casting pool, Stephen, the influencer, came up to him with a fly rod in his hand. The rod had a reel attached, orange line hanging off the tip-top. At the end of the tippet was tied a bit of red fluff to represent a fly.

"Where's Stevie?" Vincent asked.

"She's doing a meet and greet."

"A meet and greet?"

"To introduce her new line of high SPF outdoor skin-care products. But, hey, you need to try this new Kent Triple-X rod. Entirely new form of graphite—originally developed for the U.S. Space Force and only recently declassified by the Department of Defense. Rod features an exquisitely sensitive tip, persistent tracking, progressive power throughout all sections of the shaft. The Kent guys joke that it's a rod that won't take no for an answer."

"Oh," said Vincent. "Okay." He accepted the rod from Stephen. "Which one is this?"

"It's the four-weight."

"All right." He stepped up onto the casting platform, peeled line off the reel, and made false casts until he had a sufficient length off the tip-top. Then he set down a few serious casts, increasing the distance each time.

"Nice." But just as he spoke, he spotted Joan Wulff, her eyes like dark lasers as she wove her way through the crowd to get to him. Obviously having observed him from afar and detected some egregious flaw in his casting form, she meant to fix the problem. Normally, he would have contentedly—or at least resignedly—waited there for her, but this day was anything but normal, and Vincent needed to be on the move. He wasn't sure where he was going, but it was important he get there nonetheless. He handed the rod back to Stephen. "An impressive stick. Tell Stevie that Uncle Vincent said hi and good-bye."

Moving on, he passed the head of an aisle where Yvon Chouinard—a fellow Mainer—stood on a chair, talking to a crowd about the close connection between fish conservation and saving the entire planet. He next went by a table where Nick Lyons was signing books for people waiting patiently in a line. He would've said hello, but it was apparent that Nick was very busy. He reached an arena ringed with fly-tying tables, each table occupied by two tiers sitting before their vises, wrapping their signature patterns. A. K. Best and Gary LaFontaine were working nearly elbow to elbow, A. K. in a cowboy hat and string tie, Gary with bits of feathers and fibers stuck all over his short-sleeve dress shirt and clearly not caring one bit about it. He said hello to both of them.

Then Vincent burst through a heavy exit door. The door whooshed and slammed behind him, he felt a gust of icy air, and he was back out alone in the silence of the endless unpeopled meadow. He tried to reopen the door, but it was locked as if for all eternity. On their haunches, the hyenas were now together on the same side of the brook—*his* side of the brook—and waiting for him at a respectful distance. They giggled as if to greet him, then rose to their feet and resumed dogging him as he headed across the meadow and back down to the bank of the brook.

Soon, from afar, he heard accordion music, then a violin, a cello, and finally a guitar. He crested a rise, and on a wooden stage below and ahead of him were two tango dancers and a band playing Leonard Cohen's "Dance Me to the End of Love." Even from a distance, the movements of the dancers were somehow familiar, and as he drew closer, he saw that the dancer in the heels and the red dress with slits down the sides was Caroline and that the one in the pinstripe tuxedo was Naya. Vincent stood watching for a minute, and he had to admit that the two women flowed together perfectly, with neither a seam nor a riffle. He felt an unexpected flash of anger at the fact that, completely absorbed in one another, neither dancer acknowledged him or even gave a sign of having seen him, and he was nearly overcome by the impulse to jump up onstage and cut in on them. But then he realized that not only was he not dressed for tango, but he didn't even know this dance. He could accomplish nothing save for disappointing everyone and making a fool of himself. He turned away and continued his upstream journey as the hyenas followed and the music faded.

There was more music ahead—sad this time rather than merely wistful—and he came on a group playing a soulful song of the Andean *altiplano*. The singers, a man and a woman, sang the story of a distant village, a lost family, and a love they would never see again. The flutes, the *charango*, the voices, made Vincent shiver; the deep wooden pipes and the hide drum reverberated inside of him as if they'd been a part of him all along. Then a rocket whooshed upward from somewhere and burst against the stars, sending crackling streaks of blue and white toward the earth.

Vincent walked on until he arrived at his childhood home, and it was there that he reached the source of the stream. The backyard was flooded, as it had been in his long-ago dream, and it was from this unexpected font that the brook went splashing down a rocky embankment and began winding its way toward his future—and his past. Another rocket exploded overhead.

The hyenas, his honor guard, went to their haunches on the dry edge of the lawn. They laughed as Vincent, trying to keep his feet from getting wet, carefully skirted the pool until he reached the door to the basement of the house where he'd grown up. He opened the door and stepped inside.

"Hello, asshole. Welcome home." From his left. Eastern European accent. As Vincent's eyes adjusted to the darkness, he saw that the speaker was the broken-nosed striped bass being from yet another dream—the one in which he'd been loitering in the parking lot of a long-vanished topless-dancing club. Muscular, this fellow, in a hooded boxer's robe of scaly striper skin. Large fishhook piercing in his lower lip—size two-aught, the naked hook looked to be. Vincent guessed that, subjected to the corrosiveness of saltwater immersion as well as the punishing push of current, any tying materials that had once been wrapped to the hook had come unraveled and fallen away. Which was a shame because it would have been interesting to know what pattern and color of fly this pug of a fish had fallen for.

"Have you learned some lesson from your trip?" the striper being asked. Vincent was unsure whether he was talking about Río Perca or the big, one-way walking trip he had just concluded, but he decided not to ask.

Vincent said, "The lesson is, fish as much as you can. Feed your curiosity. Have sex when you're able. Try not to hurt anybody; try not to allow anybody to be hurt. When everything goes wrong, look for some humor in it. That's it. That's all I've got for you, *boludo*."

"Also," said Vincent, "Keep swimming in the salt water, and that hook will likely rust out before you know it. You'll be good as new."

Vincent moved past him and into the basement. A light shone down on a round table where Vincent's father was playing poker. The old man clenched a Tiparillo in the corner of his mouth, biting down on the plastic tip with his eyeteeth the way he always did until smoke would no longer come out of it. Then he'd crush out the damaged cigar and light another. His dad threw some chips into the center of the table and glanced up from his cards. The other players—three of them, all of whom Vincent knew by name and also knew to be long dead—stared down at their cards and did not acknowledge his presence. Vincent heard a rocket detonate in the air above the house. Then another. His father asked, "You want us to deal you in?"

"Not sure yet."

His father said, "Kid, you gotta play the hand you're dealt. But first you have to decide whether you're in or you're out." He returned his eyes to his cards.

"That's the mystery I'm attempting to solve at the moment. I'll let you know. In any case, as I don't have to remind you, a fool and his money are soon parted." Another rocket burst above them.

His father said, "So long. Write when you get work. Don't take any wooden nickels."

As Vincent continued on through the basement, curtains of darkness parted before him, one after the other. The basement was far bigger than he remembered; he found it odd that he could not see any of its walls. Sean Rideout and Sancho Nelson appeared together beside him. Sean said, "You ready to fish? We've got Olives and Hendricksons starting to hatch."

Sancho said, "*Listo para pescar?* Where there's one big salmon, there's bound to be another."

Vincent said, "Guys, I can't tell you if I'm free today."

Sean warned him, "A day you don't fish is a day you don't get back."

"I need to find out if I have a day to begin with. And you do know that the term 'hatch' is a misnomer, do you not?"

"Of course I do. It's just that 'emergence' doesn't sound as sexy. Sounds like something some eggheaded professor would say."

As he turned from them to continue onward, he heard Sancho say to Sean, "He is a good angler."

"I have occasionally seen worse," Sean conceded.

He took a few steps and found himself facing three angelic beings. Hairless, wearing robes patterned with the maps and mazes of a brook trout's back. Of course he knew them, from long ago. They were smiling at him. They lifted their bamboo fly-rod scepters in salute.

"Shit," Vincent said. "I was just talking to my old man. I forgot to ask him about you guys. That's what you told me to do."

"Don't you have a good idea already?" asked the being who carried the rod with the yellow wraps.

"I can make an intuitive guess."

"Vincent, we have for you a seat of honor," said the brook trout with the red-wrapped rod. He placed his hand on the back of what looked to Vincent like a folding camp chair webbed with green and gray camouflage fabric.

"It looks like a camp chair."

"What greater honor could you ask for? Take your seat." Three rockets in a row boomed outside. Vincent sat.

The brook trout being with the blue-wrapped rod stepped forward with a metal bowl. He said, "We have here a helmet, to protect you as you ride into battle."

"It looks like an old-fashioned barber's basin." From out of the darkness behind him, he heard Sancho call a confirmation: *Sí, Maestro; es un basín de barbero.*

"It *is* a barber's basin." The being turned it over and settled it onto Vincent's head. It fit him surprisingly well.

"Now," said the being with the red-wrapped rod. "We are ready to definitively answer your age-old question. We're going to guide you to the place we go when we're not here. We think you'll like it; the brook trout water is literally infinite."

Before Vincent could respond, two rockets exploded. Butch Cassidy and the Sundance Kid came striding toward him out of the darkness. Vincent recognized them immediately. Their faces were those of well-known actors.

Butch Cassidy said, "So, you didn't want to play poker with your old man?"

"It's not that I didn't want to."

"In that case, neither should you be in a rush to shuffle off to brook trout land. Did you forget about *el dorado?*"

"What about El Dorado? Did you guys find it? Somewhere in Bolivia, I'm assuming, before you got killed?"

"As a matter of fact, some of the world's finest dorado fishing is definitely to be had in Bolivia. We cast to them there in clear water, down in the jungle streams. Sight fishing. None of this monotonous blind casting from boats on big, muddy rivers, like they do in Argentina and Uruguay."

Vincent laughed. "I think we're talking about different dorados."

The Sundance Kid said, "Ours is the real one. And, it's on your bucket list. You've always wanted to catch one. Worth hanging around for."

Vincent stood up from the chair. He looked at the brook trout beings; he looked at Butch Cassidy and the Sundance Kid. "How can I make decisions when I don't even know which side of the bucket I'm on?"

The brook trout who carried the blue-wrapped fly rod appeared beside him. "Would you like to go out and watch the fireworks? I believe they'll only get more intense from this point onward. That might clear things up for you."

But Vincent stepped on through the seemingly endless basement. Over his shoulder he answered, "If you go out there yourself, be careful. There's hyenas all over the place. They'll eat any damn thing, even a fish."

The Allman twins approached him. They were wearing English-style riding clothes—black boots, jodhpurs, red waist jackets, velvet-covered helmets. Angela carried a leather crop in one hand and was slapping it into the palm of the other. "Well, now," said Vincent. "My two lovely, literary friends. What a nice surprise."

"Hold out your hand," ordered Angela. He feared she might whack him with her whip, but nonetheless he reluctantly did as she demanded. She pressed an icy coin into his palm. Vincent brought it closer to his eyes and examined it; it was an 1899 twenty-dollar Liberty Head gold piece.

"Why are you giving me this?" Four rocket bursts, one after the other, in the sky above Vincent's childhood home.

"You need a coin to flip. I do admire your bowler, by the way. It suits you well."

"Bowler? It's only a barber's basin."

"Hold out your other hand," ordered Gabriela. Vincent extended his hand, and she dropped in an identical coin.

"Did you steal this one from Marta? Anyway, for flipping, I only need one."

"One's to flip; two are for your eyes if you lose the toss."

"Jesus. Things are sounding grim around here."

"*Otra vez*," commanded a voice that seemed to come at once from above them and from nowhere and from everywhere, the speaker clearly addressing someone other than Vincent. Also, from beyond the basement: the sound of five rockets detonating in rapid succession.

Vincent laughed. "Second verse, same as the first." He clinked both coins together in his left hand and began sliding one against the other between his thumb and forefinger. "For luck," he said aloud. "Which I seem very much to need."

"Vicente." It was Clara, stunning in an old-style stewardess's uniform: blue, tight-fitting mid-length skirt with white gloves, buttoned blue jacket with wide white lapels, a round cap pinned in front with a badge of golden wings and perched atop her head at a fetching angle.

"Well, now, look at you," said Vincent. "I bet you got picked for a role as a flight attendant. Over in Spain, maybe. And *you* painted a moustache on me. What a lucky man I've been."

"*Despejen*," warned the unseen voice.

"Vicente," Clara said. "The time has come. Both of your horses are saddled and waiting." She took his hand and led him to the dusty, cobweb-covered concrete cellar wall, then through the wall and out into his mother's flower garden, where in the darkness a black *criollo* horse and a white *criollo* horse stood tail to tail among the blooming peonies. The moonless sky at once grew silent, thick, almost trembling, with expectation. Crickets sang in the grass.

"*Escoja, y montáte*," Clara said. A choice. She was giving him one. Vincent found himself stepping toward her, sliding an arm around her and kissing her full on her warm lips. After a moment, she leaned into him and kissed him back, then smiled and gently pushed him away.

"*Entonces, nos vemos*," she said. Vincent laughed.

"*Sí, mi vida. Nos vemos.*"

Vincent went to the white horse, kicked his foot into the steel stirrup, and lifted himself into the saddle. Then he rode off in the direction from which the sun would soon be rising.

ACKNOWLEDGMENTS

USING A DIFFERENT TITLE, I TOOK MY FIRST SWING AT WRITING *Rolling Back the River* well over thirty years ago. Like me at the time, the early version of Vincent Mapp was a much younger man and fisherman. He was also kind of crazy rather than merely impulsive. For one thing, he carried an unloaded handgun with him everywhere and didn't mind menacing people with it. He was a struggling freelance writer—again, like me at the time—and so poor that dust bunnies constituted one of his main fly-tying materials. Angela Allman 1.0, rather than being a cosmopolitan, continent-hopping, multilingual playwright, was a hot, young, blue-collar bartender who somehow had a very eccentric, extremely jealous multimillionaire uncle. She did not have a twin. Original Vincent's over-the-rainbow journey, instead of lofting him from Maine to Patagonia, led him up I-95 from Connecticut to Maine. The whole thing didn't work very well, and the manuscript ended up in a moldering box in my basement as part of a stack of other half-baked writing projects. I never forgot about it, though, and after I started traveling to Argentina in 2022, two enchanting fly-fishing lodges located on remote properties with working livestock operations—Estancia Tecka in Chubut Province and Arroyo Verde in Neuquen—began calling to me as potential settings for a somewhat similar though much more ambitious story. For their completely unwitting role in helping to reignite my imagination, as well as for their warm hospitality during my stays with them, I would like to thank the Ochoa (Estancia Tecka) and Lariviere families.

I owe a deep debt of gratitude to my generous first readers— Dave Martel, Jeff Reardon, Kathy Scott, David Van Burgel, and Ted Williams—who all eased my anxiety by assuring me I was on the right track.

I'd also like to thank my friend and fishing buddy, Master Maine Fishing Guide Sean McCormick, for his companionship, rowing skills, and wry humor over the past couple of decades.

Several Argentine fishing guides have helped me understand the angling and the aquatic ecosystems in Patagonia: Gustavo Sarthou, Diego Martin, and Federico Conesa. *Gracias, amigos.*

Big thanks as well to my Stackpole editor, Jay Nichols, for deciding that a fly-fishing novel might not be a terrible idea.